HOTEL ANGELINE

HOTEL ANGELINE

A NOVEL IN 36 VOICES

BY

Jennie Shortridge - Teri Hein - William Dietrich - Kathleen Alcalá

Maria Dahvana Headley - Stacey Levine - Indu Sundaresan

Craig Welch - Matthew Amster-Burton - Ed Skoog - David Lasky

Greg Stump - Kevin O'Brien - Nancy Rawles - Suzanne Selfors

Carol Cassella - Karen Finneyfrock - Robert Dugoni - Jarret Middleton

Deb Caletti - Kevin Emerson - Kit Bakke - Julia Quinn - Mary Guterson

Erik Larson - Garth Stein - Frances McCue - Erica Bauermeister

Sean Beaudoin - Dave Boling - Peter Mountford - Stephanie Kallos

Jamie Ford - Clyde Ford - Elizabeth George - Susan Wiggs

OPEN ROAD

INTEGRATED MEDIA

NEW YORK

FOREWORD

BY NANCY PEARL

PART OF THE REASON I love living in Seattle is that there are two strong communities—one of writers and one of readers. I think of their relationship as a kind of Venn diagram. Each group has its own uniqueness and individuality, but there is a crucial overlap where their separate existences come together. And this overlap is, I think, crucial.

Of course, Seattle is not the only city in the United States, or even the world, where this is the case. There are the Twin Cities, Minneapolis and St. Paul, and, of course, Brooklyn, not to mention Portland, Oregon (and maybe Portland, Maine, for all I know); San Francisco; Austin; and Sydney, Australia. In fact, when I think back to the places I've traveled in the last decade, and the writers and readers I've gotten to know, perhaps every city, large and small, can claim these two separate but connected communities.

The relationship between reading and writing is well documented, but I always remember that it was Ernest Gaines, author of *The*

Autobiography of Miss Jane Pitman and other novels, whom I first heard articulate it to an audience. When he was in Seattle in 1999 (his novel *A Lesson Before Dying* had been selected for "Seattle Reads"), someone in the audience asked him if he had any advice for aspiring writers. He said, yes, he had eight words of advice: "Read, read, read, read, write, write, write, write."

Another aspect of the Venn diagram that—for me—expresses the relationship between readers and writers, or reading and writing, is this: No two people read the same book, even when it appears to be identical, with the same author, same cover, same publication date, and same pagination.

When I say that no two people read the same book, I am thinking of three quotations.

Robertson Davies, the great Canadian writer, stated in "A Rake at Reading": "Reading is exploration, extension, and reflection of one's innermost self."

Jorge Luis Borges wrote: "I sometimes think that good readers are poets as singular, and as awesome, as great authors themselves . . . Reading, meanwhile, is an activity subsequent to writing—more resigned, more civil, more intellectual."

And finally, in an interview with Joseph Malia in *Bomb Magazine* in 1988, Paul Auster said, "The one thing I try to do in all my books is to leave enough room in the prose for the reader to inhabit it. Because I finally believe it's the reader who writes the book and not the writer."

This idea of no two readers reading the same book is easily demon-
strated at any book group meeting. Everyone brings to the reading of a
novel a lifetime of experiences—thoughts and dreams, successes and fail-
ures, preoccupations and habits—as well as his or her mood while reading the book in question. (Incidentally, that's why I think there's really
no such thing as rereading, since each time we pick up a book we are,
in some incalculable way, a different person, and therefore a different
reader, with the result that it turns out to be a different book.) The writer
writes a book and sends it out into the wider world, and each reader of
that book makes it his or her own. I love that.

Seattle is blessed with an enormous variety of writers who bravely
send their novels out into a wider world than their own minds. The
Novel: Live! project was a testament to this robust interconnected community, and the result of the project, *Hotel Angeline*, owes its unique
charm to the diversity of that community. Loca-readers (as I like to call
those people who especially enjoy reading books written by writers who
live in, or set their novels in, their hometowns) can come to know the
writers more fully through witnessing their literary intersection. To read
Hotel Angeline is to celebrate how this diverse group of writers (and
readers, all of them) can pool their talents and expertise to come up with
such an entertaining and soul-satisfying novel.

Here's how I suggest you read *Hotel Angeline*: straight through, trying your best not to notice which author wrote which chapter, and only
when you've finished that first read-through should you allow yourself
to go back to the beginning and see who's written what. When I read
it a second time (still not looking at who wrote what), I put the list of
contributors in front of me to see if I could figure out whom the writer of
any particular chapter was. I found this to be both fun and instructive at
the same time.

As a reader, I was fascinated and awed first by the whole idea of The
Novel: Live! project; second, by the number of writers who agreed to
participate; and finally, by the fact that *Hotel Angeline* actually came to
a delicious fruition. Whether it's mysteries, historical novels, nonfiction,
realistic fiction, novels for teens, thrillers, romances, or poetry that you

read, you'll find contributors to *Hotel Angeline* who come from each of those writerly disciplines. There are writers here whose books have been widely successful and those who perhaps haven't yet reached the popularity they deserve—names you'll recognize and, probably, some you might not know. And yet, despite their various literary backgrounds, they united to create *Hotel Angeline*.

I was having lunch recently with a friend who has written novels for a teen audience. I asked her if she wished she had taken part in The Novel: Live! project. She laughed and said that, for her, writing was hard enough when she was sitting alone in her office. She couldn't imagine trying to write a chapter with a camera and an audience focused on her as she was working.

Writing a novel as performance art—who'd a thunk it? But how exciting that it worked!

Only in Seattle.

But wouldn't it be great if other communities of writers took on the idea and made it happen in their hometowns?

Enjoy *Hotel Angeline*. I know that I did.

INTRODUCTION

THIS NOVEL WAS BORN ONE afternoon when Jennie Shortridge and I attended a planning meeting for a month-long arts festival to take place in Seattle. We had cofounded a literary nonprofit called Seattle7Writers, and so had been invited, along with a number of other people from the Seattle literary scene, to brainstorm ideas of fun events for the "literary week" of ArtsCrush.

I have to admit, most of the ideas were a bit bland, and entailed . . . readings. More readings? Seattle, ranked the nation's Most Literate City three out of the past six years (placing second in the off years), has dozens of readings every single evening at our wonderful bookstores, libraries, literary centers, and other venues. More readings? Was that the best we could do?

"Let's come up with something special," I said. "How about a reading marathon for the entire week?"

My suggestion was met with raised eyebrows and mumblings.

"Better yet," I said, "how about a *writing* marathon!"

Well, now, *that* sounded promising.

Jennie and I immediately began tossing about ideas, and soon, the kernel of The Novel: Live! emerged. We would write twelve hours a day for six days. Each writer would take a two-hour stint, requiring thirty-six authors. We would do it in a public place, on a stage, with an audience. We would simulcast it on the Internet, have a chat room function, raise money for our causes. We would bring in school field trips, auction off naming rights, and, hopefully, get it published. But best of all, we would energize readers and writers everywhere for a once-in-a-lifetime event!

People called us crazy. People called us unrealistic. People said, "This is not how books are written!" We said, "Wait until you see how much fun this will be."

The Richard Hugo House immediately joined in and offered their cabaret space, video projector, staff, and cafe facilities. Amazon.com pledged a grant to underwrite the production. Independent bookstores all over the region agreed to help market TN:L! and offer special discounts to attendees. Restaurants donated food. Local luminaries offered to host evening events. An army of volunteers answered our call for support.

And thirty-six authors laughed and scratched their heads and said, "Why the heck not?"

On October 11, 2010, at 10:00 a.m., Jennie Shortridge typed the first word. On October 16, 2010, at 6:00 p.m., Susan Wiggs typed the 73,535th word. In between first and last words, great fun was had: from Mary Guterson's record-setting stint (4,560 words!), to Erik Larson's record-setting cups of coffee (four!), from Kit Bakke's Long Distance Award (Shanghai, China!), to Susan Wiggs's costume changes (four!).

Writers are perfectionists by nature. We immerse ourselves in our manuscripts for months or years until they are just perfect. Being allotted merely two hours, and being put on stage, was liberating for so many of our authors. Part of it was the pressure: as Clyde Ford said, "I've written more in two hours than I usually write in two weeks; I should try this at home!" Part of it was the camaraderie: "No matter what happens, I'm only $\frac{1}{36}$ to blame," Kevin O'Brien said. Part of it was the craziness: "I can't believe I agreed to do this," said Erica Bauermeister.

Keep in mind, this was not a free for all. Before we began, an editorial committee was convened, composed of Elizabeth George, Robert Dugoni, Jennie Shortridge, Maria Semple, and me. We brainstormed a story idea and outlined a plot. We knew if we were going to write a complete book in six days, our authors had to have very clear goals for their writing sessions. So in addition to each author reading the text that had already been written, he or she also met with an "editor" before taking the stage. The editor reviewed the narrative arc and the themes, and made suggestions about where we had to go next. Outside of these specific plot necessities, the writer was free to let his or her imagination roam.

It was never our intention to accomplish in six days what took James Joyce eighteen years to accomplish with *Ulysses*; we knew we were not writing a literary masterpiece. It *was* our intention to build a solid, fun story that was a collaboration between three dozen writers, various editors, and an audience both live and virtual—what we wanted to create was a community. We began our project with so many objectives: make the writing process transparent to students, support our local literary causes, and raise the visibility of dozens of local writers. But in the end, one objective stood above all the rest: create connections between readers and writers, between bookstores and customers, between literary centers and libraries and their communities.

In that sense, TN:L! continues to embody everything we stand for at Seattle7Writers, for we are a collective of Pacific Northwest authors with a twofold mission to raise awareness of Northwest literature and to give back to our communities by doing good works for literacy causes. We began our nonprofit with seven of us. We grew to ten, then to eighteen, then to thirty-two, and at latest count we are an alliance of forty Northwest writers who make it our mission to inspire people with our passion for reading and writing.

After working with our editor, Julie Doughty, and all the folks at Open Road Integrated Media, we are proud to present the completed result of The Novel: Live!—*Hotel Angeline: A Novel in 36 Voices*. It is collaboration in every sense of the word—different styles, different tones, different voices all working to a common end: a single story.

How do thirty-six authors write the same characters in the same story? How does a character such as Alexis take any kind of coherent shape when drawn by thirty-six hands? Do fiction writers create their stories, or do we merely discover them and interpret what we see for others?

I believe that we who write fiction discover our fictional worlds—or at least parts of them—and do our best to bring what we see to others. I also believe that until a reader interprets a writer's vision through his or her own set of ideals, values, experiences, and expectations, a book is just a colorful doorstop, and it is not doing what it was designed to do: provoke thought and imagination.

So I hope that you will take our novel as a provocation on multiple levels. First, as a story, of course. But also, as a provocation to think about what makes a community a great place to live. Conversation and dialogue are central to our society. Give and take, listening, speaking, thinking, hearing, adapting, understanding, evolving. The act of writing a book—which necessitates that that book be read to be valid—is the epitome of conversation, and so stands at the center of our communities.

With that in mind, I encourage you to support your local libraries, bookstores, and literary centers; these are the places that help make our communities vibrant. In fact, by purchasing this book, you are doing just that: 100 percent of the proceeds earned by Seattle7Writers will be re-granted to not-for-profit literary causes throughout the Northwest.

I hope you enjoy the story and adventures of Alexis and her wacky extended family. We certainly enjoyed bringing them to you. And now, turn the page, flick your finger across the screen of your ereader, or stay tuned on your audio book, and have fun getting to know Alexis, Linda, LJ, Habib, and rest of the cast of *Hotel Angeline: A Novel in 36 Voices*.

Garth Stein, Seattle, 2011

CHAPTER 1

JENNIE SHORTRIDGE

HALFWAY UP THE BASEMENT STEPS of the Hotel Angeline, laden with a heavy stack of industrial sheets and towels, Alexis Austin was beginning to think that perhaps she'd taken on too heavy a load.

If I just keep moving, she thought. *I only have six more steps—*

The screech of a crow made her jump, dropping towels and sheets, even though she was getting used to Habib's racket coming from LJ's room. The crazy old man had rescued the crow from the alley behind the residential hotel the month before, finding it there with a broken wing, and all of the residents complained about the noise.

"LJ!" she yelled, and retraced her steps down the stairs, picking up swaths of white fabric, pungent with vestigial bleach. The stairs creaked and sighed as they had been doing for nearly one hundred years. Alexis shivered, imagining that sound in the old days when the hotel was a funeral home, morticians and grieving families treading them every day. Death had always felt close at the Hotel Angeline.

"LJ!" she yelled again, and the bearded man appeared at the top of the stairs, Habib on his shoulder.

"Yo, little sis," he said. "What's up?"

"That crow has to go," Alexis grumbled, but she knew her mother would never have made their dear friend give up his pet.

Her mother, Edith, had been running the Hotel Angeline—named for the daughter of Chief Sealth, Seattle's namesake—far longer than the fourteen years Alexis had been alive. The people who lived here now were the people who had always lived here, society's rabble-rousers and rebels from days gone by. Hippies, some people called them, but her mother said they were all heroes, and that she would always take care of them, no matter what.

Only now there was no way her mother could help. Three months ago she'd gotten sick with what seemed like the triple-whammy flu—coughing, headaches, rashes, exhaustion—and Alexis had been doing more to take care of the hotel and its residents before school and after school, making the afternoon tea in the parlor, collecting the rents. No one had inquired after her mother in quite some time, and Alexis stopped now on the stairs, sheets wound around her arms, towels spilling all the way to the basement, and swallowed back salt, then drew a breath.

"You could at least help me, LJ," she said to the old man. He was like a father to her, truly, and he was far nicer to her than she was to him sometimes. Her own father had gone AWOL before her birth, that's how much he had cared about her. Her mother didn't like to talk about him. Alexis suspected he was dead. LJ would sometimes say, "Your old man was one cool dude," and when she'd press for more, he'd shake his head. "Promised Edith," he'd say, shrugging. For as long as she'd known LJ, he'd always kept his promises.

One thing Alexis knew. Her dad had not been white. While her mother was pale, Alexis's skin was latte creamy in tone. She may have been half black, half Asian, or half Nicaraguan, for all she knew. Not that it mattered on Capitol Hill in Seattle. Everyone was some shade of coffee or another.

LJ hobbled down the steps, Habib flapping his wings and cawing, and helped her pick up the spilled laundry. "I always got your back, little one," he said. "Don't you worry."

After school, Alexis ran in through the back door into the kitchen, slung her book bag onto the table, and started to get out things for tea. Her mother's good silver tea set. Platters for the politically correct Fig Newmans (Paul Newman's alternative to Newtons) and granola bars all the residents preferred over cookies Alexis loved, like Oreos and Chips Ahoy.

She poured her mother's Fino sherry into the leaded-crystal decanter. Edith had taken it medicinally, every day at four p.m. and many of the residents had taken up the habit, some drinking it clear through to bedtime.

Alexis carried the heavy tray into the parlor, where old Ursula had already parked her knitting bag and peg leg—her choice over a more conventional prosthetic after losing her leg to diabetes. In her glory days, Ursula had been a Seafair Pirate, one of the theatrical eccentrics who dresses up in pirate garb and scares children during the city's Seafair festivities each summer. Though long retired, she still preferred to speak in pirate parlance. "Argh," she said to Alexis. "Yer two minutes late."

"Sorry, sorry." Alexis busied herself setting out cups and saucers, teaspoons, sugar, and real cream in a cracked pitcher they'd used to replace the missing silver creamer.

"My pipes arrrgh all broke up in my room," Ursula growled. "I don't suppose yer mother'll call a plumber."

"I can take care of it," Alexis said. "Is water leaking? Do I need to do it now?"

"Yes, there's water leaking! And even though I'm an amphibian of sorts, living my life on the sea"—Alexis rolled her eyes—"I still don't like getting me boot wet." Luckily for the old pirate, her peg leg had a rubber bottom.

The other residents had started to filter in, and everything was set, so Alexis ran up the stairs to 307, Ursula's apartment, and let herself in with the passkey she kept on a chain around her neck. Indeed, there was water all over the floor, and from the smell of it, Alexis suspected this little plumbing thing hadn't just happened that day.

"Jesus H. Christ in a box," she said, trying to trace the water flow to its source. It seemed to be coming from the bathroom, not the kitchen. Alexis sighed, then went in and kneeled in the muck to peer under the sink, pulling aside the skull-and-crossbones flag that obscured the pipes. Sure enough, water spurted from the hot-water supply. She reached up, pinched the bolt, and tried twisting it tighter, but water gushed out more fervently, soaking her plaid miniskirt and the vintage sweater her friend Linda had stolen for her from Value Village.

It was hard not to be pissed off at her mother, whose responsibility all this was, and who never would have let it get this far. She'd had a way of ferreting out trouble before it started, knowing when something was amiss before it got too bad.

"LJ!" Alexis yelled, hoping he would hear her, but knowing him, he'd already started hitting the sherry."Oh, for God's sake, old man!" she yelled, jumping to her feet, charging down the stairs. At the bottom, she stopped and tried to calm herself. Her mother always said "These people are our family, Alexis. Treat them with all the love and respect you do me."

And Alexis had, her entire life. She went now to the parlor, skirt stuck to her thighs, water dribbling down her shins, and saw the old friends gathered together, arguing about the two-state solution, the situation in Latin America, the tanked economy, the battle to legalize marijuana, all of them animated and excited as if they were still twenty years old and in the thick of the fight.

She wrapped her arms around her ribs, feeling lucky to have so many people in her family, in her home. If only she could get rid of the crow.

"Um, LJ?" she said sweetly. "Could you come upstairs and help me with something?"

He looked up from his conversation with Deaf Donald, the former Greenpeace warrior who'd lost his hearing in an action that required deep-sea diving in the waters off Japan.

"Yes, ma'am?" LJ winked at her with watery blue eyes.

"Never mind," she said. "You just have your . . . tea. I can take care of it."

"By the way, my bonny Alexis," Ursula said. "I ain't gonna be able to get you rent again this month. But my ship's coming in, any day now."

Alexis nodded. Her stomach churned. "I'm sure it is," she said, and went back down to the basement to search for a wrench.

Her mother had been the landlady of all time, über-efficient, unbelievably kind even under pressure. She knew how to unstop sinks and fix electrical sockets, how to calm frightened residents when the police came knocking at the door—almost always just collecting money for the Police

Charity Fund. Alexis wasn't sure she'd inherited the landlady gene from her mom, but, well, she had to be one anyway. There was nothing to be done about it.

Down in the damp dark of the basement, she looked among the old embalming tools and makeup brushes, tubing and trays. "A wrench, a wrench," she mumbled. "My life for a stupid wrench."

Squeezing between coffins, she went to look in the long pullout trays, where the newly dead had been stored years ago before being prepped for their final farewells. "Damn," she said. Where had her mother kept the tools?

"Mom!" she yelled, and then it came to her. *In the drawers, sweetheart, beneath the stairs.* Alexis walked over and pulled open the top drawer and . . . sure enough, tools of all kinds: hammers, screwdrivers, Allen wrenches, channel-locks, and yes, a small crescent wrench. Just what she was looking for.

She could do it. She could run this place, pay the bills, and do everything else her mother had always done. Alexis was certain of it.

She breathed in the dampness, filled her lungs with the musty remnants of the long, strange history of the Hotel Angeline. She would make peace with LJ's crow. She would make sure everyone was happy in this place, until nature had its way with each of the residents upon their deaths.

If only she could do the same for her mother.

CHAPTER 2

TERI HEIN

IT WAS PERHAPS SEVEN THOUSAND times a day that Alexis wondered what it would be like to have a slightly different life—you know, one with things more . . . well, routine or normal. Whatever that was—presumably something she would never quite know, not at the rate things were happening these days. There was too much to keep up with to manage normal at the same time. Alexis lived for the little moments she could steal just for herself, between school and duties at the hotel. Moments with Linda, especially.

Alexis glanced at the clock. Linda was late, as Linda always was. Linda, who always assumed forgiveness and Linda, who always got it. She said it was because she was Puerto Rican that she was always late. It was genetic or something. And Alexis said fine, because it meant she got to be with Linda. It was just another thing to get used to. Alexis's mother's code was punctuality and she had drilled it into her daughter. Sometimes it could even mean jumping the gun a bit in certain circumstances. Alexis smiled at the irony of this and fingered the bottom button on her blouse. She bit down on her tongue at the feeling that welled up—the feeling that couldn't be described. It was the thing that reminded her she wasn't a hundred percent in control, and it was the thing that every now and again made her wonder if she really could pull this whole landlady thing off.

Damn that crow, she thought, letting go of the button.

"Yoo-hoo, señorita," she heard someone call through the crack of the front door. Linda was there, having shoved the door open to where the floor had warped. Couldn't her mother have found someone with a planer to shear off the bottom of the door so it could swing open again freely? Now who was going to be doing that? LJ? *Yo lo dudo*, as Linda said, her favorite expression: I doubt it. Quite certainly Donald wasn't going to leap to the cause, and neither would Ursula. And so the door stuck anytime anyone opened it, halfway trapping people in or halfway trapping people out, depending on how you looked at it. Someone of Herculean strength could push it all the way open on the first shove, but Alexis needed a shoulder and a minimum of three pushes.

Linda slid in through the door neatly, knowing better than to put her shoulder to it. Behind her she pulled in the worn backpack she carried everywhere. Alexis's heart skipped a beat.

Like Alexis, Linda was brown, and like Alexis, she didn't know her father, although she knew more about him than Alexis knew about hers. How else could they have landed in Seattle if her father hadn't been chasing his dream of making it big in the music world? He was a big fish/small pond kind of guy who played the trumpet à la King Garcia (or so he thought). And he also thought that in order to get noticed, he should play where they least expected him—not in New Orleans, or in New York but, of all places, Seattle, Washington. Why not? So they left New York behind and ended up living in White Center, south of Seattle. It was a full two years before Linda's father riffed his way right out of town and Linda and her mother were on their own.

So much in common: absent fathers, present mothers, and that stupid governing committee they were both put on at John Marshall Alternative School before it was closed down. Their teacher Audra said the two of them could run that school if left to their own devices. The transition back to the "normal" Garfield High had been tough on both of them.

Maybe that was why they gravitated together—because things just didn't work the same for them as for other kids. Or maybe it was something else.

"Hey," Alexis said with a little wave, trying to act casual.

"Hey, sorry I'm late." Linda brushed her hair away from her eyes. "I hope you weren't waiting."

"No—"

"You want to head downstairs and fold some laundry? There must be some sheets and towels down there that need a bit of attention, yes?"

Linda's "fold some laundry" was really a euphemism for something else. Something else was really the thing that in some ways was the most important thing to her these days, the thing that made everything else OK. When they had come upstairs after that first time, they told her mother they were down there folding laundry. Now they folded one, maybe two sheets or towels—almost as foreplay—and would carry them upstairs, part of the ritual. Some might call the coffin thing sick but they called it just fine. And maybe even good clean fun.

But they wouldn't be going to the basement. That was certain. In spite of how much fun they'd had in the coffins that one time—OK, more than one time—today was not the day for anyone to go down there. Especially not to do *that*.

"We can't," Alexis said, trying to think of an excuse. "My mom's down there."

"No problem." Linda shrugged. "She won't be down there all day. We can just sit here and wait." She slumped down on the first step of the staircase and unzipped her backpack, extracting a pack of Marlboros.

"Hey!" Alexis said, almost glad for the distraction. "You can't smoke in here. You shouldn't even smoke anyway. It's disgusting. Nobody will kiss you, you know."

"Meaning you?" Linda took a smoke from the pack, tapped it on the hard case, stuck it between her lips. It bobbed there, unlit, as she spoke. "You saying you don't want to kiss me anymore, Alexis? Is that what this is all about? Because, you know, other people think I'm fine." She stood, shouldered her pack.

"No," Alexis said, "that's not what I'm saying, but—"

"But nothing, girlfriend. You don't want me around. I can take a hint." When she walked out, she left the door ajar.

Alexis hated it when she and Linda were fighting.

"Linda," Alexis called after her as she slung on her bag. "Wait up! Maybe we can find some sheets that need folding somewhere else!" She ran out the door and down the steps, then back up to slam the door closed. It took three hard pulls before the latch clicked.

Alexis turned to run after Linda, but there the girl stood at the bottom of the stoop, cigarette now sticking out from behind her ear.

CHAPTER 3

WILLIAM DIETRICH

LJ TOLD ONLY HIS CLOSEST friends that his real name was Lynn, because Lynn didn't have the manly ring of Dude or Duke or Sly or Rock or some other more heroic moniker that fit his admittedly scrambled image of himself. He *did* tell almost anyone who would listen that he'd fought through Tet in 'Nam, had partied at Woodstock, had been a bellhop at the Edgewater when the Beatles blew through Seattle, and had caught Cobain down in Aberdeen before anyone had ever heard who that fucked-up genius was. Of course the truth was that LJ had served his year at a supply depot in Da Nang and had never made it to a rock festival farther east than Sky River. He didn't remember a whole lot of the '60s besides that, but he had come of age protesting the Man, and now the Man had actually called, right here at the Hotel Angeline, and maybe it was finally all coming down.

So he had to warn Alexis.

LJ looked very much like what he was—a badly aged hippie. That glorious lion's mane of hair that had crowned him in his 1969 protest days, that peacock's tail of wiry dark plumage, had turned whitish-gray and migrated southward. His pate was bald, the surviving fringe hung to his shoulders, and too many follicles had changed address to his eyebrows and ears and nostrils. The wiry rocker's body that had once turned women wild—well, a couple chicks anyway—had long-since sagged to middle-age paunch. His complexion was that of a well-fed Keith Richards, and he smoked grass now to ease his complaining joints. But the old fire hadn't dimmed, and neither had his conviction that reality was out to get him. It was all a massive conspiracy—Bin Laden, Wall Street, Sarah Palin, Hollywood, and the Manhattan publishing industry that had rejected every manifesto he had ever written—and so LJ was like the Thin Blue Line, or the Catcher in the Rye, his purpose to look after overly mature innocents like Alexis and guide her political beliefs toward the orthodoxy of his hometown heroes of 1970: the Seattle Liberation Front, or as locals had called them, the Seattle 7. The fact that LJ's own life had gone nowhere didn't deter him from the belief he should direct others. Besides, he liked the girl.

So he caught her outside the old hotel with her lesbo-leaning girl-friend Linda and told her portentously and mysteriously to follow him upstairs. "Girl, there is something serious I've got to tell you. We've had a phone call."

Alexis hesitated. He knew she already felt burdened, caring for a bunch of crazy people.

There was Ursula the Seafair pirate, who occasionally sneaked onto Lake Union pleasure boats to loot pieces of self-esteem. She'd give a yacht club pennant or jacket crest or maybe one fine Italian shoe to street people and explain that she was spreading self-satisfaction to the dissatisfied.

There was Deaf Donald, who'd screwed up his hearing saving the world for Greenpeace and drove everyone nuts by trying to hold conver-sations when he couldn't hear anything anyone said in return. He tended to follow in Ursula's shadow, perhaps attracted by the one sound he could hear—the loud rap her peg leg made on the wooden floors.

There was Otto Kenzler, who claimed he was 110 years old and a former OSS agent who'd come within inches of killing Hitler, winning World War II all by himself, even though Edith said he was only eighty-nine, max.

There was Roberta the snake lady, who kept a python under her bed no one was supposed to know about but who explained, just in case, that snakes were lazy if you kept them fed.

LJ felt comfortable in the Angeline because, by these standards, he was a model of sanity, and the only father figure that Alexis really had.

"I'm kinda busy, LJ," Alexis said. She was wiggly with that adolescent impatience.

"*Really* busy," said Linda.

"I'm serious, Alex, we got a *phone* call," LJ said. He could almost see the hormones jumping inside the two teens like heated popcorn, but none of that mattered if his interpretation of this new threat was correct. "I think it's about your mom and the future."

That stopped her. LJ was the one other person who knew what was really going on in the basement.

"What about Mom?"

"I think we have to find some papers she must have hidden in her room."

"I could help," Linda said. She was curious. Nosy, in LJ's view. He shook his head as a signal to Alexis. Secret, private stuff.

The fourteen-year-old sighed. "We'll fold laundry later," she promised her friend. "*Hasta luego,* right?"

The Puerto Rican shrugged. "Whatever, señorita. Go with old baldy there." And she skipped away.

Alexis and LJ started up the hotel staircase. "Is this really important?" she asked.

"I think it's finally going down. I been looking for you since that phone call."

"*What* phone call?"

"I'll tell you upstairs. Don't want to yell fire, you know?"

Alexis and her mother lived on the top floor of the Angeline, up three flights of dim and creaky stairs, and as far from the caskets as you could get. Alexis had a small bedroom with a single bed, cracked window, and kid stuff that was made more precious by its rarity: one soccer trophy that every kid on the team had gotten, stuffed animals worn bare because she rarely got new ones, pop posters, a pink bedspread, and a shelf of books that ranged from fairy tales to *Rules for Radicals,* a gift from LJ she'd never read.

There was nothing to remind her of her absent father.

Her mother lived in the adjacent room, which had a kitchenette and a sofa bed. An old business desk took up more than its share of space and was crammed with ledgers, legal papers, and receipts that Alexis was now trying to make sense of.

There were some art posters and a vase of plastic flowers, but not much that would make *Architectural Digest,* or would even establish femininity. LJ had been up there occasionally and felt it was a curiously empty nest; Edith had put all her home energies into the hotel as a whole, making room for everybody but her own soul. He did see one of the perfumes he sold at Pike Place Market on the bureau. He named them things like "Aquarius" or "Penny Lane," and the teens who bought them thought they were quaint.

"So what's the big emergency?" Alexis asked. She was always in a hurry, the way all fourteen-year-olds hurry, but Alexis was more like fourteen going on thirty-eight because of the deal in the basement. Tougher than she should be because of responsibility—wiry, but tomboy pretty, too. Dark curly hair, full mouth, dark eyes with a smoke to them that could make her look older than she really was. It was no mystery why the older Linda hung around.

"OK, this is how it went down," LJ began. His speech patterns had begun to lock up in his brain when he got too heavily into the chemicals business. "The phone rang and rang, and nobody picked it up, and after a while I thought, 'It's up to you, man.'"

"To answer the phone?"

"So I picked it up, and said hello, and there was this silence, and then this formal woman who says she's working for your uncle says she has a message for your mom."

"My uncle?"

LJ knew that would surprise her. Edith had always told him how Uncle Burr was well off and remote and disapproving. Getting a call from him was as unlikely as a call from the pope.

"So I said your mom was indisposed, and could I take a message. And she says, 'Who are you?' and I said I'm the executive assistant, and she asked if I am competent to convey a message, like I'm a moron or something, and I said I was conveying and messaging before she was born."

"What was the message, LJ?" Alexis was looking impatient.

"Oh yeah." He drew himself up. "'This is to confirm our dinner tomorrow night at the Sorrento Hotel to go over the details in the papers I sent about the hearing next week.'" He nodded, proud of his memory. "You know that fancy hotel? I went there once and I couldn't even afford the free pretzels."

Her mom was to meet her uncle? In the Sorrento? That was weird.

"What papers?" Alexis asked. "What hearing?"

"That's what I would have asked. Except I'd already pretended I was an executive assistant, and I didn't want to admit to the bitch on the other end of the line that I had no idea what she was talking about. So we need to find them. Because you know as well as I do what must be going down here, Alex."

"What?"

"Your mom got sick, and your uncle smells blood. He wants the hotel. He wants to shut it down and get rid of us all, and head off the revolution."

"*What?*"

"Maybe. I'm just trying to think this through. Why else do we suddenly hear from him? This is valuable real estate, and making us homeless would make him rich."

The girl sat on her mother's couch, looking sick and stunned. She was a chameleon, going from young girl to harried woman and back again in an instant, trying to take responsibility when most kids were just trying to grow up. LJ wanted to protect her, and figured the first way to do that was to warn her, but he felt bad about the way his message had made Alexis look. Talking about legal papers and hearings was like showing a gun. It scared him, and it scared her.

He thought again about the secret in the basement.

"We'd better look through her desk," he suggested. "I don't think your mom would throw papers like that away."

"If they were from Uncle Burr she might," Alexis said. Not only did she not have a father, she didn't have an extended family to help. Unless you called LJ and Ursula and Roberta and Otto and all the rest of them her family. Which reminded her. It was almost time for afternoon tea, and she needed to get to that as well. "But I guess we'd better look."

So they prowled through the desk. As before, much of it seemed as incomprehensible as Mayan code to both of them—a bunch of numbers and accounts that gave no clue as to whether the Hotel Angeline was solvent or bankrupt. Chewed pencils, stubby erasers, a stapler with no staples. Alexis looked like she was ready to weep in frustration. "I don't know what to do," she said.

"We need to hang together like we did in the sixties," LJ counseled. "We gotta have our conspiracy that's better than *their* conspiracy. We got to"—he put a hand on her shoulder—"serve afternoon tea and get the Hotel Angeline brain trust to outfigure the figurers."

CHAPTER 4

KATHLEEN ALCALÁ

WHAT IS THIS? THE EMPRESS HOTEL? Alexis thought as she went to the kitchen to prepare afternoon tea. But her mother had started a tradition, and she was bound and determined to follow through.

Alexis began pulling cups and saucers out of the cupboards. She rummaged through the pantry for a fresh bottle of sherry. They seemed to go through a lot of sherry.

As she lined up the cups on the counter, Linda wandered back in.

"What was that all about?" she asked.

"Oh, LJ wanted to look for some papers in my mom's room."

"Why can't your mom look for the papers?"

"She's really sick. I told you."

"Why don't you take her to the hospital?"

"She doesn't believe in regular doctors." Alexis was improvising now. "A special sort of doctor, skilled in the Caribbean ways, will be stopping by later."

"Hmmm." Alexis could tell that Linda did not believe her. "That's the first I've heard she was interested in Santería."

"She gets interested in lots of things. Right now it's a spiritual thing."

Just then a goldfish fell into one of the teacups. It was accompanied by quantities of water.

"Hell. Not again."

It was not from Ursula's room. Alexis bounded up the stairs, fish in hand, to the room with the best exposure, which happened to be directly above the kitchen. She knocked on the door of #209.

"Kenji? Mr. Kenji?"

The door opened onto a scene out of a tropical forest. Everywhere she looked were palm trees in pots, *schefflera*, and avocado starts in paper cups. She waded through all this to the bathroom, where she found Mr. Kenji painting.

The younger brother of a famous Seattle artist, Mr. Kenji was also a vet of some war older than the Iraq war. He was the director and the only employee of the Wabi Sabi Correspondence School of Watercolor. He sat at a rickety wooden easel propped in the doorway to his bathroom, painting the koi he kept in his bathtub.

"Mr. Kenji, it's time for tea," said Alexis, returning the goldfish to the tub.

"Just finished!" he said, putting a flourish on his damp painting.

"That's amazing!" cried Alexis, who took the painting and tacked it up with the hundreds and hundreds of others that lined the walls of the apartment.

She and Mr. Kenji made their way downstairs, where Linda had started the tea. They were out of cookies, so Alexis passed around a box of Ritz crackers as the residents began to gather.

"Late again!" said Ursula.

For a pirate, thought Alexis, she was awfully conscious about time.

Mr. Kenji took his place next to Otto on the couch, while Ursula took a chair that was easier to get in and out of with a wooden leg.

Close to the now-defunct fireplace there was a chair that no one ever sat in. It had been the seat occupied by David the poet, who had always had his head in the clouds and his hands full of drafts. He'd moved out ten years earlier, and it was rumored that he'd won a Pulitzer Prize.

LJ came into the parlor. He had smoothed his fringe back into a ponytail. Alexis recognized this as his "formal" look. LJ cleared his throat. Only Donald noticed.

"Ladies and gentlemen," LJ began. Someone handed him the Ritz crackers.

"Ladies and—"

"Oh come on, matey!" said Ursula. "Speak your mind and be done with it!"

LJ really did like a bit of ceremony once in a while.

"Oh, all right. I—I mean, we—need your help. You see, I—I mean, we—are in a situation, a pickle if you will, with the Man, the Law, the Other Side, if you know what I mean—"

"Oh, stop," Alexis said. She stepped up in front of LJ. "What he is trying to say is, we might lose the Angeline."

"What?" said Donald, cupping his ear.

Alexis soldiered on. "My mom received a call and has to go to a meeting tomorrow. But since she's sick, I'm going." LJ gave her a look. "Yes, I'm going to meet with Uncle Burr about signing some papers."

There were noises of protest.

"They can't do that," said Mr. Kenji. "This is our home!"

"Argh!" Ursula said. "I've lived here for a dog's age, and longer!"

"Well, we're not absolutely sure that's what will happen, but if you know other people who know about the history of this house, or want to share any of your stories with me that will help us keep this history and this family together, now is the time to call on them, call them up, muster our forces." Alexis knew better than to ask if they knew anyone rich, or a good estate lawyer—if the residents here knew anyone like that, they would have called in their favors long ago.

Just then Roberta came in, the python hanging lazily around her neck. "I should have known something sinister was going on," she said. "Pluto here woke up for no reason at all. I could tell he was agitated."

"I've got a story," said Otto. "A long time ago, there was a poetry contest in this very room, where my good friend David the poet and Theodore Roethke and Richard Hugo and . . . I forget who else stayed up all night reciting verse to each other. It was epic!"

"Good, good," Alexis said. "Who else?"

Her friend Mia came in the front door. Mia was a few years older and done with school. She was a violinist with a band that practiced in the Panama Hotel, where she stayed in exchange for cleaning the other rooms. Mia was full of big dreams, and when you were with her, you always felt like they were possible.

She was tall, with wild hair, and dressed in vintage clothes that on anyone else would have looked terrible. On Mia, they looked divine.

Mia caught the anxious looks on everyone's faces. "What's wrong?" she asked, looking around the room. "Who died?"

Alexis burst into tears.

"Oh, honey," said Mia. "I didn't mean to upset you." She gathered Alexis into her arms for a hug.

"It's just that, my mom has been really sick, and now LJ says that my uncle Burr called and there are some papers to sign and the ceiling leaks over the kitchen and I tried to fix Ursula's sink but it still leaks and we're out of cookies."

Linda walked up to them. "But we've got it under control."

Just then, the first riff of "In-A-Gadda-Da-Vida" came blasting through the room. LJ looked guilty. "I'll just step outside and take this," he said, taking out his cell phone.

Alexis rolled her eyes—LJ was always tinkering with a phone when she needed him to pay attention.

"How much would it take to buy this place outright?" asked Alexis.

"Why?" Mia said. "Is it for sale?"

"It might be. Or my uncle might be thinking about it. I don't know."

"Maybe a million dollars?" Mia ventured.

Alexis's heart sank. "Where would we ever get a million dollars?"

For the first time, Ursula looked interested in the conversation. "There's ways, matey, and there's ways."

"I mean, legally."

"How about a bake sale?" Roberta offered.

"How many cookies do you need to bake to make a million dollars?" Alexis asked. They all looked at each other, unsure whether she really expected them to answer.

"How about a concert?" Mia asked. "I don't think you can get more than fifty people in here, but maybe we could find a bigger venue."

"And who would pull that together?" asked Linda.

"Now, wait a minute," Alexis said. "We need every idea we can muster to get us out of this situation."

Pluto curled thoughtfully around Roberta's body, a Möbius strip of meditation, as the group concentrated all of its powers on the problem at hand.

Two more residents came trickling in. They were twins, Kevin and Kato Borealis, and for the life of her, Alexis had never been able to tell them apart. Each wore a beret. Each wore an identical pin on one shoulder, a different one every day. Each completed the sentences of the other.

"We were outside—"

"Smoking."

"But we heard what you said—"

"And we have been thinking."

"Because two heads—"

"Are better than one."

The twins did not talk all that much, so when they did, everyone paid attention.

"If there were a concert—"

"We could publicize it ahead of time."

"We could get our story out into the papers, and covered—"

"By radio and television."

"Hmmmph!" Linda said, crossing her arms in front of her.

What was her problem? Alexis wondered.

Mia spoke up again. "I've got the band, if you've got the stories."

"Aye, we've got stories, matey!" Ursula said.

"We only lack one thing," Mia said.

"What?" Alexis asked. A teacup? A wrench? Clean laundry? Her head was spinning.

"A violin."

Again, the residents of the Hotel Angeline looked at one another.

"A violet?" asked Donald.

"A violin!" yelled Ursula. Everyone could hear Ursula. She was used to yelling over the hydroplanes at Seafair.

"What happened to yours?" Alexis asked Mia.

"Had to hock it," Mia said, shrugging.

"I've got one," Mr. Kenji said. He had been quietly doodling in the corner.

"You do?" Alexis asked. All she could imagine was a violin with a plant sprouting out of it. She could not imagine that a musical instrument could survive in that environment.

"I used to be quite good," he added. "Before . . . well, before." Mr. Kenji bowed his head. "Then I just could not make music anymore."

"In that case, I will look for a venue that will accommodate more people," Mia said. She tossed back her hair and grinned.

"I'll go get it," Kenji said, and made his way back up the stairs.

"That was—," Kevin or Kato said.

"A good idea," the other one said.

"My idea."

"No, mine."

"No—"

"It was everyone's idea," interrupted Alexis. "Without all of you, I don't know what I would do." She started to get a little teary.

"Can it," said Ursula. "You'll have plenty of time to behave like a landlubber after we ride out this storm."

Otto stood up suddenly. "I will send postcards," he announced.

To whom, about what, no one else knew. But Otto loved to send post-cards. He even played chess by mail, with people in obscure countries who spoke obscure languages, except for the language of chess.

Tea was over. They began to gather up the cups and saucers, saving the Ritz cracker crumbs for Habib. Alexis noticed that the sherry bottle was empty again. Mia and Ursula stepped outside for a smoke.

Linda sidled up to her. "I don't trust Mia," she said. "I'm just not sure that she is, you know, someone you can depend on."

Mr. Kenji appeared with a violin case. He held it lovingly before giving it to Alexis.

"I should tell you something about this," he said. "It was a gift. From your father."

"My—my father?" Alexis asked. She must have misheard him. There was no scrap of anything about her father in the hotel, or in any of her mother's belongings that she had ever seen. She had never even seen a photo of him.

"Yes. He seemed to have a feeling that—that things would be lost. So he gave it to me for safekeeping. In case of an emergency. And this seems to be that emergency."

Alexis put her arms around Mr. Kenji. Now she was going to go ahead and cry. "Oh, Mr. Kenji. You are so sweet!"

All this was interrupted by the furious cawing of a crow. LJ and Habib were back. "I've got work to do at the perfume factory," said LJ, "so I'm going now."

"Oh, LJ, we've got a plan," Alexis said. "These are the bravest people I have ever met in my life."

"What's the plan?" he asked. "Now that you think you can meet with your uncle by yourself—"

"I *will* meet Uncle Burr by myself! You know he can't stand you." She was determined to not let LJ bring her down. "I'm going to do it for Mom."

"Edith trusts me," he said. "She knows that I have always had your best interests in mind."

Alexis wilted a bit. "I know you have. I trust you. I've just got to do this. And the crew here has decided to put on a concert. Mia is going to organize it."

Alexis was blue-skying now. "We're going to rent the Paramount Theatre and sell tickets, and Mia's band is going to play, and the residents of the Angeline are going to tell stories. Just like *A Prairie Home Companion*. Or *The Vinyl Cafe*. Mr. Kenji even volunteered a violin that he had been keeping for me."

"For you?"

"From my dad. Oh, LJ—he actually left me something! A violin!"

LJ stopped moving. Even Habib fell silent. "A what?"

"A violin. It's mine. Mr. Kenji has kept it all this time."

LJ began to tremble. He started walking around in circles, Habib flying a bit to keep up with his shoulder. "A violin."

LJ whirled around and focused on Alexis. "Do you know how long I have been looking for that thing?"

"What? What are you talking about?"

LJ tried to get control of himself. "It's just . . . it's not that important. It was just something—actually, do you think I could borrow it, just for a little while? I need it for a project I'm working on."

Habib let out one of those long crackly noises that crows make.

"Um, sure," Alexis said reluctantly. "Well, anyway, it's just the right time for it to surface—just in time to help save the hotel. Mom will be so proud of me."

"Well, I think I might just go out and see to a couple of things," LJ said. "Thanks for the tea."

"But you didn't have any," Alexis pointed out. "You were outside."

"Yeah, but it's the thought that counts." LJ and Habib left. In a big hurry, it seemed to Alexis.

Linda helped her put everything away in the cupboards. "Well, that was exciting," she said.

"Sometimes I feel like the Mad Hatter, caught in a perpetual mad tea party."

"And LJ is the Caterpillar," added Linda. They both giggled.

"Thanks for the help," Alexis said. "I'm going to go talk with my mom right now, see if she is OK."

"Can I help with anything?"

"No, I've got it."

"Well, just let me know when I can help. You know how to reach me." Linda hesitated. "Babe, I'm sorry to burst your bubble, but you do realize that this building is worth more than a million dollars, don't you? And that they won't rent you the Paramount Theatre? And that if they did, we'd never get enough people to come to even pay the rent. Don't you?"

Alexis couldn't think of anything to say to that. She hung her head.

"I'm sorry, Alexis."

"Thanks, Linda."

"I'll call tomorrow." Linda leaned over and gave Alexis a smooch, smoothing her curly hair out of her eyes.

Alexis leaned into Linda's hand but couldn't meet her eyes. It would be so great if they could have a plan and have it work for once. Wouldn't it?

CHAPTER 5

MARIA DAHVANA HEADLEY

WATER DRIPPED ON ALEXIS'S HEAD as she made her way toward the stairs that led to the basement, trying to look like someone who actually planned to do laundry.

She opened the door, called a happy good-bye to the residents, and closed it quickly behind her, locking it with the old-fashioned key she kept on a chain around her neck.

What kind of basement locked from the inside? Alexis had always wondered, thinking about ghouls rising in the mortuary supplies below, but today she was grateful for the quirk.

She made her way down the stairs, automatically skipping the steps that creaked.

"Edith?" she called.

No answer, but somehow it made Alexis feel better to say her mother's name. She sat in the little chair she'd hauled down days before—a vanity stool from the '30s. The chair, a find from Deluxe Junk in Fremont, made her feel better too. Her mother had loved it.

Alexis couldn't believe that no one had figured it out.

This was a house filled with family of a certain kind, but it was a family that did not pay much attention. Sometimes, Alexis felt like the oldest person in the place. She flattened her hand on the coffin, feeling the smooth polish of the wood. It had not seemed like a good idea to place Edith inside one of the fancier coffins, although that had been Alexis's first impulse, so they'd chosen a plain coffin of good quality.

She wanted to cry, just thinking about it. Dusty and unadorned. Her mother would have hated it.

"I wish you'd told me about the problems with the hotel," Alexis said.

"Don't worry," an imaginary Edith replied, her imagined voice as soft and melodic as it had been in life.

"Everyone here is going to be out on the street if I don't worry."

Alexis pictured her mother, her fake pearls around her neck, the way she'd count them with her fingers when something serious was being discussed.

"You're too young to worry about this," said the imaginary Edith, but she'd been saying that for years. She'd said it the night she died, and Alexis had believed her.

Now it seemed so stupid—all of it. The weeks of illness that had led up to this point, Edith's refusal to go to a doctor. It hadn't occurred to Alexis to force her. It *had* occurred to LJ, but his medicine took the form of pot, and though Edith was not opposed to marijuana, she hadn't wanted any this time. Alexis had watched LJ leave Edith's room, shaking his head.

"Your mother is an exceedingly stubborn woman," he'd said, and that was obviously true.

Mercury poisoning.

Alexis smacked her hand on the coffin, and tried not to swear. Edith would hate it, but Edith was dead. Still.

A broken thermometer months ago had not seemed like a big deal. Alexis had been wandering through Capitol Hill, doing her usual rounds, and when she got home, Edith was in the midst of vacuuming up the mercury.

"The Internet is full of people who are smarter than you," Alexis told her mother now. "Would have been nice if you could have fucking consulted them."

"What did you say?" the imaginary Edith replied. "Did I hear the F-word?"

"No," said Alexis. "You didn't hear anything."

"Maybe I'm dead, but I'm listening to everything you say." Edith's voice sounded peevish. Most mothers washed mouths out with soap. Edith washed a mouth out with bourbon and vinegar, convinced that it would get the taste for alcohol out of Alexis's system, along with the taste for swearing. Neither thing was true.

Alexis now knew that you were not supposed to vacuum up mercury. You were not really supposed to do anything with mercury other than look at it from far, far away while wearing a face mask. But Edith, who took her own temperature typically seven or eight times a day, her sole hypochondriacal indulgence, had broken the thermometer while shaking it down.

She'd managed to inhale the mercury, Alexis now suspected. The last three months of Edith's illness had been increasingly worrying, and in the last week of her life, her memory had grown so spotty that she was unable to remember Alexis's name.

"We're going to save the hotel," Alexis said now. "I wish you hadn't died, but you did. You wish I didn't swear, but I do."

"There are things you don't know about me," Edith informed her. Alexis looked around in frustration. This was true.

"Maybe you'd like to tell me who my dad is? Any thoughts on that, Mom?"

Edith had long claimed that Alexis did not need to know her father's identity, but who had given that violin to Mr. Kenji? And why? The violin existed. Normally things that appeared out of Mr. Kenji's room were less than substantial. He'd been known to make rabbits appear out of hats, twist them into complicated knots, and then turn them into scarves again.

"Was my father a violin player?"

"How should I know?" the imaginary Edith responded. "This coffin could be lined in a much better shade of silk for my coloring."

"Did my father live here? Did he leave his violin when he left?"

"I have no answers," said the imaginary Edith, sounding suspiciously like Mr. Kenji's performance persona.

Alexis looked around the room. She thought about the day her mother had died. There'd been a note outside Edith's door.

"Don't come in, honey. Get Lynn, and have him come see me."

Alexis felt doomed the moment she read it, but instructions were instructions, and bourbon and vinegar awaited a daughter who disobeyed.

It took a moment for her to figure out who Lynn was, but once she had, Alexis located LJ and followed him upstairs. Did they really think she'd stay outside? This was her mother. She'd followed him all the way into the room, stopping only when LJ started to cry.

It was shocking. Normally, if LJ cried it would only be because he'd managed somehow to lose his copy of Tom Robbins's *Even Cowgirls Get the Blues*.

Alexis knew exactly how he'd lost his copy of said novel: to Alexis. She'd heard that *Cowgirls* was the most stolen item in the Seattle Public Library system, and that it had to be kept behind the counter like cigarettes. No wonder.

This time, though, LJ's tears had been genuine. Alexis had never seen him so upset, and then she'd turned the corner, and there.

Was.

Edith.

In her bed, her hair and makeup done more beautifully than she'd ever done it in life.

LJ knelt beside the bed and held Edith in his arms while Alexis stood, paralyzed. She knew it was bad, of course. Her mother had been very sick. But she had not imagined this could happen. How could Edith die? She ran everything, all the time.

LJ turned to Alexis and asked her, "What are we going to do?"

She was appalled.

"Why did he ask *me*?" Alexis asked her imaginary mother now.

"You're the grown-up now," Edith said, and in Alexis's mind, she smiled. Her mother had the kind of smile that could persuade a person to do anything.

"Fuck," said Alexis, but under her breath so that no one, dead or alive, could hear her swearing.

"We'll put her in the basement," Alexis had told LJ, after she'd gained control of her voice. Her words echoed inside her own head, sounding foreign. She acted without giving herself time to grieve. She couldn't think about the fact that her mother was gone. There was no time. She knew what would happen if the police found out, if *anyone* found out that her mother was dead. She'd be screwed. Foster care, or something like it. Homeless. They'd lose the Angeline.

No one could know.

Alexis was thinking fast when she told LJ to send everyone out of the house. Gas leak, she said. It would not be surprising. Such things happened in the Hotel Angeline about once a week. Alexis sometimes felt amazed that the whole place, with its crow, with its pirate, with its goldfish falling from the ceiling, hadn't blown up yet.

She and LJ bundled Edith—Alexis couldn't think about her as her mom, not at that moment—into her favorite silk nightgown, and then into her blankets. LJ carried her down multiple flights of stairs, all the way to the basement.

"Like a bride," he said.

"You have it backwards," Alexis said. "You're carrying her out from the threshold, not in."

"The kid's got it right for once," said LJ, and then he wouldn't speak to Alexis any further on the subject.

She waited at the bottom of the stairs, dancing from foot to foot. In truth, LJ had trouble navigating the steep staircase, as he didn't understand which treads were unreliable. Alexis herself had spent plenty of time lurking in the basement. Some of the makeup used on corpses was immensely flattering on teenage girls who wanted to make strangers worried and friends impressed.

LJ lurched. Edith's blankets were snagging on the banister, and her foot, pale and pedicured, was revealed.

There was a sound behind the upper door, which was only half shut. Alexis had failed to lock it for this, the most important use of a lock in the door's history.

The door creaked open.

"Who is it?" LJ managed. He already had a couple of small time offenses in Seattle.

Was it illegal to carry someone down a set of stairs? Of course not. The parts of Alexis that were not filled with grief filled with righteous indignation.

"This is a business establishment," she shouted up the stairs. "And we're closed!"

She clenched her fist, looking at her mother's silver toenails. There was another creak which resolved into a *crawk*, and then the crow flew down, making what was already a morbid scene worse.

Now and forever, Alexis would be forced to think of Habib when she thought of Edith. She would also think of how Habib had flown down to peck at her mother's shining silver toes.

"Get away!" she'd screamed, and the crow flapped his way up to the ceiling, looking down on the room with a baleful glare.

LJ placed Edith gently in the coffin, when they'd finally chosen the one they would use.

"Are you sure we should do this?" LJ asked again, clearly uncertain of anything. He looked collapsed. Even his hair seemed shriveled. "There might be other options. We might find some of her family, look through her papers . . ." His voice trailed off.

The imaginary Edith interrupted her daughter's thoughts. "You have no other family," she informed Alexis.

"I know," Alexis said. She could easily recite the list of family members, times and dates of death, even which mortuary had laid them out. Growing up in a house like the Hotel Angeline did that to a person.

"No other family," the imaginary Edith repeated, and although Alexis had begun to question her on this point, she did not feel like arguing with her mother, dead or alive.

"There are no other options," Alexis had informed LJ, and now part of her regretted it. She'd expected him to turn her down, expected him to solve the problem somehow, but he hadn't.

"I'm going to run this hotel, and you're going to help me," Alexis had said, and he'd believed her.

For a moment, she thought wistfully about what it might be like to go into foster care. Someone might take care of her. She would not need to fix staircases and find wrenches, nor would she need to fish goldfish from out of the stairwells. Most important, she would not need to figure out where the money to keep the hotel operational was going to come from.

"There's going to be a concert," she tried again. "Mia's going to play the violin. We're going to make a million dollars to keep the Angeline."

Somehow, of all the stories of the hotel her mother had told her, one stuck in her head: the time the twins, Kato and Kevin, had fought and decided to separate from each other, only to find that without Kato, Kevin could only talk in half sentences, and without Kevin, Kato could only walk backward.

She thought of how her mother had always said—

And the imaginary Edith said it again: "The Hotel Angeline is your family, and you have to take care of your family."

Alexis thought about Linda for a moment. If Edith were truly here, what would she think about that? Would Linda become part of the Angeline family?

It was horribly hard not to tell Linda about Edith's death. It was hard to do anything without telling *someone* about Edith. Alexis felt herself starting to cry, but she swallowed her tears.

"We're going to save the hotel," she said again, but this time she believed herself.

"I never doubted you for a moment," said the imaginary Edith. "Except for the moment when the bird got to my pedicure."

Alexis sighed. She was doing the best she could, and it was never quite good enough for her mother. She wished she had a father. It seemed like a father might be more understanding of imperfections.

She thought about what might truly startle Edith, but nothing startled Edith—not crow droppings, not twins wandering forlorn and talkative through the hallways, their brooches shining like tinfoil diamonds.

She thought about Linda, and how *she*, at least, loved Alexis's imperfections.

"Everyone's a disaster, chica," Linda had said. "Everyone's crazy. It's no big deal."

This while Alexis was examining the enormous zit that had overtaken her nose—a blinding beacon of disappointment, right in the middle of her face.

"I think you're beautiful," Linda had told her. "That zit just improves your bone structure."

Then she'd cackled her distinctive laugh and gone on with drawing a portrait of Alexis. All this was back in the glory days before Edith's death.

Edith would not have approved of it. How could she? Her daughter, fooling around secretly with a girlfriend? There had been sleepovers. Edith believed that girls should stay virgins.

"For how long?" Alexis had asked her.

"As long as you can stand it," Edith had said. "And then another three years."

"How long is that?"

"Twenty-seven, twenty-eight, I don't know, and please, if you love me, don't lose your virginity to any of the tenants."

"I have something to tell you, Mom," Alexis said now. Her skin prickled with nervousness.

"Tell me you have everything under control," said the imaginary Edith. "Tell me there are no leaks."

"No leaks," Alexis said. "I fixed them."

"Illegal pets? Extra pirates? Twins have a new sibling?" asked the imaginary Edith, and Alexis pictured her with the fake pearl necklace between her fingers. There was no help for it.

"I'm gay, actually," she said. "I'm sorry I didn't tell you while you were alive."

Alexis pictured her mother's necklace breaking and plastic pearls being flung all over the basement, scattering into the dark corners and rolling like marbles over the tiled floor. Still, she felt better.

"That's not so bad," said the imaginary Edith.

"Really," said Alexis.

"I thought you were going to say that you'd let Habib into my jewelry box," the imaginary Edith said. "I love you, but don't let the bird eat my pearls."

"It's Linda," Alexis said.

She waited for a response, but realized that she didn't know what her mother might say to that news.

She was a girl talking to a dead woman, a girl in charge of a hotel, a girl who needed to make a million dollars. A girl with a girlfriend who was waiting somewhere outside, trusting Alexis to deal with her life.

Alexis stood up from the coffin and made her way up the stairs with a skip over the creaky ones, with a leap over the broken one.

"Bye, Mom," she whispered over her shoulder, and then she unlocked the door and left the basement. She had things to do, and though she had spent the previous hour living in the past, the future was waiting for her.

Habib landed on her shoulder as she walked into the upper part of the house.

The bird nibbled her ear, and she imagined him telling her that all of this was going to be fine.

CHAPTER 6

STACEY LEVINE

ALEXIS STOOD LEANING ON THE stone stairs outside Garfield High School. She felt the breeze playing with her hair. The past few days had brought tension enough to swirl her head and block out teachers' voices—those daily commandants who were after her about her recent absences. High school seemed the proverbial dream for some giddy teens, yet they were in another world; Alexis simply was not one of those. Swarms of students passed by. As the tide lessened, a confused-looking admin woman from the school's front office appeared outside with a clipboard, a beeping radio device on her belt. Alexis leaned down such that her hair fell across her face. She was vaguely aware of guilty feelings about letting her academic work slip. However, the admin woman was not looking for Alexis; glancing at her radio, she disappeared.

Alexis waited for Linda, who had texted her as soon as Alexis had switched on her phone after the final bell. HEY U CUTIE. MEET ME SOUTH DOOR, the text had read.

Linda appeared. "What's with you? You look like you've seen a ghost," she said, smiling.

"Naw," said Alexis. "But I've got to get back home. Want to walk?"

"I was thinking something else," Linda said, toying with her phone, from which dangled at least three tiny bright charms on chains. She dropped the thing, which was frankly, Alexis thought, overadorned, and then scooped it up, looking embarrassed. "Don't go home right away. Let's go over to Moonlight Phở on Jackson."

"Sounds great, but, um, I've got an English test tomorrow, for one thing." Alexis couldn't bring herself to mention the whole clotted rest of it, although the "conversation" with her mother the night before had brought some relief.

"When have you ever cared about English tests before?" Linda quipped. "Besides, you can get Bs without even studying. What's all this, girl? Distance? Excuses? At arm's length?" Linda drew close and closed her eyes a moment. "You know you want . . . phở."

"Well, when you put it like that. I mean, just for a little while, OK?"

She was bearing and covering so much. Was life always full of so many complications, details, spells of worry, fear, and even remorse? Alexis suddenly wondered if she would ever live past the age of nineteen. It didn't seem possible. *What will I be, if I'm really an adult someday?* It was not quite imaginable. If she grew older—old—that would mean, for one thing, her hair would turn gray, for sure. Her mother's left eyebrow (as well as the rest of her hair) had turned fully gray. The eyebrow was pretty peculiar, for sure, although Alexis had gotten used to it. Her mother's self-consciousness about her appearance had of course dictated the ongoing and meticulous use of hair color.

Alexis sat down on the stone steps. "Ah, fuck it," she said.

"Fuck what?" said Linda.

"Gray hair," said Alexis.

"Sure thing. Hey, you are quite the mystery chick. But that's why I love ya! Why, I friended you first of anyone. Gray hair—what the hell? Now, come on. Quit brooding about imaginary stuff and let's get to Moonlight Phở."

"Well . . . yeah, sure. Sorry."

The two walked slowly down the stairs, winding their way along the path to Twenty-third. The wind was strong. Two boys, probably seniors, were teasing a freshman kid about his books and folders, which had dropped to the ground, and papers were swirling everywhere in the afternoon wind.

"No, no. I can't go," said Alexis. "I gotta know what's going on back at home."

"You're going. You promised," said Linda, a hand lightly on Alexis's shoulder. "You're in high school—you're not supposed to want to go home. I know you have responsibilities, but, jeez. Relax."

"Linda," said Alexis as they walked, "do you believe in ghosts?"

"Absolutely," said Linda without a trace of hesitation, which surprised Alexis. "I've seen one, once. No, twice. And I've heard voices—me, my uncle, and my sister did one night on a road near home. I'm sure it was our grandmother."

"Really? Amazing. I'm glad you're not a skeptic—I didn't think you were. It's kind of a cliché, but there's so many things we don't know about. I mean, like Mr. Smiley said in bio, ants don't know it when we stand over them, look down at them. That's us—the human race."

"Totally," said Linda. "I don't know what ghosts are made of—maybe a little bit of matter, a little bit of soul, but they exist. Did you see one? Someone who died at the hotel?"

"Yeah, it was that," said Alexis.

"Well, who? What did they say?"

"Oh, not too much."

"What, Alexis? Spill it."

"Just that they were happy where they were."

"Was it a man or woman?"

"A woman."

Once at the restaurant, they were seated at a quiet table, facing each other. After ordering, the girls watched the wind blow plastic bags in the parking lot outside. It was the kind of dark, blustery day that demanded dreamy contemplation. Linda picked up a lime wedge from the condiment plate. Breaking the moody silence, she held the lime up in front of Alexis and squeezed it. Droplets sprayed Alexis's face.

"You bitch!" Alexis laughed and threw a bean sprout at Linda. She picked up another bean sprout and, instead of throwing it, she crushed it between her fingers in front of Linda's face.

"That's a beautiful sight," said Linda. "A flattened bean sprout. Its life is over, Alexis. You murderer."

The teens fell into laughter so loud that the man at the next table glared at them.

Alexis did not care. It was amazing—the afternoon had suddenly become a lovely break, an oasis. Linda was great for that.

"So what about your grandmother's ghost?" she asked Linda.

"Yeah, right. This was my stepdad's mother. They were really a rich family. My stepdad inherited a boatload—well, enough to go to law school anyway. My grandma was happy about that. But she was pissed as hell about my dad's brother. We called him Al. My uncle was in charge of my grandma's estate and he basically cheated my other uncles and aunts out of beaucoup bucks. So that night her ghost appeared, and she was hella mad. I swear to God this ghost was chasing us down the front road of my grandma's house. I heard something like music. It sounded like wind, but more whistly than wind could ever be. So my uncle fell down with this pain in his stomach! That was grandma's ghost, too. God, she was mad.

"Anyway, the week after that, my stepdad landed a huge case. It totally made his career. He's one of the most well-known probate attorneys in Seattle now. Don't mess with him. He just bought our family a second house—in the Bahamas."

"Jeez, why didn't I know that, Linda? What other things are up your sleeve?"

"What other things are up yours, Alexis?" Linda's eyes were shining.

CHAPTER 7

INDU SUNDARESAN

BACK AT HOME, ALEXIS STOOD at the very top of the stairs that led to the attic at the Hotel Angeline, on a small, sunlit landing. She looked up at the skylight in the roof. A few years earlier, LJ had been walking her back from school and he'd seen a glint of silver on the Angeline's roof.

"What's that?" he said. "A skylight? There's no light on my landing."

Alexis shaded her eyes and peered upward. "I don't know," she said. "Could be, but . . . it's odd."

"Come on," he said, pulling her by the hand as they ran back to the hotel. He raced downstairs to the basement, grabbed a hammer, and sped past her up to the top floor, where he had his apartment. At the landing—this landing where she now stood—LJ set up a ladder and began pounding away. Drywall flaked down, bits of insulation swirled through the air, and Alexis watched in horror as LJ wrecked the ceiling. "What is Mom going to say?" she whispered.

Just then, Edith appeared at the top of the stairs, holding a hand over her heart to ease her breathing. "High time," she said breathlessly. "The roofers threw in a skylight for free, but I've never had the time or the energy to open it up from inside."

In time, because Edith insisted, LJ framed out the opening with pieces of plywood (to keep the rats from falling into the house, he said) and also patched up the other spots he had thrown his hammer into in an effort to locate the skylight from below.

Alexis stood now in the light of a fitful Seattle sun, which bathed her like a benediction and gave her a moment of peace from the riot of the past few days. She had her hand on LJ's doorknob, and the metal had grown warm under her palm.

She knocked softly. "LJ? You there? Can I come in?"

No answer. She waited and knocked again. She hadn't seen him all day and desperately wanted to talk . . . about everything.

"LJ?" Alexis took her passkey and let herself into LJ's apartment, shutting the door softly behind her. This apartment, on the top floor of the Hotel Angeline—the same floor she and her mother lived on—was L-shaped, with the shorter arm leading to the doorway and the far side of the longer a bank of warehouse windows, floor to ceiling.

Alexis tiptoed into the main room. At some point during his stay at the Angeline, LJ had convinced Edith to allow him to install a small kitchenette in his room. It ran lengthwise, on Alexis's left—cabinets below and on the wall; a tiny sink barely big enough (or so it seemed to her) to hold a teacup and a saucer; a camping stove on the countertop with two burners, attached to a gas cylinder; a glass-fronted wine fridge under the counter.

The kitchen was scrupulously clean, the countertops wiped down, the sink gleaming steel, flowers (flowers!) in a glass bowl on one of the burners. Habib roosted on the countertop, head drooping in sleep. He opened one black eye, gave her a good stare, and then closed it again. Where was LJ?

Alexis turned right and saw the bed against the far wall and for a moment her heart stopped. LJ lay on the floor at the side of the bed, his arms splayed out, his toes pointing outward. Like a corpse.

"LJ!" she shouted and ran to him. She put her hand over his heart; surely, there was a tiny beat? But his chest barely seemed to rise and fall. Was he dead? Had he died also? Was she going to be alone in the world?

Just then he blinked, his pale blue gaze capturing the anxiety on her face. "What's up, kiddo? Thought I was dead, too?"

She pushed his shoulder feebly. "Don't do that. Don't ever do that. Not now, after all that's happened in the past few days. Not ever! What were you doing on the floor?"

"Yoga," he said, stretching his arms overhead, wriggling his toes and then curling up on his side to bring feeling into his arms and legs. "It's called the Shavasana. 'Corpse pose.' Looked real, didn't it?"

"Yoga? Since when?"

"Since a long time, pet. Lots of people around here practice yoga. It's been in the papers lately, did ya see?"

She pulled her shoulders up to her ears. "I don't read the papers, LJ."

"You should, kiddo, it's the duty of every good citizen to keep themselves informed. Yoga's un-Christian now, so the article says. But—duh —it originated many years before the advent of Christianity, in India. And saying a few Oms during Yoga class ain't going to make anyone a Hindu."

Alexis rose from the floor and put a hand out to haul LJ up. He stood towering above her. "Why the disconsolate face?"

"Have you been ingesting a dictionary?"

He raised a withered eyebrow. "Ingesting? Who's been now?"

"I have nothing to wear for tonight, LJ," Alexis moaned, going to sit on the deep old windowsill. LJ had colored glass bottles along the length of the sill, and the fragile sunlight glowing behind her sparkled their many colors onto the floor, onto the ceiling, in a kaleidoscope of light. Most of the bottles were empty; only one—tiny, purple—was corked. She moved the bottles aside to sit down. "You know, the dinner tonight with Uncle Burr."

"Ah," LJ said, coming up to her and putting a hand under her chin. "The eternal lament of all womankind. You really have nothing?"

"This stuff," she said, indicating her black tights, her black T-shirt, the bangles on her wrists, the blue nail polish on her fingernails.

His hand touched her hair lightly. "When did you color this red? Is this from one of Edith's many bottles?"

"A mix of two colors," Alexis said, pulling her crimson hair over her eyes. The world before her was suddenly red, diluted by the sunlight from behind. "You like it?" she asked.

"Very much," LJ said gravely. "Now"—he turned to his kitchen— "can I make you some tea, coffee? My turn now, after all the teas your mother and you have fed me downstairs in the parlor. Look around if you want; I know you're thrumming with inquisitiveness."

Alexis did, going to the far wall behind LJ's bed. It was decorated with a mammoth collage of photos—all in black and white—of all sizes. There was a ten-foot two-by-four nailed on the wall, just below the ceiling, studded with nails. Thin cords hung from the nails and were threaded through paper clips that were pinned onto the unframed photos.

"Did you take these, LJ?" Alexis asked, stopping in front of a picture of Mount Rainier from Kerry Park, downtown Seattle in the foreground, the Olympics to the west, the massive cranes on the docks leaning over the waters of Puget Sound as though searching for a fishy meal.

"Yeah, pretty good, aren't they?" Coffee bubbled in the percolator, filling the little apartment with its aroma. He poured some out. "Some are old"—he came up to her with a cup and put it in her hand—"and some new. I've been taking photos in Seattle since I moved here, with this." He pulled out a tiny camera. "Never needed anything more."

Alexis took a sip of the coffee and watched through her red hair as the strands became damp and shredded in the steam from the cup. LJ had a sense of humor, she realized—a wry one. Here was a photo of a dog with his leg lifted over a fire hydrant (on Broadway, perhaps?), marking his territory, and in the distance, at the traffic light, a policeman looking at the dog in disgust. Everyone else around was laughing, but the dog and the policeman were perfectly framed.

"Who's this?" Alexis asked, pausing in front of a collage of eight or nine photos of the warehouse in Fremont where LJ housed his perfume business. He sold his wares from a stall at Pike Place Market; the colored bottles on his windowsill had been originally used for his early efforts at making perfumes.

"Just photos of the factory, kiddo." LJ put a hand under her elbow and tried to guide her away.

"No, I mean this one," she pointed at a photo in the middle right of the collage. It showed a close-up of the sandwich board for the warehouse—rain shower aromas—and a man stopped in front, his head bent, his hands cupped around his mouth. His collar was drawn up near his ears. Though Alexis could see neither the cigarette nor the lighter held in his hands, a plume of smoke weaved its way upward through the man's fingers.

"Nothing," LJ said, pulling her away with real force now. "Nobody. Just some man who had stopped outside the shop; someone on the street. I've no idea who he is. Is it important anyway? We have other things to do."

Just as Alexis was beginning to wonder at this plethora of negations (why explain so much; she'd asked a casual question), a bell chimed and LJ's laptop screen lit up. It was lying on the bed and had been hissing and humming in hibernation mode, but now the background came to life and a bubble appeared on the screen. A calendar reminder, it seemed. Alexis had the perfect vision of a fourteen-year-old and could see the words *"D-Day! Tonight's the night to go to the warehouse"* before LJ pounced at the laptop, turning it firmly away from her interested gaze.

"You going somewhere tonight, LJ?"

LJ frowned. "Didn't your mother teach you not to read other people's stuff?"

Alexis smiled in an impish way. "Only mail. But I thought you might walk me to the Sorrento to see Uncle Burr. I know I said I'd meet him alone, but I need some coaching. What will I say to him?"

"I can't come, pet. Have to be at the factory tonight; something big. Maybe it'll make all our fortunes and you won't have to worry about your uncle or anything else. You'll be fine." He grinned. "Just talk like his fancy secretary, all pebbles in her mouth, words escaping around them, and he'll understand you perfectly."

"I still have nothing to wear!" Alexis wailed.

"OK," LJ said, "let's go to Buxby's on Broadway and get you something for the dinner."

She pulled back. "I could never afford anything at Buxby's."

"It's on me, kiddo. I have enough for whatever you want tonight." He slapped at the pockets of his jeans, checking for money and his camera. Just as he was shutting the door, he said, "Wait a minute," and ran back inside.

"OK," he said again when he was back. All the way down the stairs, out into the watery sunshine, down Broadway, a thought strummed through Alexis's head. She'd seen the man in the photo before. Nothing much of him was visible, but his eyebrows—thick, unruly—and his slicked-back hair were distinctive. Who was he? And why did LJ not want to talk about him?

They pushed open the door to the vintage clothing store and a jangle of brass bells, hung on a jute cord, clanged violently, announcing their arrival.

Alexis and LJ stood just within, the last of the light escaping from the room as the door shut behind them. In a few minutes, their eyes became accustomed to the gloom inside. The store was small, and most of the floor space was crammed with clothes racks. It smelled a little dusty, a little musty, although a sign under the cash register proclaimed that all of their clothes—genuine antique/vintage—were dry cleaned before being displayed.

An inner door opened and a woman put her head into the shop. She had a round head, a round face, fleshy cheeks red and blooming with happiness. "Let me know if you like anything; I'll ring it up for you," she said before disappearing into the back room again.

"She's very trusting," Alexis said. "Mrs. Buxby?

"No," LJ said, his eyes very bright in the darkness of the shop. "His mistress." He moved unerringly through the racks, his fingers brushing over the clothing lightly. The spotlights on the ceiling were all direct-ed toward the walls, but there was enough reflected light in the store to make the sparkles and spangles on the dresses gleam as his hands moved through the fabric. He pulled out a silver lamé top and a long skirt that seemed to be made entirely of blue feathers. "This," he said triumphantly, "will wow your staid uncle."

Alexis fingered the skirt doubtfully. "I'll look like a peacock in this, and it's just not my style, LJ."

"I insist," LJ said, propelling her toward the fitting room. "Try it out at least; it'll match your nail polish beautifully. And"—he pulled out a pair of silver knee-high boots from another rack—"these will match the outfit perfectly."

The skirt wasn't as long as Alexis had feared it would be—just above her knee. If she'd had the time, she would have taken the hem up a few more inches, but she had to leave from the shop to make it on time to the Sorrento Hotel for the dinner with her uncle.

She wore the clothes to the cash register and waited patiently as the lady snipped off the price tags, the metal of the scissors cold against her skin.

"You're a lucky girl," the lady said, nodding toward a beaming LJ. "To have a father like this."

"He's not—," Alexis began to say, but stopped, her heart thumping painfully in her chest. And why not, she thought? He was the only father she had ever known.

She tried on a pair of old-fashioned glasses at the counter. They made her look older—wise and sophisticated. Perfect for making Uncle Burr take her more seriously, particularly when she drew her hair back into a sensible low ponytail. She added them to the pile.

The bill came to an astounding $352.23. LJ dug the money out of all the pockets of his jeans and laid it out on the counter as if it were an offering. Alexis reached up and kissed him gently on his cheek and he instinctively brushed it off, his face crimson.

"Here, something else," he said, opening her hand clumsily and putting a bottle in it. It was the corked purple bottle from his windowsill.

"What is it?" she asked in wonder, turning the little bottle around in her hand, the liquid inside swirling around the glass.

"The first perfume I ever made. Bergamot, sandalwood, cassis, all dissolved in hundred-proof vodka."

"I'm supposed to drink it?" she asked, laughing.

"Wear it, kiddo."

"What did you name it?"

"In Seattle, what else?" His smile was wide. "Rain Water."

When they stepped outside, LJ took three photographs of Alexis near a newspaper stand, the sunlight setting her newly colored head to a red blaze, glittering off the silver of her top and her shoes, the blue feathers of her skirt iridescent against the newsprint. Alexis would find these photographs one day and treasure them as a happy, innocent memory.

She held her hand up in a tiny wave and, to her surprise, LJ came bounding up to ruffle her hair. He bent close to her ear and said, "Love ya, too, kiddo. Be brave."

And then he was gone, loping toward the Angeline through the crowds, his white hair streaming behind him.

Alexis pushed her shoulders back, took a deep breath, and started the walk toward the Sorrento and her meeting with her uncle. She patted the papers in her bag, to gain some confidence from them and to reassure herself that they were still there. Later that night, when the dinner was done, she thought, she would go to LJ's factory to find out what he was really up to.

CHAPTER 8

CRAIG WELCH

ALEXIS FOUND HERSELF ALONE, COMPLETELY alone, for the first time in days.

She moved along Broadway, an occasional gust whipping the skirt around her hips. The denizens of Capitol Hill busied themselves along the sidewalk, basking beneath the glittering sun. No one paid her any attention, but she still felt awkward, a child in her new-old clothes, walking alone on a street that suddenly seemed unfamiliar. She remembered clearly the last time she'd felt this strange and out of place in her own neighborhood. It had been Christmas, and her Uncle Burr had come without warning. He'd insisted on taking Alexis and Edith to dinner, urging them to dress as he did, talk as he did. Alexis had felt like an impostor then in her egg-colored skirt. The whole night had been uncomfortable, her uncle trying to learn how she was "faring" at school, about her friends, whether she "enjoyed" the Angeline's residents. She'd been just ten years old, but she'd sensed something between the two adults, an old argument just below the surface.

She remembered the drive home, her face plastered against the rain-splattered window in the back of the BMW, her eyes scanning the red brick of a Capitol Hill still lined with construction cranes. The bits of old Seattle were more visible then—the cracking plastic video store marquees, the remnants of car dealerships, the litter. The big boxes were going up, yes, but they hadn't yet taken over. The night had ended with her walking up the stairs and hearing fierce whispers between her two family members.

Alexis moved toward Elliott Bay and the Sorrento, her eyes on the people she'd lived around her entire life. She'd been so preoccupied for so long, she hadn't noticed them lately, but the events of the past week had settled in her heavily and she found herself happy for the distraction.

At the 7-Eleven she saw the corner boys—the white kids not much older than her who sold dope to the drive-bys, the outsiders who cruised in from the big homes on the plateau. The dealers all thought they were Eminem, with their finger snaps and their yo-yo-yos. She spied one just then, holding court, shooting spittle at a middle-aged guy in cream khakis. The dealer pointed at the guy's shoes and elbowed his buddies— "Dude's wearing slippers, man." The man stared off, beaten down and oblivious.

Alexis had overheard LJ telling people that marijuana was getting tougher to find, something about how the border patrol's crackdown on terrorists seemed to bring down mostly dope runners instead. Alexis didn't know anything about that, but it sure didn't look like there was any kind of drug shortage.

LJ . . . LJ liked his secrets, no doubt, but Alexis couldn't recall him ever being quite so mysterious. She wondered, not for the first time, if she should be worried—not just about what he might be doing but about him, about his stability. What was he up to? She quickly let it go. LJ was LJ. He'd be OK. She'd never been able to figure him out anyway. She had to trust that he could take care of himself.

She'd trust, all right, but she'd verify, too. Tonight.

Alexis hugged her bag closer and moved past Rudy's Barbershop and the poster-strewn poles outside the Comet Tavern. She watched a father grab his toddler by the hoodie just before the child darted into an intersection. Would her father have done that for her? Her father. He'd been on her mind a lot lately, thanks to Mr. K's gift of the violin. Then again, what hadn't been on her mind?

She could see the hospital up ahead, which meant she was just a few blocks from the Sorrento. She could already feel the mahogany beams beneath her fingers. The hotel was nothing like the Angeline, and its clients were another species altogether. The men wore sweaters tied around their necks. They ironed their jeans—or, more likely, had someone ironing the denim for them.

Thinking about the Sorrento now brought back memories of Mia. It had been Mia who suggested, back when Alexis was in sixth grade, that they wander the halls and try to hunt down the ghosts. The kids in their neighborhood knew the stories about the hotel, about the couple that had been gunned down on the third floor by a burglar in the '20s, about the bride who'd fallen to her death on her wedding night. They'd all heard about the rooms with doors that slammed shut by themselves. Mia had insisted Alexis come with her to investigate.

They'd made quite a little team back then—Alexis so young that the cleaning women barely noticed her, especially when she was with Mia. No one missed Mia. Tall, thin-nosed, with a dancer's grace, Mia was fearless and breathtaking. She lied with such ease that the girls always managed to gain access to a room and they would spend hours rifling through drawers, the thrill of the illicit making Alexis's skin tingle.

They mostly found other people's secrets—receipts from Nordstrom, dog-eared scraps of paper with scribbled directions. But in a drawer by the bed in every room, the Sorrento kept a book of hotel history. Mia didn't care much for reading—she didn't have the patience—but Alexis liked flipping the pages, taking in tales of President Taft's first visit or the stories behind the carvings etched into the woodwork. The last time they'd been there together Mia had found a gold hoop earring beneath the bed. Alexis had found herself suddenly wanting it. She reached out and Mia, an odd smile curling her lips, had held it aloft.

"It's gonna cost you," Mia said, teasing.

"What do I have to do?" Alexis asked. But even then, she had an idea.

Mia, without warning, leaned in and kissed her. Alexis, startled, pulled away. She'd never been kissed by anyone who wasn't her mother or LJ. She flushed and looked at Mia, but Mia just smiled and stared back, one eyebrow slightly raised. Alexis felt the redness in her face deepen. Her mind was a blur. She grabbed the earring from Mia's hand and, without another word, bolted from the room and the hotel.

Walking now, toward the iron gates of the hotel's entrance, Alexis thought about how many times she'd come back to the Sorrento alone. She wasn't sure she could explain what drove her. Mia's kiss, of course, was always on her mind. But something else, too, drew her to the hotel. She'd wander the halls, trying desperately to carry herself as if she belonged, trying to mimic Mia's confidence, pretending she was a guest's child. Alexis would search until she found an open room and another copy of the hotel's history. For hours she would sit below a window in that room, studying the stories of former guests, as if their stories somehow held a key to her own.

There was the alcoholic who'd had his last drink near the fireside lounge, who'd returned thirty years later clean and sober. She read about the Air Force pilot who'd broken his back in a fall. He'd spent sixteen months in a hospital in Seattle and recuperating at the hotel—away from friends and family and everything he knew—before he eventually returned to active duty. There were weddings and funerals and Thanksgivings and vacations, and even the sad stories gave Alexis a little lift. These were rich people, sure, and she detested this world. (What would LJ think if he knew she came here? Oh, God, what would her mother think?) But these were families doing what families do, living the kind of lives Alexis only knew through TV. She hated them for that. But she loved them a little, too.

Inside the lobby, Alexis tried to shrink. Men wandered about in the same black vests she remembered. The women still wore those dark, somber suits. She was supposed to meet her uncle in the lounge, and she wanted desperately to get there without having to speak with anyone. She feared what might tumble out of her—about her uncle, about LJ, about her mother still tucked neatly inside her coffin, about their silly plan to raise all that money. (Had she really thought they could do it with a concert?)

Alexis slipped into the lounge without opening her mouth and moved quickly to a chair by the fire. She turned it to face the door. She was early, but she knew her uncle would be, too, and she was there less than a minute before she saw him.

Uncle Burr's hair and beard had gone white, and he looked like he'd lost weight. He saw her and tried to smile, but he looked like he'd bitten down on a pickle. Alexis had always hated the weakness in his features, the way he seemed filled with worries bigger than her world. Seeing him, she felt all the old anxieties returning. She recalled the overheard arguments with her mother, the formal way he always spoke to them both, and she knew right then that she needed to trust her instincts. Alexis knew she was right to hate him.

CHAPTER 9

MATTHEW AMSTER-BURTON

"SHALL WE SIT?" ASKED UNCLE BURR.

Alexis nodded and turned up the corners of her mouth, a fake smile to match the old man's. A waiter led them to a table in the dining room and left them with menus.

Burr patted his jacket pocket, looked upward as if remembering something, and picked up his menu. "It's good to see you, Alexis," he said stiffly.

Alexis sniffed. "Mmm-hmm." She made a show of studying her menu, which did, in fact, resemble a final exam on the twin subjects of Northwest agriculture and French culinary terms. It was nearly indecipherable from top to bottom, and Alexis wondered whether she would want to eat any of it even if she could crack the code.

"When will your mother be joining us?" Burr inquired smoothly.

"She can't make it. She's not feeling well, so she sent me as her representative."

"Oh, really?"

"Really. I'm fourteen, you know—plenty old enough to help run things," Alexis said a little defensively.

"Hmmm. I really have business I need to discuss with your mother. I came to town just for this meeting."

"Well, you'll have to deal with me." Alexis said firmly.

"We'll see. I suppose we may as well enjoy our dinner," Burr said grouchily.

Alexis went back to studying the menu, but the type swam before her eyes.

"If I may," said Burr, "the crab salad is perfection."

"Thank you." Alexis had been practicing the art of saying "screw you" in the guise of "thank you" for years, and this was one of her finest performances. OK, then, she would have the crab salad, for twenty-three dollars. She thought about slinking back to the kitchen and cutting a deal with the cook: He could have the crab salad and half the money, and she'd take the rest and get the hell out of there.

But no. For one thing, she was no criminal mastermind. She'd long noticed that the criminals in her favorite detective novels were suave intellectuals, unlike the real criminals in her neighborhood, who wore ripped jeans and smelled funny. They were idiots.

Who was the idiot here, though? Burr knew what this meeting was about. Alexis didn't. She'd read once that people fear public speaking more than death. Well, her fear of death was long gone, but here, facing off with this tired-looking rich man, she felt like she was expected to give a speech, and she had lost her note cards, and the speech was about the mating habits of ocelots, and she'd missed that day in health class.

"For you, miss?" asked the waiter.

"I'll have the crab salad, please," she said, grateful for the interruption.

"And for your entree?"

"Huh?"

"Your main course, miss?"

He couldn't possibly mean the twenty-three-dollar salad was an appetizer. Alexis knew that rich people ate expensive food, but did they always do it in massive quantities? She looked around the room and saw a disappointing lack of gorging, vomiting, and slugging directly from wine bottles. She couldn't help it. She imagined the woman on the far side of the room, the one stuffed into a black dress that might have fit her in a past life, guzzling red wine and puking. She laughed.

The waiter, unperturbed, waited patiently.

"Just the salad for me. I'm not very hungry," she said.

"I'll have the langoustines, and the filet," said Burr, "and do you have a bottle of the Haut-Brion open, by any chance?" The waiter shook his head. "Then sell me a bottle, pour me a glass, and give the rest to the kitchen."

This act of charity made Alexis hate her uncle three times as much. There's nothing worse than watching someone you dislike do something unequivocally nice. The mind casts around for a way to transform an act of kindness into something else, and Alexis told herself that Burr would be abetting some poor cook's slide into alcoholism.

"Care to let me in on the joke?" Burr asked.

"What joke?"

"You were laughing."

"I was coughing. So why are we here?"

"You always did get right to the point. I admire your philosophy, but mine is: dinner first, business later."

A hardwood chair with no padding is uncomfortable. A mattress with a defective spring is uncomfortable. The silence while Alexis and Burr waited for their food was more like an iron maiden. Alexis let an ice cube melt in her mouth and avoided eye contact. She listened to the elevator music they had piped into the dining room, and found to her surprise that she recognized some of the songs, and felt an inexplicable indignation at the fact that Led Zeppelin's "Thank You" made good elevator music.

"The crab salad, miss," said the waiter, setting down a plate that, to Alexis's relief, had no claws on it. She couldn't identify anything that was on the plate, but she took a bite.

Wow. Oh, wow. This was not right. This salad was going to melt her steely facade. Salad! Roberta liked to watch this show where, as far as Alexis could tell, people competed to make the most weird, complicated, and improbable food. As she chewed, she felt her world rearranging itself and coming back together in a new form. It was as if she'd learned that monsters were real—this wouldn't have surprised her—but were also cuddly.

The salad tasted like a ferry ride, like a rainy day that washes the roads clean. It was going to be very hard to go on hating anyone while eating this salad. Was this part of Burr's plan? Maybe this concert idea was all wrong. Instead, they should set up a tent and sell this salad.

"You like it," said Burr, and it wasn't a question.

Alexis nodded. Burr, she noticed, was eating something that looked like a plate of crickets. *Say nothing,* she told herself.

Fat chance. "Are you eating a plate of crickets?" she asked. It was the salad talking.

"They're crayfish," said Burr, laughing. "Would you like to try one?"

"No."

"More for me, then." Why did adults always say stupid things like that?

Alexis did her best to make the salad last while Burr consumed a steak the approximate size and shape, though not the color, of a blueberry muffin. He ate dutifully, like he had eaten this same muffin-shaped steak dozens of times before and had maybe enjoyed it long ago. He patted his jacket again and sighed. Alexis kept herself busy trying to blot the last molecules of dressing from her plate with a piece of bread. Then, just as she resigned herself to the fact that she'd eaten it all, she looked down and the plate was gone. Petty thieves, she thought, could learn a lot from waiters. Or maybe fancy waiters were all former petty thieves.

People who buy you dinner want something. Alexis knew that much. The more expensive the dinner, the more they want. That was basic math. But what did Uncle Burr want? He wasn't leering at her in a sleazy-uncle way, which would have been almost reassuring, since Alexis knew how to deal with that kind of problem: Kick it in the nuts and run.

No, this problem required a detective. In Alexis's favorite mysteries, the breakthrough in the case always came in one of two ways. Either the detective would question the suspect until she broke down, starting off with easy questions, circling around the matter of the murder, or the— well, it was always murder. Then, suddenly, without understanding how it happened, the suspect would admit everything. "Yes, yes, I killed him! I couldn't stand his snoring anymore!"

Or the detective would sift through case files. She'd put photos up on a wall and connect them with string (actually, Alexis realized, this was something they did on TV, not in books, and she had no idea why they did it). She'd read through the files and study the photo of the crime scene. "Something isn't right here," the detective would say.

Since there had been no murder and Alexis doubted her powers of cross-examination, she searched her memory like it was a cold case. When had her mother last crossed paths with Uncle Burr?

She shivered. Her mother was never at her best in the presence of Uncle Burr. Mostly, her memory served up a tape loop of Mom shouting into the phone. Details? None. It was funny how memories melted into ingots of pure feeling over time. Alexis was a perceptive child and knew she'd paid attention to her mother's words, not just her tone, but now, it was like watching someone pick up the phone and shout, *"I'm angry! Are you angry? Then we are both angry!"* Not helpful.

"Dessert, miss?" asked the waiter, who had appeared stealthily at Alexis's elbow. This made her want to sneak up and surprise him, just to see if she could do it. She did want dessert, although she didn't want Burr to pay for more expensive food, especially not after she'd been caught enjoying the salad. But she ordered the tarte tatin, even though it was twelve dollars, because she was hungry and someone had once ordered it in a book. She wasn't sure what it was, other than some kind of tart, but because it was on the dessert menu, it probably didn't contain crickets. Probably.

It was about the house, of course. That's what they were always fighting about. It was very simple, according to LJ: Burr wanted to sell the house. Mom didn't. The rich get richer. An old story, and not very interesting even when you're the poor-get-poorer part. Why would a guy rich enough to spend hundreds of dollars on dinner need even more money? Alexis didn't know, but it seemed like the sort of thing rich people did all the time, just out of habit, like the way they ate a fifty-dollar steak without even noticing that they'd done so.

Alexis was sure of one thing: if Uncle Burr asked her to sign something, she wasn't going to sign it.

"Alexis," said Burr, "I'm happy to buy you dinner, but it's very important that I speak with your mother."

"I need to go to the bathroom." She excused herself, spotted their waiter across the room, and sidled up to him. "Pardon me," she said loudly, and the waiter jumped. Success! "Where is the restroom?"

When she returned to the table, Alexis found her napkin neatly folded, and this made her feel like crying. *Great, crying over a napkin,* she thought, biting her lip. Very *mature.* The waiter appeared, raised his eyebrows at Alexis to acknowledge that they now shared a joke, and set down the apple tart.

Please, don't be as good as the salad.

It was—thick with caramel and not too sweet. Damn. If Burr had passed a contract across the table asking her to sign over the deed to the Angeline, her mother's body, and the few dollars in her purse, she would have signed it. She ate faster. Burr drank some sticky-looking wine from a small glass.

"I hate to be dramatic, Alexis," said Burr, "but if I can't speak with your mother soon, we're going to have a serious problem. She is not an easy woman to reach. Never has been." When he saw Alexis's glare, he softened. "Never mind, that's between her and me. Now, do you like to play cards?"

"Cards? Like poker?"

"I'm not trying to induce you to gamble, if that's what you're getting at. When your mother and I were young, we used to play this card game. If you'll come with me to the lounge, I'll teach you, and then, if Edith is truly unavailable, you and I will have to speak about certain pressing matters. Did you get enough to eat? Good, then please follow me."

On the way to the lounge, Alexis elbowed the waiter. "Hey," she whispered. "This place may be full of rich jackasses, but the food is good."

"I know. Todd, by the way."

"Alexis. Get used to me; when I hit it big, I'm going to eat here a lot."

"Hit it big doing what?"

"I don't know. Rap. Roller derby. Chef."

"Then best of luck in all three." Todd crept silently off to surprise another table, and Alexis found Uncle Burr sitting in the lounge, shuffling a deck of cards. With his narrow eyes and soft features, he looked like a seal, Alexis thought. She laughed again. What could be less threatening? But he handled the cards deftly, like he could swindle you. Maybe this was how he'd made his money, cheating people at cards.

"It's a solitaire game," said Burr, "but I find it works as well for two as for one. Watch what I do." He built several columns of cards, then arranged and rearranged them. At first it looked random, a game with no rules, like watching a baseball game, but with hoops and soccer goals and horses. Then the detective in Alexis's mind woke up, and it assembled Burr's moves into a list of rules, and she knew how to play.

"Deal me in," she said.

"You've played this before," said Burr, once she'd beaten him. "Your mother taught you." His way of posing questions as accusations infuriated her.

"She didn't," said Alexis, and promptly beat him again.

"Then I'm impressed. Here, try this." He laid out a sequence of cards. "What's the next card in the series?"

"I've already been to school today, thank you."

"We can start off with an easier one, if you'd like."

"I didn't say it was too hard. Queen of diamonds."

"Very good."

"Here's one for you." She laid out a two, three, five, and seven.

"Jack. Any suit." Alexis frowned; she'd thought that was a tough one. She was thinking in patterns when Uncle Burr said, "As much as I enjoy mathematical puzzles, we have some business to attend to."

CHAPTER 10

ED SKOOG

OFTEN THE THING YOU'RE LOOKING at becomes the lens through which you see the world. She'd heard that somewhere, somewhere good—not school, she didn't think—maybe on the radio that afternoon they cleaned the high gutters of the Angeline, all that muck coming out in handfuls, tar-black goo to her elbows, streaking her clothes, clotting in her hair, and her mother holding the ladder below. She'd looked out of proportion down there, distorted, and not very good at holding the ladder steady, more intent on the radio propped in the window for the duration of the task—the lens through which you see the world—though it may have been another radio, or not a radio, and anyway hadn't she fallen from the ladder that afternoon? Not all the way down, but a slight misstep as Edith turned away to watch a stray cat cross the street into the park? Now she would have to clean the gutters herself, of course, all the work of the Angeline, grim and meaningful.

She did not want to play cards, but she would rather play cards than talk about the house, because cards were a real thing she could shuffle, examine, move, hide, restore. You could count them, you could fold cards back into their pack and carry them in your hip pocket. You could leave them behind. She didn't know what to do with the invisible. Business, love, grief, algebra II: this was not accustomed terrain, and she resented not having her mother there to hold steady this complicated set of gestures.

"Yes," she said. "Let's get down to it."

Burr took an envelope from the inside pocket of his jacket—egg-colored, she noticed, like the skirt she'd worn that uncomfortable Christmas Day when Burr had picked her and her mother up in his BMW and they'd gone to dinner. He had been stuffy and pompous then, too. "How are you faring?" *Faring.* She'd known even then what he meant, what was unsaid in that antique phrase about the difference between Edith and what a mother was supposed to be, according to some gingham sentimentality. He slid the envelope across the table and did this thing with his eyes.

"There's a check in there, so take care of it. It's for your mother," he said. "She'll know what it's for."

It was just another card, she thought, and he was playing it. Then he went on with the caring-uncle bit, asking about her college plans, what did she want to do when she grew up, things he wanted to be when he grew up, the names of the colleges he attended and how he'd be happy to "be a resource" in a few years when it was time to think about the future. "Not just financially," he said, "but someone who's been around the world a bit and has some idea how things work."

"And my mother's not?"

"Your mother is . . . Your mother is your mother."

And she almost lost it there, half from hate, half from hope.

"Go to hell," she said, and threw the check and the cards in the fireplace. She got up, her lamé shirt glittering righteously. The Sorrento lounge fell quiet except for a few couples talking at the far end, and crackling fire.

"I'm trying to help!" Burr shouted from his chair. She was surprised and almost deterred by his frustration, which was the closest thing she'd ever seen to emotion from him, but all it resulted in was a hurried, apologetic smirk as she turned and walked away.

"One way or another, this thing will be resolved at the hearing next week."

"Can you hear this?" she shouted back, flipping him the finger.

"Alexis," he shouted back, and shambled up out of his chair, nodding assurance to the hotel staff, who were beginning to gather.

She paused by the concierge stand. A limousine idled just outside the door.

"Alexis," he said, his face softening to a conciliatory sadness, one she'd seen pass across her mother's face at certain times.

"What?" she demanded.

"Your mother has to be at the hearing next week. Even if she's still sick, even if she hates me, even if you hate me, she has, has, has to be there."

Alexis was blocks away before her fury began to ebb back in to the numb grief she'd been carrying around like a child. It wasn't like she'd read, this feeling about her mother—nothing beautiful or bittersweet or fond or even human. No, more human than she'd ever felt before, but not in a good way. It was grotesque, an unasked-for carnival ride that kept going past the thing that was no longer her mother in the basement, and then the plunge.

She looked around. Freeway Park, a complex of landscaped concrete, forms shaped well for skateboards and seclusion, a no-place place right in the center of the city. She used to love the park, had taken her first steps there, played with nameless other children, then had her first drink there, at twelve, a little bit of someone's stolen peppermint schnapps mixed with grape juice. One time she found a stack of unemployment checks from the State of Washington, all made out to different names, in a Safeway bag along with a perfectly good tangelo. Only last year she found a bullfrog in the weeds and made three wishes before she noticed it was made of plastic, an Archie McPhee novelty.

But now she couldn't avoid the emotional information the park was showing her—an industrial vista, a dead afterthought, an abandoned idea. It was a park, but there was nothing below it, nothing to hold it steady. What had seemed novel and unconventional now looked like a bad joke. It was the bottom of the world.

"I am the Regent of Freeway Park!" she shouted to nobody. She looked off the edge into an apartment all decked out for Halloween, with a big-screen television showing a blizzard. She thought she felt an out-of-season snowflake on her cheek, but when she looked up, the sky was dark and uncommunicative.

It would be good to see LJ, regardless of whatever perfumed complications he would bring to bear. He would be a secret fellow mourner, as he was the only person who would miss Edith remotely as much as she would.

She needed to talk to Linda. Although the rest of her life had disintegrated, and not only her past but also her future—there would be no more cleaning the gutters of the Angeline when her uncle stole it and sold it, as he certainly would after the hearing next week, and turned it into whatever mean people turn good things into—maybe it wouldn't be so bad. Maybe she could be turned into something new as well. She and Linda could hop a bus to anywhere, change their names, find some cabin, some garret, and be together always. Perhaps take Habib, crowing into the broad sky. It was a comforting story to tell herself, and it gave her peace to think about it as she walked toward Linda's place, not realizing at first that she was heading there, further and deeper downtown, using the spire of Smith Tower as a guide, keeping her eye out for landmarks that she increasingly needed as usual bearings and safety of workday hours were long since rolled up, darkened, shuttered, disappeared. During the day Seattle seemed like a pony—safe, humorous, miniature, its hair braided and everyone laughing. At night Seattle grew into an unpredictable crocodile, and now it was walking alongside her. No pet. Alexis didn't know all the details, but what she gathered from Linda was that her stepdad was as restless as he was rich, and that since her mom had hooked up with him they'd moved every couple of years from one ostentatious domicile to another, usually just after Linda had formed attachments to neighbor kids and came to terms with the creaks and corners. Alexis tried to understand, but felt only sympathy, unable to fathom having to divide her sense of self from the building she lived in. She and the Angeline were one. Leave the Angeline? Sooner die. Or at least dying was as hard to imagine as leaving. Linda's current bedroom window faced out directly on the Alaska Way Viaduct. From the bed one could see the faces of inbound passengers, drivers on cell phones, whole families eating dinner, the flashing lights of the Seattle Police. The police were always around her apartment, making the homeless move from one slight comfort to another. Linda said she heard gunshots from time to time. "Drug dealers?" Alexis had asked during a late-night phone call.

"No, that's the cops. It's some sort of ethnic cleansing going on down here."

"I'd better be careful, then."

They had the top floor of an old building slightly damaged by the Nisqually earthquake, which is how Linda's dad got it for a steal, and planned to develop and sell it for a bazillion dollars, once the viaduct came down and the view would become the grandest in the city.

No one answered the buzzer. Alexis craned her neck to see the windows dark. Hadn't Linda said she was going to be home tonight? Or was that yesterday? Hadn't she said to come by? Wasn't there some exciting promise in those two syllables? Come by. Come by.

What did it mean that Linda wasn't home, Alexis wondered. The way things were going, it wouldn't surprise her if Linda abandoned her, too. Alexis would understand. Forgive her, probably thank her for proving that her worst thoughts of the world were true.

She sighed. She had been hoping to fold some laundry. She stood under the viaduct and waited for the bus. All around her people seemed bound for great nights, romance, adventure, richness. Even the homeless guy dozing against the facade of the old OK Hotel seemed to be having amusing, clever thoughts.

CHAPTER 11

DAVID LASKY AND GREG STUMP

CHAPTER 12

KEVIN O'BRIEN

WITH A WHOOSH, THE DOOR closed behind her as she stepped off the bus. Alexis felt the October night air whipping through her long, curly hair. The feathered skirt ruffled around her legs. On the street corner, a huge, seven-ton statue of Lenin towered over her, watching the traffic on Fremont Avenue like a stern crossing guard.

The bus started to pull away. Alexis glanced up at the window and saw a woman and her daughter in one of the seats. The mother fussed with the little girl's dark, wavy hair and smoothed it back.

For a moment, Alexis remembered when she was a child, riding on the bus with her mom. Every Christmas, they took a trip downtown to the Bon Marche and gazed at the decorations in the store windows. She remembered her mother telling her, "You need to thank the bus driver for taking you this far, sweetie."

Watching the bus churn down Fremont Avenue, Alexis felt tears stinging her eyes. She'd forgotten to thank the driver.

In fact, she'd forgotten to thank her mother. She should have sat down with her sometime in those last few weeks and told her how grateful she was—to have such a cool mom who had taken her this far.

But it was too late. Right now, more than anything, she needed to talk with LJ.

Alexis gazed down the street. She'd been to LJ's perfume "factory" in Fremont only once. She'd gotten off the bus too soon. "Oh, shit," she murmured. "Smooth move, Alexis. . . ."

Clutching at the top of her shirt, she shuddered and then headed down Fremont Avenue toward Leary Way. She had at least eight blocks to go.

Her cell phone rang, and she dug into her purse to retrieve it. She checked the lighted screen, but didn't recognize the number. She clicked on the phone. "Hello?"

There was no response. It sounded like someone breathing on the other end.

"Hello? Who is this? Hello?"

She waited to hear a response on the other end, but there was nothing. Then a sigh.

"Warmongering, Establishment sons of bitches," she heard LJ mutter. At least she thought it was LJ. Sure sounded like him. "They'll never know what hit them. . . ."

"LJ, is that you?" she asked .

"Alexis?" It *was* LJ. He sounded surprised.

"Yeah, you called me."

There was a click on the other end of the line. He'd hung up on her.

Alexis stared at the cell phone in her grasp. "What the hell?"

Her mom used to say that LJ could lapse into these crazy spells, and he'd be in his own little counterculture, '60s-radical world for a while. "Uncle LJ blew out his pilot light again," she'd say, "He forgets it's 2010. Just leave him be, let him ride it out, and he'll be on track again."

Swallowing hard, she clicked off her phone and then forged on down the sidewalk, leaving the store and restaurant lights of Fremont's commercial district behind her. She glanced over her shoulder at the tall rocket perched above the store entrance to a squat building on the corner. It was silhouetted against the darkened sky.

On the sidewalk below it, she saw a man with a baseball cap hiding most of his face in the shadows. Even so—she still felt his eyes on her. He shoved his hands in the pockets of his army fatigue jacket and crossed the street to her side.

Alexis quickly turned and started walking again. She guessed the man was about a half-block behind her. Not looking back, she picked up the pace. She saw a lamppost ahead and hurried toward it. She'd feel safer in the light, where the passing cars could see her. She thought she heard his footsteps behind her, but she wasn't sure.

She still had at least four or five blocks to LJ's.

As she moved farther down the street, the houses and storefronts along the way became more and more rundown. The lights were farther apart. It was easy to get lost in the darkness. Maybe that was what that guy had done, because when Alexis glanced over her shoulder again, he wasn't behind her anymore.

Catching her breath, she stopped and stared for a few minutes. She saw something move behind a telephone pole, but then realized it was just an old flier that had come loose, flapping in the wind.

Alexis sighed. How did she get so paranoid all of a sudden? Simply because he'd crossed to her side of the street, it didn't mean the guy was Jack the Ripper, for God's sake.

She decided to try LJ again. She speed-dialed his number—Lucky #7—and anxiously counted the ring tones. He picked up on the third ring, but didn't say anything.

"LJ? Lynn? Are you there?" she asked.

There was a long pause, and then he cleared his throat. "The wingspan of a Boeing 757 is 125 feet . . ."

"LJ? What—"

"So—how could it punch a hole in the Pentagon that's only sixty feet wide? It doesn't make any goddamn sense. Even if the wings broke off on impact, there would have been a lot more debris outside. It doesn't make any goddamn sense at all. . . ."

"LJ, what are you talking about?"

"I'm talking about how they pulled the wool over the public's eyes, honey!" he replied loudly. "For Christ's sake, if the wings broke off, why didn't we see that in all the photos they took of the Pentagon on 9/11? You didn't see any plane wreckage in any of those pictures. It was all a lie, goddammit, all a lie. . . ."

"LJ, please, just calm down. You're scaring me. . . ."

"The people have been duped," he went on, "just like they were back in sixty-three. Back then, they all bought that lone-gunman theory. No canisters, then ventured down the gloomy corridor. LJ wasn't picking up, but she followed the sound of his ring tone. Photos and posters lined the unpainted walls. One showed an Asian man shooting another Asian man in the head. The victim wore a slightly geeky short-sleeved checkered shirt and had a horrible grimace on his face. Another photo was of a thin little girl, running down the street, naked. She was crying. LJ had other photographs, too—Lee Harvey Oswald posing with a rifle, and shots of the Twin Towers.

She clicked off her phone, and the "In-A-Gadda-Da-Vida" ring tone ceased. "LJ?" she called.

There were also several photos of the Fremont Troll statue under the north ramparts of the Aurora Bridge. The hulking sculpture was perpetually posed as though ready to crush a near-life-size Volkswagen in his hand. On some of the photos, LJ had drawn what looked like a time bomb. Arrows showed how a bomb could be planted inside the Troll's Volkswagen.

Staring at those pictures, Alexis thought of what he'd said earlier: "We gotta have our own conspiracy that's even better than their conspiracy."

She glanced back toward the stairs at the bag of fertilizer and those canisters of gasoline. She thought of something else LJ had said—when he didn't know she was listening: *Sons of bitches, they'll never know what hit them.*

"Oh my God," she murmured. "He wants to blow up the Aurora Bridge. . . ."

She looked at her phone and scrolled through the recent calls. She found the incoming phone number she didn't recognize. Highlighting it, she pressed redial. After a moment, Alexis could hear the opening strains of Wagner's "The Ride of the Valkyries" sing out.

She saw an open doorway at the right, near the end of the gloomy hallway. The snoring came from in there. It was almost drowned out by the Wagner ring tone. As she stepped inside the room, the Valkyries got louder. She smelled marijuana smoke and saw LJ curled up on a sofa, dead asleep. "LJ? Wake up!" she said, hanging up her phone.

He muttered something under his breath, then sat up and rubbed his

f. Like why would Oswald—when he's
get an untraceable gun just about any-
from a Chicago Sporting Goods store?

e told you before, 'We gotta have our
er than their conspiracy.' It's time. We

up.

se, Alexis hurried down the sidewalk.
or loopy or both. But she had an awful
himself or someone else if she didn't get

l she spotted the dilapidated building LJ
ly more like two adobe shacks side-by-
a sign on the front lawn: YOLANDA THE
YOUR FUTURE! A small sign was posted
ck: LYNN'S ORGANIC PERFUMES & OILS—WE
teller was long gone, and LJ had expanded
rely sold perfume anymore.

mont Avenue, Alexis scurried across the
hedding from her skirt. She ran up to the
and pounded on the door. "LJ? Are you
nd listened.

dn't hear a sound, just traffic noise on the

heard it click as she gave it a twist. Biting
d peered inside. The small, darkened room
g perfume bottles of all shapes and sizes.
mbating scents, but it wasn't unpleasant.
e door behind her. LJ had an old fashioned
e counter—along with a scribbled sign: if
ff! Behind the counter was another room
d see a dim light filtering from that annex.

eyes. "Hey, honey. I was just thinking of you." He grabbed something off an end table. At first glance, it appeared to be a silver poker chip. "Look at what I've been holding on to," he said. "I found it earlier tonight."

Alexis gazed down at the cheap little silver disk that had both their names on it. She remembered him getting it at one of those imprint machines at the Gayway fair by the Seattle Center. LJ & ALEXIS AUSTIN, HIS FAV GAL, it said in a circle around the token's edges.

She worked up a smile for him. "I was trying to call you," she said.

He let out a little laugh and quickly shook his head. "No, no, you couldn't call me, not now. I'm in the middle of an experiment, and the phone—"

"Is that what the gasoline and fertilizer are for, an experiment?" She glanced around the cramped, windowless room. "What is this place anyway? I didn't even know this basement was here."

Across from them was a beat-up wooden desk. On top of it, he had a lava lamp, a bong, two fat candles—and in a cheap frame, a photo of her mom and her from when she was about five. They were on the beach, building a sand castle together. Alexis still remembered the pale blue one-piece swimsuit she wore in the photograph. Her mother had on a peasant blouse and jeans. Edith was laughing, and her hair was blowing in the wind. She was beautiful.

Beside that framed picture was something that looked very much like the bomb LJ had drawn on the photo of the Fremont Troll under the Aurora Bridge. Three sticks of what must have been dynamite were bound together—with colored wires and some little gizmo black box displaying a digital countdown: 1:39 . . . 1:38 . . . 1:37 . . .

A wire attached to the box led to a cell phone.

"What's going on here?" Alexis asked.

"This is where I work," he replied. He gave her a stoned, sleepy grin and scratched his head. "And I—nah, I can't tell you, honey. I can't let you get involved."

Her eyes wrestled with his. "What are you up to, LJ? When you called me, I heard you saying all sorts of strange things—I've been trying to call you back, but you were asleep."

"You phoned me?" he said, his bloodshot eyes widening. "When?"

"Just a minute ago. But you changed your ring tone. It was that opera song they used in *Apocalypse Now*. You know. When they were surfing—"

He bolted off the sofa. "'*Walkürenritt*'? Oh, Jesus, we've got to get out here!" he cried.

"Why?"

"That's a dummy phone! It's a detonator. It's set to go off with a delay. You called that number?"

Paralyzed, Alexis stared at him. She couldn't move.

"A bomb!" he shouted at her. "Get the hell out of here! C'mon, c'mon! I'm right behind you."

"But can't you just dismantle it or—"

"Jesus Christ, go!" he screamed.

Without thinking, Alexis swiveled around and raced down the corridor—past the poster of that screaming little girl. She could hear LJ's footsteps behind her.

"Go, go, go!" he cried.

Breathlessly, she weaved around the gas canisters and the bag of fertilizer, then raced up those creaky old steps, and through the door. Jane Fonda's poster was torn off the secret doorway as she ran into the annex.

She headed out the store's entrance. "Hurry, for chrissakes!" LJ yelled.

She sprinted across the street, dodging between cars, and then turned to see him in the warehouse's doorway.

Suddenly, there was a blast. Alexis put a hand up to cover her eyes from the blinding light. She felt the ground shake beneath her. Glass popped and shattered in the explosion. It rained shards along with smoking cinders and debris.

Car alarms wailed.

With a roar, black clouds plumed up from the inferno that was once LJ's lab. Traffic on Fremont Avenue screeched to a halt.

She couldn't see LJ past the thick smoke. "LJ?" she screamed. "LJ!"

"I saved it!" she heard him say over all the noise.

Alexis blinked and saw him in silhouette, hobbling through all that soot and smog. LJ came into view. He had a dazed smile on his dirt-smudged face. His clothes were burnt and torn. Dust matted down his long gray hair, and blood dripped from a cut on his forehead.

In his hand, he showed her the cheap silver disk souvenir.

Alexis gasped.

LJ didn't seem to realize that a spear of glass was protruding from the side of his throat—just where his neck met his shoulder. But then his smile waned, and he collapsed on the street at the edge of the curb. She ran back across the street to his side.

"Go away!" she heard him gasp. "You have to. Please . . . Alexis. You—you don't want to get involved. Your mom would never forgive me. You . . ."

But words no longer came out—just a strange, gurgling sound. He sighed, and then became very still.

Stunned, Alexis stared down at him. Tears clouded her eyes. He'd urged her to flee, but she hesitated. Part of her couldn't just leave him there—though she knew he was dead. Already people were climbing out of their cars to look at the fire—and the charred, bloody corpse at the edge of Fremont Avenue.

"Are you OK?" she heard someone ask. Alexis numbly gazed at the middle-aged woman approaching her. She had auburn hair, glasses, and a fisherman's sweater. In her hand she held a cell phone. "Did you know him?" the woman asked loudly—over the crackling fire and the car alarms.

Alexis opened her mouth, but she couldn't get any words out. She saw the car's headlights reflecting off that silver disk in LJ's hand.

Her name was on it.

But she couldn't go back. There was no way she could ever go back.

Sobbing, she ran as fast as she could—in the other direction.

CHAPTER 13

NANCY RAWLES

MERCIFULLY, IT STARTED TO RAIN. She felt the water on her face, and it seemed as if the sky had seen her grief. She kept on running until her legs let go, and she found herself on the ground near a bed of ivy. She knew this trail. She remembered walking past ivy when she was a small girl, holding her mother's hand. It had been snowing that day. The city had closed down. Buses were stuck on the hills, cars skidded through the ice, sirens sounded in the distance. Edith decided they should walk. They would take the Burke-Gilman Trail all the way home.

That day in the snow, Edith had been red with cold. She'd forgotten her gloves, and her hands were hard to the touch. On a patch of ice near the university, she'd suddenly fallen, pulling Alexis down with her. Edith laughed, so Alexis laughed, too. But whenever she revisited that day, she remembered it as the first time her mother had fallen. The fall had frightened Alexis. In her tumble, she had lost her mother's hand.

Now she found herself, weary and disbelieving, on that same lovely trail. A runner stopped to ask if she was all right. It must have been ten o'clock by now. The rain was coming down in sheets. Alexis looked at him but didn't answer. Her eyes were glazed with tears. When he touched her shoulder, she shook her head. He smiled weakly, then went on his way.

She pulled herself up and continued walking. She had seen too much. Too many people had fallen away. She couldn't comprehend all that had happened.

Some people look better in winter. And are the dead so different? We were walking and you fell. A sheet of ice hidden under snow. We were walking and you fell. A crack in the sidewalk I didn't see. Next time me.

Fear gripped Alexis. Eyes were staring at her from the darkness. Despite the late hour, students passed on their way home from Friday night dates. Skateboarders, cyclists and, as always, the runners. Where were they all going at this time of night? What had they seen that caused them to flee?

LJ's body. A flash of light. Smoke and heat. Had they heard the sirens? Had they called 911? She could see Edith, sleeping. The hotel crumbling, collapsing into dust. And Linda, running away from her.

She stumbled along the trail for what seemed like hours. By now, she was drenched. Her new silver shirt clung to her body. She thought about stopping one of the strangers and confessing all that had happened to her. But she didn't know what to say.

Once, when one of the hotel residents had come crying to Edith about a cat who had died, Alexis, then four, looked up at the large sad face and offered, "So what? Everybody dies."

"Ah, the existential response," Edith had commented. Years later, when she recounted the story, she marveled at her young daughter's wisdom.

But death was different now. Alexis was old enough to understand the end. Still, sometimes she forgot. She forgot that her mother was dead. She forgot that both of her parents were dead. She had no parents left. Death was the ending of childhood.

She wanted to lie down. *If you lie down in a snowdrift and fall asleep, you won't even realize you're dying.* Maybe it's better just to fall asleep. Who would miss her?

The noise of the traffic beckoned. She had reached Twenty-third. Cars streamed by with their headlights glaring, searching her face like massive eyes. She hid herself behind her shaking hands. She could smell the soot on her fingers. And there it was again, the blinding light of the explosion. Alexis felt frozen with fear. She struggled to regain her stride.

If she walked to the Montlake Bridge, she could catch the #43. She could see people waiting at the bus stop. She would go and wait with them.

As she approached, she could hear someone singing. A woman waited with a guide dog. She was wearing an orange rain jacket and singing. *"Heaven, I'm in heaven. And my heart beats so that I can hardly speak."* Alexis looked at her and felt an overwhelming need to talk to somebody. The woman wouldn't judge her. When the bus came, she sat in the front, next to this woman and close to the bus driver, but she didn't say a word.

She'd left something behind. The trinket from the fair, a small medallion with both of their names pressed upon it. Worth almost nothing, and now worth everything. She reached into her pocket, in case it had magically claimed her. Nothing.

It was still in his hand. The evidence of her knowing him was in his hand. The police would find it when they found him. She was the last person who had seen him. And they would come looking for her.

She had to protect herself. Whatever LJ was doing wasn't good. He'd always made her nervous, but he'd never really scared her before. She was desperate to see him alive again.

The bus passed a man standing in the rain talking to himself. It could have been LJ. One more step, and he could have been that man on the corner talking to himself. Not too long ago, the police had killed such a man—a man who was drunk and carrying a knife. A danger to himself and others. LJ.

The bus had turned the corner and was rolling down the hill to Nineteeth. It came to a screeching halt at the tennis courts. They were soaked, with puddles gathering near the nets. The tall streetlamps bathed them in a surreal light.

Alexis needed air. She rose abruptly from her seat and hurried down the steps, away from the prying eyes. The wind had picked up, and the rain hit her back at an angle. She bent her head and hunched her shoulders.

It was a little more than a mile to the Angeline. What would she do when she got there? *Maybe Mr. Kenji will find me. I'll tell him what happened. He'll keep my secrets like he kept the violin. And Edith. I'll wake Edith up and tell her what happened.*

She walked toward the Safeway on Fifteenth. She was aware of being hungry. The dinner at the Sorrento seemed as if it had taken place days before. If she slipped into the supermarket, maybe she could grab something warm. No, someone would see her, someone she knew from the hotel. She kept walking.

Something told her to take the back streets, so she headed south on Seventeenth. She could see the hospital complex and the Christian Science Church. She moved like a cat, ducking in and out of doorways to get out of the rain.

That's when she saw them—Linda and their friends from Garfield, turning onto Pine in a sleek black VW Bug. They were on their way to the midnight showing of *The Exorcist* at the Egyptian. She was supposed to have been with them. No wonder Linda hadn't been home earlier. Alexis couldn't believe she had completely forgotten, but Linda had asked her to come to the movie two weeks ago—before all her problems began. It had seemed like a good idea at the time.

Now her life was like a horror flick. Nothing Hollywood could dream up could compare with what she had lived through in the past few weeks. For some reason, when she saw Linda, shame washed over her. Would Linda want her now?

Sometimes, in class at Garfield, she would listen to stories of classmates who had seen relatives die in front of them or descriptions of parents lost to drugs. She always felt sorrow when she heard such stories, but she also felt *At least . . . At least, I have a secure place to live . . . a mother who loves me . . . at least, I have a huge adoptive family . . . we keep each other going . . . at least.*

She wanted to run after Linda's car. She wanted to pull her girlfriend away from the others and tell them they needed to run away, somewhere far from Seattle, somewhere far from the reach of parents and ghosts.

Maybe it wasn't real. Maybe she had imagined it. Linda. The explosion. Edith. The hotel. LJ. This night.

But here she was at the Hotel Angeline. Its sad Victorian face was sullied by tears. Ursula would be complaining about the leaks. Alexis went around back to the basement door. She didn't want to run into any of the residents.

She needed to get to LJ's room. Something in his room would help her make sense of it all. She could hear the sounds of the television coming from the parlor. *Law & Order: Criminal Intent.*

She climbed the stairs and rounded the corner. Several residents were sitting in front of the TV. Mr. Kenji wasn't there. She headed for the stairs that would lead her to LJ's room. Just then, the announcer's voice stopped her cold.

"Breaking news on the Fremont Inferno: Seattle Police have discovered evidence of a terrorist bomb-making lab in the abandoned warehouse where a chemical fire has been raging for the past hour. KGNU-TV will bring you updates as they develop."

She was aware of feeling hot. Just then, Habib appeared by the window with a pretzel in his beak. She gasped. Ursula called from the parlor, "Is that you, baby doll?"

She hurried up the stairs, noticing that the skylight was open a crack and that rainwater had pooled on the floor. So, that was Habib was getting in and out. Alexis wondered if LJ had opened the skylight on purpose before he left, to give the crow its freedom. She fished in her shirt for her passkey and used it to open LJ's door. The flowers were still fresh, everything laid out neatly like the whole place was waiting for him. What was she looking for? Something that would give her an idea of who he really was. Some evidence, some opening.

She searched his desk. His mechanical pens were lined up in a carved wooden box from India. The side drawers held papers and newspaper clippings. In the top drawer were several neatly labeled discs.

One of them read ALEXIS: LISTEN.

CHAPTER 14

SUZANNE SELFORS

ON THE QUIET BIRCH-LINED STREET, something sparkles, gliding between raindrops. Night has descended. The familiar and soothing rhythm of rain beats against the windows and rooftops of the Capitol Hill neighborhood. Sleep has enticed most into its depths. But not the girl who sits at the edge of a bed, shivering.

And not the shape, which lingers outside the Hotel Angeline, hanging in the mist like a whisper.

Why am I here?

Thoughts are scattered, difficult to grasp. The shape pulls its edges closer. Awareness gathers.

I am Edith.

And then she remembers. This is her hotel. Angeline. Named after the eldest daughter of Chief Sealth. She remembers the story of the daughter who refused to leave her land at the edge of the sea. Of the princess who chose a shack and a life as a laundress rather than a life on the reservation. Poverty and isolation became Angeline's roommates, but she worked hard, supported herself, and kept her home.

Just as I have done, Edith thinks. *I worked hard, supported myself, and this is my home.* Her thoughts drift again, as hazy as her formless body. She looks down. What body? *Where is my body?* Panic surges and she twists and writhes, trying to find what is lost. *Where is my body?* It hadn't been a perfect body. She'd always regretted her soft thighs and her wide feet. But an imperfect body is better than no body at all. She looks back at the building. A deep longing to be reunited with her physical self draws her forward. She moves, a mere essence, finding her way through the cellar doors and into the basement. City light follows, trickling after her like mercury. The light points with silvery fingers at the center of the room, where a plain dark coffin sits, a stool next to it. Is this the reason she's been summoned to this place? She circles, then dives through the lid. A corpse's face greets her, eyes closed, skin pale despite the heavy makeup. She shoots out of the lid and hovers below the ceiling.

My name is Edith and I'm dead.

A sudden rush of indignation hits her. Why had they stuck her in the plain coffin? Why not the fancy one in the corner, with its glossy veneer and red-satin lining? And why had no one given her a funeral? Maybe her life hadn't been the most exciting on the planet, but it deserved some sort of ceremony. Stories are supposed to be told, prayers said. A priest, a rabbi, a shaman, a ferryman to take her across the river. Something, for God's sake. Not stuck in the basement!

Edith sweeps through the room, a tornado of emotion. Where was the gratitude for all that she'd done? She'd kept the place spotless. She'd treated her tenants like family, letting them be late with the rent, listening to their tragic histories, holding their aged hands. She'd brought tradition to their weary lives with afternoon tea. *These people are family*, she'd often said. *Treat them with love and respect.* How many times had she spoken those words? She'd opened her home and her heart and they weren't even going to give her the satisfaction of a funeral.

Stashed away in a coffin in the basement. Only one person could have come up with such a stupid idea.

Lynn, she thinks, hovering over her tomb. *You're behind this. You and your crazy ideas.*

And to think she'd slept with him all those times, sneaking between bedrooms after the other tenants had turned off their lights. Whispering secret longings, secret regrets.

He was handsome in those days. His rebellious nature charming. But the years gradually soured him and paranoia scarred his features. Initially, she'd felt that motherly instinct to care for yet another lost soul, but when Lynn began to see conspiracy at every corner, when his whispers turned delusional, her desire for him died. She had more important things to focus on anyway.

She turns and looks toward the stairs. Something pulls at her, urges her forward. Someone is whispering her name.

Up the stairs she moves, without footsteps, to the second floor. A crow sits on the banister. It cocks its head and looks directly at her. *You see me*, she thinks. It clicks its beak. They are alone on this floor, the scent of sherry in the air. The others have gone to bed—the woman with the peg leg, the Greenpeace warrior, the snake charmer. *Where is the girl?* she asks the crow. *Where is my daughter?*

The crow takes flight and disappears up the stairs. She follows, up one flight, then the other, until she comes to the fourth-floor landing. The voice calls for her again and she flies into the room. There is pain in this room, sorrow as thick as the night. A girl sits at the edge of a bed, which has been stripped of its sheets and blankets.

"Mom," the girl whispers, wringing her hands—a gesture much too old for one so young. Her shoulders are hunched and she is shivering. Her hair is a new color. Curly locks fall over her eyes. Though it's night, she hasn't changed into her pajamas. Hasn't brushed her hair or teeth, all those rituals she'd been taught. A silver blouse clings to her skinny frame, a rain-soaked skirt of blue feathers is matted against her legs. Why is she dressed this way?

Alexis, I'm here. But the words have no sound and the girl continues wringing her hands.

Edith floats above the bed. No one has bothered to make it. The striped ticking of the mattress is stained from sweat and sickness. *This is where my life ended.* The memories wash through her.

She'd refused to see a doctor. When the symptoms began—the sweating, the aches, the pain in her gums and tongue—it was easy to tell herself that it was a bout of flu. She'd been sick off and on for years with assorted ailments. She'd been called a hypochondriac, and maybe there was some truth to that. So when the new illness came on, she'd decided to deal with it on her own. Why visit a doctor just to be told it was all in her head? Why add a doctor's bill to the pile of unpaid bills that already littered her desk?

By the time she began to lose her balance and the tremors took over, the mercury had already poisoned her brain. The heavy metal had invaded her nervous system, every organ, every cell. She should have gone straight to the hospital, she should have asked for help, but her brain was muddled, starved of oxygen.

Lynn should have known. He should have taken her. But doctors were part of the system, part of the Establishment he distrusted. His own brain was as warped as her mercury-poisoned brain, from a lifetime of chemicals he'd chosen to ingest. So instead of doing the right thing, the rational thing, he'd carried her body to the basement.

Edith screams, a silent gust that shoots around the walls.

"Mom."

The whisper draws Edith back to the moment, the reason she's been summoned to this place. She settles on the bed next to her daughter.

I'm here. Alexis, I'm here.

Edith wants to hug her with arms that no longer exist, arms that are imprisoned in a plain coffin in the basement. *I know you're afraid.*

"I don't know what to do," Alexis says. As she speaks, she stares at the crow that now stands across from her on the dresser. "We're going to lose the hotel."

The crow offers no words of advice. It gazes upon Edith with its black bead eyes. *Tell Alexis that I'm here*, Edith says to the crow. But it turns its attention to its once-broken wing, grooming the feathers. Time is running out. Edith feels herself evaporating like a puddle in the sun. But she isn't ready to leave. She must help her daughter. The Hotel Angeline was supposed to shelter both of them. Edith had done everything humanly possible to hold on to the hotel, but it wasn't worth this terrible price. If only she'd realized that and acted sooner, been able to prevent this. Instead she'd left a huge mess, the proof scattered atop her desk and all around the hotel. Debt and more debt. Crazy tenants who rarely paid rent. A father figure with a drug-soaked mind.

A small sob escapes her daughter's lips. "I won't let anyone take the hotel," Alexis says, tightening her mouth in stubborn determination. Edith knows that look. She's worn the exact expression for most of her life. *We're both so stubborn*, Edith whispers.

Then Edith understands why she's been summoned. She must guide her daughter. But in what direction? Alexis is alone. She has no one. If she gives up this fight to keep the hotel, her future could be bright. She could live with her uncle. He's not so bad. At least he'd keep Alexis safe. Buy her whatever she desired. Send her to the doctor when she gets sick. She'd have the chance to make new friends, go to a good school. She could leave the burden of this place behind.

The crow clicks its beak, then flies from the dresser and lands on the bed. It curiously nips at one of the blue feathers. "I miss her," Alexis tells the bird. "But even though she's gone, I don't want to leave. This is my home. I love it here. I don't want to live with my uncle. But I don't know what to do."

The apple doesn't fall far from the tree, Edith thinks. These are her walls. This is her home. Alexis will not give up. The spirit of Angeline is alive and well.

"Mom? What should I do?"

Edith winds around Alexis's shoulders, weaves between strands of hair. *You must get help*, she whispers, rippling down her daughter's arms. *Get help, Alexis. You can't do it alone. Get help.*

Alexis looks up. For a moment she stares right at her mother. Then her gaze travels through Edith, focusing on the open doorway. She stands. "There's no one to help," she says.

Edith sighs like a wind chime.

Then she is gone.

CHAPTER 15

CAROL CASSELLA

ALEXIS LET HERSELF SLUMP ONTO the pillow; the smells of her mother's perfume, a vintage LJ mix of chamomile and rosemary with a wisp of spearmint, lingered in the down. Suddenly it felt like Alexis had swallowed half the pillow, a thick lump in her throat that was a mix of loss and grief and terror. She had been alone for so much of her life; no siblings, no father, a mother vaguely distracted on the best of days and a bit loony on the worst. A soft-bellied hippie for her other stand-in parent. But at this moment, she was discovering the bitter roots of that word "alone." Not one living person in the world knew she was now, officially, an orphan. All her conviction to grow up overnight and manage this rotting hotel vanished in a wish to be eight, to be five, to be a baby in her mother's arms.

The rain pelted against the window and the shadows of the streetlight fell on the worn floor in flickering streaks. Winter was arriving with this storm; she could feel it, as if the room were dropping by degrees with each moment. If she stayed here she would lose her grip, she thought. If the world was going to leave her this abandoned, then she would have to find her own help. She would have to give up on her stubborn determination to save the Angeline and herself through her own single-minded grit. But who in this crazy hotel could she trust? *Linda*, she thought. Linda was the only living person who might even claim to love her.

Alexis pushed herself up and wiped her eyes on the edge of the pillow, pulled her cell phone out of her bag and dialed Linda's number. Her heart skipped once when she heard it pick up, but just as quickly it went silent again. Linda had hung up. Alexis dialed again, and this time she heard Linda's harsh whisper, "I'm in the movie. *Exorcist.* And you're not, in case you didn't notice!"

"Linda, I'm sorry. I couldn't . . . I need to talk to you. I need to see you."

"So, like, if you'd come to the movie, like you were supposed to, we'd be talking. Right?"

Alexis ran her tongue across her salted lips. "Look, I'm kind of desperate here. I want to see you." She waited through a long pause. "Please. Please, sweetie."

Maybe it was the endearment, but she could almost hear Linda's heart soften. "Yeah. You don't sound so good. I'll see if Jen and Lisa are ready to go." She let out a short laugh. "It's not like we don't know how the movie turns out."

Forty-five minutes later Alexis saw the lights of Linda's car sweep across the ceiling of the hallway and she slipped out the front door, knowing none of the residents would even turn over in their sleep. In fact, it was two o'clock on a cold, rainy night and no one in the world cared that she was sneaking out of her house, nor would they miss her in the morning if she didn't come home. In fact, as much as Mr. Kenji and Ursula and Otto and the twins considered themselves friends, as long as she left the sherry bottle out for afternoon tea they'd go for days without noticing her room was empty, her bed not slept in.

The car smelled like fake buttered popcorn and stale beer, and pot; Alexis's stomach churned. The girls were yabbering away, imitating the green-pea-soup scene and Satan's voice coming out of Linda Blair's pudgy mouth. Lisa and Jen didn't even seem to notice Alexis had gotten in the car. Linda turned the stereo on and they all three started singing to Lily Allen: *"Ever since he can remember, people have died . . ."* It seemed to take hours, days to get to Jen's house in Ballard and drop her off. *God,* thought Alexis, *don't her parents even care that she's coming in stoned at two thirty in the morning? Doesn't anybody care?* Lisa stumbled out of the car next, her small, rundown house in Crown Hill lit up like Grand Central, the garbage can spilled across the front lawn.

At last the car was empty except for Alexis and Linda, and Alexis climbed across the front seat to sit next to Linda, snagging her silver blouse on the seatbelt buckle. Linda glanced over at her once, then a second time and turned off the radio. "You don't look so hot."

That was all it took for Alexis to burst into tears. Linda reached over and took her hand, the car swerved across the center line and then righted. "Just pull over, would you?" said Alexis.

Linda steered the car with one hand onto the narrow shoulder just at the entrance to the Aurora Bridge. Alexis stared through the rain-streaked windshield at the long bridge, deserted at this hour, still intact despite whatever fantastic conspiracy theory LJ had conjured in his last delusional hours. How ironic that Linda had stopped here, as if to remind Alexis of the last friend she'd lost.

"What is it, babe?" Linda asked.

Alexis tried to answer her; she *wanted* to answer her, tell her everything and let somebody else worry about it with her for a while. But then she was pushing open the car door, the wind shoving it back against her body so she had to throw her weight into it. Rain hit her in the face and the cold was already stinging. She started to run, going forward, wherever forward was, finding herself on the narrow raised walk that rimmed the high bridge across the Ship Canal. She thought she heard the waves slapping against the massive concrete posts that held the span, but when she stopped for breath and looked over the railing she knew, in a dizzy rushing wave, that the water was much too far away to hear. A few small boats anchored below lifted and slapped onto the water with every gust of wind. Farther out the lights of a tug wavered, and she heard the moan of a foghorn calling across the sound. Her dress clung to her legs, the synthetic feathers crawling on her skin, the soles of her silver boots soaked with water.

Then a hand was at her shoulder, gripping her, pulling her, and she would have screamed except that she hardly cared whether someone hurled her off the bridge. It was Linda. Her Linda. Turning her around and wrapping her in her own coat. Suddenly the story was pouring out of Alexis, so fast that Linda put two fingers against her lips, shook her head and said, "Slow. Slow down. You're not making sense."

Alexis choked for a moment, rain and tears running into her mouth. "My mother. My mom. And LJ. Everyone's gone. They're all gone."

"Alexis, sweet thing, you are talking crazy here. I know your momma's sick and all, but nobody's goin' anywhere. And least of all me. I'm right here. I am right here for you. Always."

For the first time since running away from the blinding, shattering blast that took LJ, Alexis felt her heartbeat begin to slow down, could hear her own breath take on a measured, even flow. Linda looked so beautiful to her now, the rain and the night making her coffee-colored skin even warmer, smoother. Alexis had a flash of that scene from *Casablanca*, where Ingrid and Humphrey stand in the fog outside plane, all the pent-up love they've tried to suppress bursting through the screen, Ingrid's eyes going big and glittery with tears. Edith had always been a crumpled mess of sobs by that point, every time they watched it. Alexis took Linda's hand and pulled her farther along the bridge, finally starting to talk as they headed toward the center of the span, the lights of the shoreline dimming. "Linda, LJ died tonight. It was on the news—you must have been in the movie. He was in his lab, in Fremont, and there was an explosion."

Linda stopped walking, stunned. "Oh my God. . . ."

"Wait. That's not even . . . Linda, my mom isn't sick. My mom is dead. She died nine days ago." Even in this gloomy light Alexis could see the color wash out of Linda's face. "It's true. She's in the basement. My uncle's trying to take the hotel away from me—I'll end up in foster care."

Linda crossed her arms over her chest. "So, your mom's in the basement, or she's dead? Let's get this one straight."

"Both," said Alexis. "She's in the basement. Dead. In one of the coffins."

"Not the coffin we . . ."

"Linda, don't you get what I'm saying? My mother is dead! I can't tell anyone—I'm hiding her in the basement. Only LJ knew, and now he's gone, too."

Something shifted in Linda's eyes, a little shadow. "You know what a nine-day-old dead person smells like? You're telling me all those folks livin' right up the stairs are just eatin' their breakfasts same as always? Just a little LJ perfume to cover it up?"

Alexis felt like she had been punched, a big fat hollow place opening up in her gut as she listened to her last friend, her last refuge pulling back from her. "Hey . . . Those coffins have really good seals. Do I have to show it to you . . . her to you to make you believe me? Look, I need help. I'm begging you. My uncle is going to sell the Angeline and I'm going to be thrown out onto the streets. I'll run away before I'll let the state tell me where to live. Or if I even have to keep living." Even Alexis was shocked to hear those words come out of her own mouth, but suddenly suicide felt frighteningly possible. "I'm out of choices here. I'm asking for your help. Look . . . your dad. Or stepdad, I mean. He has money. Can't you ask him? For me?"

And then Alexis saw panic spread across Linda's face. Alexis realized she wasn't even shivering anymore, standing out there in her shiny metallic shirt and feathers, like some gawdy stuffed bird soaked to her bones. Her body was rigid. Linda's mouth twisted between a pitiful smile and a sneer. She said, "This is insane. I'm sorry. Really. I'm sorry for you, if this crazy talk is all true. But I don't have so many choices either. My dad hears this, finds out about you—you and me—and we'll be on the streets together."

Alexis didn't answer. Waited, willing to take that leap together if they had to.

Linda shook her head, "I'm a lot of things, Alexis. A gay rico with bad hair, bad grades, and bad reputation—at least when I'm hangin' out with you at the Angeline. But as far as my stepdad knows, I'm an angel. And I need his money. I like his money. Being a street person isn't in my plans, if you know what I mean. And if you don't want to wind up on the streets, too, you'd better cut this out. I don't know what game you're playing, but I don't want any part of it."

Alexis looked Linda straight in the eye for long enough to understand that she would not back down. Linda, her last friend, for all intents and purposes, didn't believe her. Alexis turned away and walked farther out onto the bridge, one small corner of her heart still hoping to hear Linda following. But there were no footsteps behind her, and then there was a car—Linda's car—pulling up on the roadway beside the narrow sidewalk.

"Alexis, please, come back to the car. Let me drop you at the police station." Linda called.

Drop her? She had *that* right. Alexis didn't even turn to look at her. Finally, Linda drove away.

The rain had turned to the steady, oozing mist that would last from now until June, colder than the deepest snow. Headlights approached from the south and slowed beside her, a black Mercedes. The window slid down and she heard a man's voice ask what price she'd take for a car ride down the street. Her fingers were so cold now her hands felt thick and clumsy, but she managed to shoot him her middle finger. As soon as he pulled away she began to cry, leaning on a light post that rose above her and wept rain onto the railings and her hair. The water below her was blacker than any object she'd seen in her life, only the smallest crescents of silver when the lamplight glistened off the waves. It looked warm to her, comforting, like the surface of a deep warm bed. Suddenly she heard something ringing in her ears, taking up the entire space inside her head. As if waking up from a dream she realized she was standing next to a telephone strapped onto the lamppost—one of those emergency phones they'd put out here to stop the torrent of suicides that made this bridge famous in Seattle. Ringing. Ringing. She picked it up. "Miss? My name is Susan. I'm calling from a hotline—we're here to help you."

Alexis held the phone out in front of her face as if she might see a pair of lips moving in the mouthpiece. "What?" she asked, putting the plastic to her ear again.

"The hotline. The suicide hotline. Someone called in about a kid walking along the bridge. Talk to me. We're here to help you."

Alexis pressed the phone harder against her face and knew exactly what she wanted to say, as if she had heard a voice as clear as her own mother's saying the words inside her head. She knew exactly what she was going to do. "You want to help me? Here's what I want. Here's what you and the Man can do for me. You tell them all to go fuck themselves. I'm buying the Angeline, and no one's going to stop me."

CHAPTER 16

KAREN FINNEYFROCK

FOR THE FIRST TIME IN a week, Alexis got lucky. The stop for her bus line was a short walk away and her bus was only a ten-minute wait. The other riders—a shifty-looking man with a Seahawks hoodie pulled low over his brow and another lonely seeming teen—didn't look at her twice. Actually, they didn't look at her once.

It must have been nerves, that knee-jerk sleep that wakes you up hours before your alarm goes off on a big day. Something kept Alexis from snoozing past her stop. She stepped down, said thanks to the driver, and turned her feet in the direction of the only home she knew. If there was anything Alexis needed more than food, sleep, or love, it was the feeling of safety, a door to close on everything.

Capitol Hill knows nightlife. There is barely an hour of the morning that doesn't see kids in tight jeans trying to get home from the clubs or the bars before the rain ruins their hairstyles. Alexis passed six groups bustling home from various after-parties, looking for a few hours of sleep before breakfast, but she wasn't really aware of any of them. She was barely aware of anything. She was a body, walking.

It was still dark out, the night that you could almost call morning, when Alexis turned her key in the Angeline's front door. The first sound she heard was the TV. Even at this hour, it was still on.

"Reports are rolling in slowly on what police are calling the largest explosion in Seattle in twenty years. The Fremont Inferno has claimed one life and more than twenty businesses. Police are following leads about the blast, but no suspects have been named."

So the explosion was huge, Alexis thought, but at least LJ hadn't killed anyone. Well, anyone but LJ.

The television was whispering in the common room, the volume nighttime low. The light from the screen flickered on the door the way sunlight strobes through trees. Alexis walked toward it and into the living room.

Mr. Kenji, legs crossed on the couch, a bonsai and a pair of pruning shears in his hands, sat watching the reporter. He turned to Alexis as she entered but didn't say a word. He held the shears raised in his right hand as if he were caught mid-snip.

His look was knowing and sympathetic. His look was vacant and dark. Alexis was tempted to spread her arms and fall into the sofa like it was a swimming pool, to go under and never surface.

"Terrible night in Fremont," Mr. Kenji said, the shears still held at the ready. "LJ's business is in Fremont. The police might come here, looking for information." His voice was steady and firm. His eyes were still hard to read.

Of course. She was wasting time. It would be hours, minutes maybe, before the police arrived, looking for LJ's next of kin, looking for someone to inform, looking for LJ's computer files, looking for her. She owed it to LJ to protect him. She owed it to herself to know as much as she could. From the couch, Mr. Kenji said, "I'll just stay up a while longer, in case anyone knocks."

Alexis turned toward the stairs, forcing her shaky legs to take them two at a time. Fingering the passkey around her neck, Alexis stopped outside LJ's door and took a nervous look right and left before stooping over to slip the key in the lock. She slid through the door in the thinnest way possible, the way a letter slides into an envelope. The door clicked behind her she raised a hand over the light switch.

It had only been hours since she had seen LJ's apartment for the first time, and now it wasn't even LJ's apartment anymore. It was a dead man's house, a shell on the beach, a museum dedicated to one man. The sadness was crushing. There was LJ's bed he would never sleep in again, his sparkling kitchenette he would never use, flowers he could no longer smell.

Life felt so small to Alexis then. She touched her own arms to confirm she was still living, still warm and intact. Life felt thin and fast, an elevator ride to the top floor that eventually returns everyone to the basement. She ran her hands down her arms to her torso. The feathers. That absurd silver-and-feather outfit. Stupid excuse for a good-bye present. Pathetic, pointless inheritance.

"LJ?" she said out loud into the room. She cleared her throat. "LJ?" she repeated louder, hoping another ghost had come to populate her family of specters. "Mom?" she added, waiting for her mother's voice to float from the basement and direct her actions correctly. "Anyone?" she said desperately to the air, to the room full of photographs, to the silent, unforgiving house. No one was answering. Maybe even ghosts have to sleep.

Alexis pushed herself back from the wall, struggling with the weight of the task at hand. She went over to LJ's desk.

Lots of things are hard for a normal fourteen-year-old to resist. Pizza. Staying up all night. Texting over the limit of her cell-phone plan. But chief among the list of teenage temptations is discovery. The events of the past ten days were forming themselves into a line, and that line seemed to be developing an arrow and that arrow must be pointing toward something. Alexis felt like some necessary truth was burned onto that CD, a truth currently more important than sleep.

She opened the drawer. There it sat. ALEXIS: LISTEN. She moved the mouse on LJ's computer, hoping to wake it up. A message popped up from the sleeping screen. It said:

Sorry pigs. This computer's been scrubbed. If you're looking for information on the people working to liberate our nation from the terrorism of endless war, then start by reading A People's History of the United States. *I have lived among you, but I have never consented. I have worked alone and am entirely to blame for this action. Sincerely, Lynn J. Robinson.*

Alexis read the screen again. Then again. Then she just read the word "Robinson." Then she said it aloud. "Lynn J. Robinson." Then she turned to the bank of windows lining the apartment and said to the new sun, "Is everything a lie?"

She turned back to the screen and punched a few keys. Same message. She slid the "Alexis" CD from its pouch and attempted to insert it into the thin slot on the hard drive. The computer spit it out without fanfare. She tried to push the CD back in, but it was a futile battle of wills. LJ left fresh flowers in his apartment, but his computer was locked as tight as a jail.

Exhausted, hungry, numb from being hit by a battering ram of grief, Alexis dropped her head into her lap. An observer would have guessed she was practicing to be in a plane crash. She hugged her knees and wished that crying would relieve something, if only the desire to cry more.

That was how she was sitting when she heard the knocking on the front door, and the voice rising up from the street saying, "Seattle Police," and Mr. Kenji shuffling from the living room, bonsai still in hand, to answer the door, and her mother's voice saying, *"Alexis, take the CD and get to our room."* And she did. But before slipping out the door, taking as many fingerprints as possible with the edge of her skirt, she reached over to the wall of black-and-white photographs and she snatched the one LJ refused to tell her about—the photograph of the mysterious man with the collar up around his chin.

CHAPTER 17

ROBERT DUGONI

ALEXIS SLAMMED SHUT THE DOOR to the apartment and turned the deadbolt. She grabbed the knob at the end of the chain lock and attempted to fit it into the slot, but her hand shook so bad she couldn't get it in. She missed. Missed again. Swore under her breath.

Watch your language, young lady. Edith's voice was as clear as if she were in the room.

"Not the time, Mother."

Alexis found the slot, slid the knob to the right. She turned her back to the door, fell against it, heart racing, mind swimming in mud. She couldn't think. Downstairs she heard Mr. Kenji ranting at the police and their retorts. Good God, she hoped he'd put down the gardening shears.

She heard someone say her mother's name. "Edith. Edith Austin."

They were coming. Without an elevator they would have to take the stairs. That would buy her some time, but not much. Not enough.

Now what?

What to do? What to do? What to do? What to do when the whole world is crashing around you? What to do when everything you've known no longer exists, no longer is true? What to do when you are alone, no one to help, no one to care? What to do?

Hide it.

"What?"

Hide the disc.

Of course. First thing. Hide the disc. Where? She surveyed the apartment, the clothes on the floor in piles, plates and cups in the sink, pots and pans on the stove with sauces stuck to them.

Pigsty.

"Really. You try, Mother. You try running this hotel, doing the laundry, folding the clothes, collecting the rent, fixing the plumbing, saving goldfish for God's sake. You try doing it and keeping the room clean on top of everything else."

You're wasting time, dear.

And she was. Hide the disc.

The couch. She'd hide it under one of the cushions.

Good God, girl, that's the first place they'll look.

And of course it would be.

She looked to the kitchen. The refrigerator. Could she hide it in the refrigerator? She didn't know. Does cold hurt a disc? Didn't know. Didn't have time to find out. OK, not the refrigerator. And not the oven. If the cold hurt a disc, heat certainly would. Couldn't take that chance.

She heard footsteps on the landing down the hall. Heavy feet. She could hear everything through the thin walls, and she knew the residents' footsteps. She'd spent years identifying them. These did not belong to anyone she knew.

They were coming. They'd want the disc.

She looked again. Under the plant? No, the water and dirt could ruin it. The mattress!

That's the second place they'll look.

"You come up with a place, then," Alexis said. "You're so smart. You come up with one."

Switch it.

"What?"

Switch it with one of the movie discs.

Brilliant. Brilliant. They'd never know. She hurried back into the living room, nearly stumbling over a pile of clothes. Her mother had bought one of those entertainment centers at a flea market in Fremont. It had a center section for the TV and side compartments for all the movies. She thumbed through them. All classics her mother had made her watch.

Casablanca. On the Waterfront. Cool Hand Luke. She pulled out the first one her fingers touched. *Gone With the Wind.*

As she switched the discs, another thought came to her. She had her answer to her first question. What to do?

A heavy fist on the door. A policeman's knock. Hard enough to rattle the door in the frame. Wake the dead . . . maybe not.

She had time. They'd expect her to be asleep at this hour. She had time.

What to do? Do what Scarlett did. Do what Scarlett did when her world crashed, when everyone abandoned her, when she had to fend for herself, fight off the Yankees, bury her mother and her father, run the farm.

Fake it. Fake it so no one knows you're vulnerable. Pretend everything is just peachy.

Another knock. Louder. A man's voice. "Edith Austin? Seattle Police Department."

Scarlett got all those men to fall for her, got them to love her. She fooled them all. Surely Alexis could fool one police officer.

"Coming," she said, trying to disguise her voice as if she were just waking.

She slipped the CD into the movie case and put the movie case back on the shelf. Now she had to get rid of the movie CD. Part One. Screw it. She rushed into the kitchen and put it in the oven.

"Ms. Austin. I need you to open this door now."

Alexis moved quickly to the door and raised onto her toes to look through the peephole. She was startled and nearly called out. The nose was huge—a big bulbous thing like the snout of one of those huge sea lions, the nostrils like two black caves, hairs protruding from each.

"I'm sorry, but who is this?"

"Seattle Police. Open the door Ms. Austin."

"I'm sorry but she's indisposed." It was a word her mother had taught her, a polite way of saying she was on the can, or in the shower.

"Who am I speaking to?"

Alexis looked down at her silver dress and boots. "Damn." She couldn't answer the door like this. She was supposed to be asleep, getting out of bed. She needed time. Needed to stall. She hopped on one leg, struggling to pull off the boot.

"This is her daughter, Alexis." She got the first boot off and flung it across the room, hopping on the other foot and repeating the process.

"Alexis, I need you to open the door."

"I'm not allowed to," she said. "My mom won't let me."

She looked back through the peephole as she struggled to shimmy out of the silver top. The man had stepped back from the door, but he still looked distorted, like one of those images you saw in a circus carnival mirror. He wore a suit and tie and ran a handkerchief over his forehead and head, red in the face. The climb up the four flights looked like it had nearly killed him.

"I'm Detective Hillary Francolini and I'm with Seattle Homicide."

"You're still a stranger," she said, the skirt falling to the floor. She kicked it away. "I'm not supposed to open the door to strangers. I'm not even supposed to talk to strangers."

"I'm not a stranger. I'm a police officer. Didn't your mother tell you that it was OK to open the door for police officers?"

"You could be lying. It could be a trick. Then when I open the door you knock me on the head. Then you kill me and cut my body into pieces and put me in Ziploc bags and stuff me in the freezer. I read that one time."

"OK, kid. Here's what we're going to do. I'm going to hold my badge and identification up to the peephole for you to see, OK?"

She found a pair of basketball shorts in one of the piles and slipped them on. "OK."

She looked through the peephole and saw the badge, but couldn't read anything on it. "It could be fake," she said. "With the Internet people can fake anything."

He pulled back the badge, his face contorted in a scowl and red again. "OK, how about I slide it under the door and you look at it that way?"

"OK."

She heard something sliding on the hardwood and looked down as the black wallet came under the door. She opened it and looked at the identification. Hillary Francolini. What kind of a name was Hillary for a man?

She looked through the peephole again. She had thought the man's image distorted, but after viewing the picture in the wallet she was no longer sure. Francolini was shaped like a bowling pin, or one of those Russian nesting dolls her mother collected and kept on the shelves of her bedroom. It wasn't all distortion. Part of it was poor genetics and likely overeating. He had a face like a basset hound, ears as big as two iceberg lettuce leafs, jowls that hung to the collar of his shirt and bags under his eyes as big as suitcases. He had one of those bad comb-overs, the kind that started just above the ear and revealed more scalp than hair.

"Well?" he asked.

"OK. I guess you're all right." She had put on a gray Garfield High School sweatshirt to go with the shorts. She pinched her cheeks. She wasn't sure why, but Scarlett had done it in the movie, so what the heck.

She undid the deadbolt and pulled the door open just far enough for the chain to catch.

"Alexis Austin?"

"Hi. Sorry about that. You can never be too sure, my mother says."

"No, you can't. May I come in please?"

"Um, what's this about?"

"I'm going to need to come in."

She knew she had stalled as long as she dared. She closed the door to remove the chain and pulled the door open, stepping back.

Francolini stepped forward, then paused at the threshold, surveying the interior of the apartment.

"Sorry about the mess," she said. "My mom's been sick and I've been taking care of her."

"Can I speak with her, please?"

"She's not home."

Three lines formed on Francolin's forehead. "I thought you said she was indisposed."

"I did. That's what I say so the person doesn't know she's not home. Like you said, you can never be too sure."

"Where is your mother?"

"She's . . . she's at the doctor's office."

"The doctor's office?"

Alexis realized her mistake. At just seven in the morning it was doubtful too many doctor's offices were open.

"She works downtown," she lied, "and she has to go to the doctor before work because her boss is really mean and he said he'd fire her if she missed any more time at work."

"What's wrong with your mother exactly?"

"Exactly? Well, I wouldn't know exactly. I am only fourteen, Detective. But I think she has that thing, you know, the gout."

"Gout?"

"And amnesia."

"Amnesia?"

"You know, she doesn't have enough iron in her blood so she gets really tired all the time."

Francolini thought about that a moment. "Oh. You mean anemia."

"Isn't that what I said?"

"You said amnesia. That's when someone can't remember something. Anemia means not enough iron in the blood."

"Anemia, yeah. Sorry." She slapped her forehead. "Amnesia . . . I guess I forgot."

"You were asleep?"

"Uh-huh."

"What time did you go to bed?"

"Regular time, you know. About ten."

"So you weren't out."

"Out?"

"Yes, out. The opposite of in."

"It's a school night, Detective. My mom doesn't let me go out on school nights."

"Do you know anyone named Lynn Robinson, Alexis?"

"Lynn Robinson?" she asked. She furrowed her brow, the way Scarlett had when she wanted to look like she was thinking hard about something. "I don't think so."

"No? He's a tenant here."

"A tenant here? I don't think so . . . wait. LJ?"

"LJ?"

"We have a tenant named LJ. He lives in a room on the top floor. He makes perfumes. I think his first name is Lynn."

"Right. Well his real name is Lynn Robinson. So you know him?"

"Sure, of course."

"When's the last time you saw Mr. Robinson?"

She scrunched her face again. "I'd have to think about that. I've been pretty busy with school and all. Maybe a week ago. I think he came to tea."

"Tea."

"Yes. It's sort of a tradition my mother started here. Every day at four she serves tea for all the residents. It's a way to stay in touch, to find out if there are any problems, you know, like leaks or something. That way my mom says they won't report us to the health department and stuff."

"So you think that's the last time you saw Mr. Robinson?"

"LJ."

"Yes, LJ."

"I think so. He doesn't always make it to tea. But that's what I remember. Why do you ask? Is something wrong?"

"I'm afraid I have some bad news, Alexis."

"Bad news? Should I sit down?"

"You might want to."

Alexis moved to the sofa and sat, trying her best to keep a blank face. She leaned forward. She thought that would make her look interested. Somebody says they have bad news, you want to look interested. Otherwise the police will think it's suspicious.

"There was an explosion in Fremont tonight at a warehouse. Have you heard anything about that?"

She shook her head. "I was asleep."

"It was a big explosion, Alexis. It caused a lot of damage. Mr. Robinson was in the building. I'm afraid he's dead."

Alexis didn't have to fake this. Just hearing the news again caused the tears to well in her eyes. "Dead?"

"I'm afraid so."

She lowered her head and covered her eyes. After a moment she looked up. "I guess I'll have to let my mom know."

"I think you should. I need to get into Mr. Robinson's apartment," Francolini said. He pulled out a piece of paper. "I have a search warrant here, signed by a superior court judge, to search his room."

"I don't have a key," she said. "My mom keeps the keys."

"And she's never told you where she puts them? What if there's an emergency? What if a tenant gets locked out of their room?"

She shrugged. "I'm only fourteen, Detective."

"Right," he said, but it sounded almost as if he didn't believe her.

He reached into the pocket of his suit coat and pulled out a plastic bag. Inside, Alexis recognized the silver charm, the one that LJ had in his hands just before the flash of light and the fireball. The last time she ever saw him.

"Have you ever seen this before, Alexis?"

She shook her head.

"Never?"

"No."

"We found this at the site of the explosion, Alexis." Francolini stood over her, waiting, and Alexis realized he wasn't as stupid as those men in *Gone With the Wind* who fought with each other over who was going to get Scarlett her pie. He was smarter than that. He had evidence. It wasn't what he thought, but what he thought was worse than it actually was. What he thought, she knew, was that the charm belonged to Alexis and that it had come off at the warehouse. That it proved she had been at the warehouse.

"I've never seen it," she said.

"And if anyone told me that they saw a young girl outside the building just before it exploded? Would that be a lie?"

"I don't know. I wasn't there. Maybe there was a young girl there."

"But that wasn't you."

"I told you, I was asleep. What kind of mother do you think I have, Detective? Do you think she'd let me stay out all night? How would I even get to Fremont? I don't drive, you know, and I wouldn't get on the bus. There are weirdos on the bus and crazy people on drugs."

Francolini turned his head, surveying the room again and Alexis looked with him. She knew he was considering the garbage can overflowing with empty cans of Chef Boyardee and tuna fish and boxes of cereal. What kind of a mother? Not a very good one by the looks of things, that was for sure.

"When do you expect your mother home, Alexis?"

She shrugged. "Tonight, I guess."

"Where does she work, exactly?"

"She works for the water department. I don't know exactly what she does. She does administrative-type stuff."

"You have her phone number at work?"

"Of course," she said and made up a number. That would buy Alexis a bit more time but not much. She couldn't underestimate Francolini, not anymore. Alexis had been stupid to say that her mother had a job at the water company. Now he would follow up, and it would reveal another lie.

"Alexis, I'm going to leave now, but I'm going to come back and I expect to talk to your mother and get into Lynn Robinson's apartment. In fact, I'm going to go back and get another search warrant, and when I come back here I'm not just going to search Mr. Robinson's apartment. I'm going to ask the judge for a warrant to search the entire building. Do you understand? So if you have anything you want to tell me about Mr. Robinson, I'd suggest you do so now."

Alexis shook her head. "No," she said. "Nothing." She looked at the clock on the wall. "Are we almost done? I'm going to be late for school if I don't get going."

"We're done," Francolini said, slipping the charm back into his pocket. "For now."

He walked to the door and opened it, but he didn't immediately leave. He turned and considered the mess again. Then he looked at Alexis.

After the door shut, Alexis hopped to her feet. Her heart was pounding and she felt lightheaded. She took two deep breaths. Now was not the time to panic. Now was not the time to faint. Francolini was coming back, coming to look for evidence that Mr. Robinson was some kind of terrorist, that he had chemicals stashed all over the building, and that included the basement. They'd look everywhere and it would be a thorough search. They'd open the casket and—surprise!—there's dear old Mom, lying there. And that would lead to a whole lot of other questions for Alexis. They'd likely think she murdered her own mother and was trying to hide the body.

Too much. It was too much to take. Too much for an adult. How was she supposed to handle it at fourteen? She was supposed to be worrying about things like the math test she didn't study for or what color to dye her hair next. She was not supposed to be worrying about dead bodies in caskets in the basement and terrorists blowing up buildings in Fremont.

"Enough," she said. "Enough whining. Now you're really starting to sound like Scarlett. One thing at a time."

You have to get rid of me, she heard her mother say. *I've liked being so close, but it's time for me to go. Kind of morbid anyway, dear, don't you think? I mean, you knew it couldn't last, right? You couldn't keep me in the basement forever.*

"OK, so what do I do? It's not like I can just open the back door and put you in a garbage can at the curb."

No, that wouldn't do. The garbage men would report it.

"Maybe I could donate your body to science."

They'd have to ask a lot of questions, first. You can't just drop off a body at the science lab.

"I'm open to suggestions, Mother."

You're a clever girl. Think. Surely you can think of someone who knows what to do with a dead body. This was after all, at one time a mortuary. . . .

And then it came to her. Of course. How could she have not remembered Clovis? Clovis Lynch, the cremator. He'd owned the building when it was a mortuary and had stayed a family friend after he sold the building to Edith's parents. Where had he gone? Some little Podunk town in the country, her mother said, where he ran a cemetery. She rushed into her mother's bedroom and fumbled through the desk, opening and shutting drawers. Her mother kept a Rolodex with everyone's name and personal information. The computer age had never been for her. She moved a stack of books and found the black metal box and flipped it open. The cards were on a spinner. She spun the knob to the L's, then went through them by hand. Lamont, Lowman, Lupes, Lynch.

She pulled out the card. Clovis Lynch. Her mother's neat handwriting included an address and phone number. She rushed back to the living room and picked up the phone, then stopped herself. Clovis Lynch had been ancient the last time she saw him when he came to visit. He might not even be alive. One way to find out.

She dialed the number. Waited. It rang twice. Someone answered, interrupting the third ring. A groggy voice. "Hello?"

"Yes, hello. Is this Mr. Clovis Lynch?"

"Who is this? What time is it?"

"Sorry to call so early, Mr. Lynch, but I have . . . I have important information?"

What? What information? She couldn't very well say "I'm looking to ditch my dead mother's body, can you help?"

"Well, what is it, dammit?"

"It's . . . it's . . . you've won the lottery. You're a millionaire."

"Damn kids," Clovis Lynch said, and hung up.

Alexis breathed a sigh of relief. OK. So he was alive. He was still alive. She looked at the address on the card. San Piedro Island. Now she just had to find a way to smuggle her mother's corpse . . .

Linda. She'd call Linda. Except Linda wasn't speaking to her. Linda had let her down. She thought for a minute. What would Scarlett do? She'd lie, of course. She'd lie if she had to. And boy did she have to.

She picked up the phone and felt just a tinge of guilt. But it couldn't be avoided, no it certainly could not. Francolini was coming back, and he'd be bringing an army of police officers with him.

She dialed Linda's cell phone. It rang three times. "Pick up. Please pick up."

"Hi," Linda said, in a small voice.

"Linda, I know you're afraid and think I've lost it, and I'm probably the last person in the world you want to talk to right now, but I need a friend."

What she really needed was a friend with a car who could drive, but she wasn't about to say that. No, Scarlett would never say that.

CHAPTER 18

JARRET MIDDLETON

THE BACK ALLEY BEHIND THE Angeline was filled with a monologue of lonely debris and terse, silent brick walls. Alexis crouched off the step to spit in the street. The mists of the last shower and the narrow encasement of the back-facing block of buildings trapped Alexis's thinking and it made her feel malignantly low. Like an ulcer palpitating on the back of a massive cancerous throat. She was breathing it out when the street coughed up a black Escalade, creeping behind a blinding field of light.

The driver's window lowered just enough for secrets to float out or for a fat stack to be passed in, but Alexis was brazen and stepped up to peer inside the car.

Linda was perched like a captain high above Alexis and the street.

"I can't *fucking* believe you talked me into stealing my stepfather's car. I don't even know what I'm doing here. . . ."

"Well the Bug is too small for a body; that's what you're doing here." Alexis twisted her shoes into the wet gravel underneath the car. "Look at the size of this thing. It's perfect."

"*Body*. What body, Alexis?" Linda sat up in the driver's seat. "What the fuck are you talking about? Answer me, there's no way. We're not going to—"

"Take my mother to a family friend's on San Piedro?" Alexis nodded.

Linda climbed down, all readied with disagreement. The tableau of Alexis, the glimmering brick, and the idling Escalade was awkward. Having Linda so close in front of her caused Alexis to draw in sharp little breaths that stabbed her lungs, which she immediately tried to remedy by staring at the line of Linda's neck. They hadn't been this close since the bridge. One of her brows rounded in an angry knot that looked like some diminutive hand had twisted the clay of her face into a permanently exaggerated position. It slid back to the normal elasticity of youth as Alexis spoke.

"If we don't do this right now, it's *all* over. Understand?" Alexis spoke with a strength that temporarily disallowed the coercion of Linda's interpretation. "Just follow my lead. Please?"

The basement of a funeral home-turned-hotel smelled as you might think it would: like dust and embalming fluid. The whole industry once built up around the dead didn't seem to disappear with the presence of living tenants. It was cold and severe like any institution. Passing through the storage hall, Linda said, "It looks like Garfield." They laughed as they rounded two sharp corners, stepping through three distinctly steep shadows that opened into the large chamber at the far back corner.

Alexis's mother was on a waist-high metal table in the center of the room within the confines of her coffin. Concealed forever by mahogany. Though she was still utterly pissed at Alexis, Linda's mood appeared to have decompressed into something more somber and essential. Her knuckles stretched to embrace the varnished box. Alexis came around the other side, flipping a red switch on the left wall. A loud shudder shot through the basement as a roller train dropped onto a casket track that weaved freely through all the concrete rooms of the foundation.

The girls grabbed hold of the coffin. Leverage was best at the widest part where the box bowed out to contain the shoulders. "One. Two. Three!" They lifted at the same time and got their cargo up an inch.

"Man, Edith's one heavy bitch."

Alexis blew out a breath of hot air.

"Sorry," Linda said.

Minor scrapes and some shoulder nudging got the coffin locked onto the track. Then they walked the body down the rollers, both conscious of each other's hesitation under the clicking cylinders. *Tick, tack.* Edith's coffin turned the corner. *Clap, clap.*

"How're we going to get her in the car?" Linda asked, completely disgusted with her complicity. *Tick, tack, clap, clap, CLACK!* Alexis widened her elbows to help slide the metal plate into place. "There's an elevator."

"Of course there's a *corpse* elevator." Linda shook her head, ducking out of the basement and back up the stairs.

The body was on the street and the girls still weren't speaking, despite working together so well. Given the grand secret, Alexis rushed to wheel her mother into the car. The black alley seemed to smoke and bend in on them like a cathedral. This was a sacred act, complex enough for the Popol Vuh. She wouldn't get to creation myths or funerary rites for two more years in school, but she felt quite aware of the grotesque responsibilities she continually bore.

The Escalade steered like a boat through neighboring streets, the back end sagging down from the weight of the exquisite corpse.

"What time is the ferry?" Linda asked.

"Can't do the ferry. Sniffer dogs."

"Bombs. Drugs. Dead bodies."

Alexis nodded. "We have to drive around. Take the Narrows up to Poulsbo."

Linda guided the black ship onto I-5 South. And their death carriage had officially begun.

Once they knew they were under way, frenzy filled the car. "Listen." Linda commandeered the massive wheel. "I trusted everything you told me, and I couldn't have even *guessed* how messed up things were with you. I mean, it's *severe*, Alex."

"You left me on the fucking bridge in the middle of the night! I told you I'd been dealing with her death, and then all this craziness followed." She mustered what she could. "I mean . . . it wasn't just her dying. It turns out I didn't know anything about her, and now suddenly it's too late for everything. Your mom remarried, Lin. Mine's in the backseat." Linda's face was bisected by passing cones of yellow light.

The gravity of Alexis's life could be felt between her bones, still living and quaking. The reality of her abandonment was starting to unfold—a black flower blooming on the ruins of her heart. LJ was dead. Mom was dead. The cops had raided the Angeline. It occurred to her then that she'd basically fled the whole scene with Linda, and the dark corridor of the highway was the first time she was able to gain any perspective on the recent insanity of her life. She wished she had more strength to fend off the attacks she knew would keep coming from Linda, especially after the previous night, but Alexis's face grew uncontrollably warm and welled up with pressure, then the cracks began to show. She searched for her motherly connection, but there was no warm beacon underneath that wood. It made heavy, water-logged noises when the flat bottom hit the backseat with every bump on I-5. Each tear called forth the next from behind her eyes, and she let go. Bawling.

Linda kept it at seventy and fought to keep herself from consoling what was quickly becoming a wrecked Alexis. She held the wheel and spoke softly. "I've never driven to San Piedro. I've only taken the boat. How do we get there?"

"Get on Highway 16 at Tacoma, then take 3 North at Bremerton. Look for signs for Poulsbo."

"Who do you know in San Piedro?" Linda asked.

Alexis gulped down the moisture in her throat. "We're going to see a cremator."

The word "cremator" petrified Linda, but the word was numb for Alexis. She thought of the expanse of the Pacific and wished for each incinerated flake of her mother to float across and sink into it. She knew deep down her mother always wanted to join the sea. Alexis sank within her angled seat. Her breathing came deep from the bottom of her lungs, past the earlier stabs and pinches brought on by the nerves of seeing Linda again. It was like the burn from running a long distance. Her stomach jerked and pulled in like a closed fist. Bile worked at the bottom of her throat. The rolling hum of the car went mute and nothing was to be heard but conscience opening the emptiness she already felt into a crater. One tragedy collided with another and she heard her own sadness for the first time since it all began, banging from one side of her skull to the other. From the skull down the neck and each chasm between bones, bones to joints, joints to ligaments, and skin to body, to name, time, place, the past, and the swinging blade of guilt.

Her slender shoulders twitched under her gray sweater and jacket. Linda reached for the heat. "You know," Alexis said, chattering, "it's like . . ."

"Easy, babe, don't say a word if you don't want to," Linda assured her.

Alexis continued, "It's like I don't know what's . . . going to happen next anymore. She's dead, Lin. And LJ's dead. The cops raided my house for Christ's sake. . . ."

It wasn't until these simple facts were stated out loud that she allowed them to be linked to the sick explosion inside her body. She clung to her duty of carrying the weight of her lie and its grief a little while longer, to exhaust the few options she had left before everyone found out.

"When I was a girl at the apartment with Mom"—Alexis paused—"I would play with this handmade silk monkey she made me for Christmas. Every night before bed I would stand on my small stool and perch the monkey up in the corner of the armoire so it could watch me while I slept. When I woke up each morning the monkey would always be there, still dangling at the edge, almost smiling as it kept an eye on me. Then I'd rush to play with it again."

Linda listened and kept an eye on the road signs. They had just passed Bremerton and the gray battleships. "Now," Alexis continued, "well, now that I'm older and all of this happened, nothing is that simple anymore. I don't know when the doll stopped watching me sleep, and I don't even know where it is now. I feel like my childhood is a dream that teases me with the idea of the world being simple."

"I hear you," Linda commiserated.

"Nothing's that simple anymore. I just got tossed into this world that I don't agree with, where everything drastically changes in an instant." Alexis glanced over and Linda returned a look of recognition. "It feels like thirty-six authors are somewhere writing my life," she said. It made Linda laugh.

"Like how Mrs. Crimson told us people think Shakespeare was

written by a bunch of authors writing in secret, or over the course of time, or something."

Linda's eyes went wide at the odd depth of Alexis's dread. It continued.

"One day, I awake in a fairy tale. Then I'm a real-life teenager that goes to school and gets good grades. I meet you, and the next moment I'm madly in love. A minute later, I'm gripped by some murderous rage. My mother dies. There're secrets that come to light, then next there's terrorism. My world spirals down. My head expands like a green balloon that nearly floats away if I don't hold on to it with everything I've got, all with some sick degree of humor. Like I'm being drawn into some comic book. I fear turning the next corner because each shadow is as dark as the inside of that . . . coffin. *Her coffin is in the backseat. How is that normal?*" she insisted.

She couldn't hear her mother's voice anymore. The way they spoke clearly, and the way they'd joked about her burial and funeral seemed a world away now, mocking her with that simplicity of everything else that had been lost. She didn't hear Mom now; she only heard that awful crashing inside and the rush of being ripped away from the world.

In an attempt to be sincere and diplomatic, she curled over in her seat and tried to offer Linda the last scraps of her sentiment. "I say things lately I wouldn't normally say. It's like I said . . . sometimes I don't know who's speaking, and I'm sorry for that."

That's why she didn't tell me, Linda thought. She didn't want any of it to come out as a lie. Linda's eyes locked up with the overwhelming portrait of Alexis having shielded the unraveling side of her life from Linda in order not to *lie* to her.

Alexis held a narrow twist in her side. "I'm so glad you helped me . . . I just don't know what I'm doing." Her eyes were a doe's, perceptibly alone. And they worked Linda to tears. "I like you so much . . ." Alexis writhed and muttered while Linda thought it out.

She was so furious at Alexis for the lies. But they were lies to avoid lying. She remembered being Alexis's age, and the logic seemed to make perfect sense. Everything had been fucked up from the moment she met her. Her parents disapproved of it. Her friends disapproved of it. And she knew there was something she always distrusted. It was a macabre sort of drama (they were driving her mother's dead body to a cremator, seriously) that showed up since before Moonlight Phở and never left. But she put herself in the shoes of her frail, sweet girl. Linda could see she was so scared and decided to drop the act. There was no way the two of them could act like their thing was sweet and innocent, but they could take it slow, and first get out of the trouble they were in.

Highway 3 languidly rolled through the evergreen hills and farm flats that eventually reached the tip of the isthmus. Their lonely car sped through the foggy aggregates between groups of black and densely clustered trees. A lone seaplane wobbled in overhead as it approached Liberty Bay, the small red lights signaling high above from underneath. Then again it was quickly quiet. Alexis slumped toward the door half-asleep with a permanent wince pulling her face apart. Her eyes were closed and Linda maintained the tiring drive through the Suquamish Indian Reservation, past the casino thronging with gamblers' cars slick and rusting in the rain.

Twenty minutes off the highway and Alexis went from a dreary slump to an upright incision of pain.

"Al, what's wrong? You feeling OK?" Linda was concerned.

The muttering picked back up, only this time more forceful. "Fucking . . . hate you . . . Ma, jus' stop it . . . we'll get you to Clovis, he'll do . . . Why didn't you name me Angeline? All the ones gone live in me, just like the hotel . . . do Ma. *Shush.* It's OK. On the ocean floor there's a door to the sky . . . you're all gone and I'll never, ever know why, we never know why." Alexis turned and grabbed a fistful of Linda's jacket and twisted it up tight around her hand. *"Stop the car!"* she yelled, and Linda slammed to a stop.

From the side, the passenger door shot open and Alexis rolled to the steep drop to the roadside. Linda looked over the wheel, then got out and ran around the warm rumbling hood the other side along the shoulder of the road. Alexis was bent over. Her vomit was hitting the tar in waves of wet splats. A wave, and then another. Alexis was folded over, holding her stomach, when she glanced up with green strings of saliva running from her chin to the ground, staring up at a worried Linda, her dead mother, and an idling car smoking from the back and glowing red. She darted from the road's edge down the embankment and straight into the forest.

Linda sprinted through the trees, yelling after her. "Alexis! Alexis, come back!" The chase steadied, and Linda was taller with longer legs and lean muscles. She accelerated quickly through the trees for a few hundred feet, then stopped, her ears tuning out the patter of rain on the hundred tiers of skyward leaves floating on the soaked thin limbs extended over and above her body poised in the chase. Footsteps scattered in the roughage ahead, and she followed.

The girls ran blind, the forest floor was heavy and wet. Linda gained on Alexis's explosive but labored path. And she remembered yelling one last plea when her breath quickened as she came down the bank of a ravine to see Alexis stumbling and losing speed. She came up on her right side and tackled her roughly to the ground. Alexis struggled to pry herself away by holding the bigger shoulders at bay. Then she punched Linda in the jaw. They rolled in the sopping leaves together, twisting legs and pulling hair and jackets. A stronger knee gained its way to the inside of a smaller, more petite thigh. A strong fist pulled the sweet angle of hair on the back of the younger head straight. And the body weight shifted. A more curved, mature pelvis nailed a younger thrusting torso hard to the wet dirt.

"*Stop.*" Linda breathed heavily over Alexis's raw mouth. Alexis's breast heaved in a dirt-covered sweater, her jacket pulled up over her side, exposing the milky pool of her stomach dredged by red lines. Her eyes fierce, wild, jejune. Face was flush and fat from crying and puking in the cold. Linda took her free hand and wiped it down across Alexis's mouth, clearing the dried ring from the edge of her lips, then she kissed them. Hard. Alexis breathed deep the sweet taste of Linda's mouth, which soothed the remaining burning in her stomach. She wrapped her legs around Linda, whose weight rubbed up the middle of Alexis's torso, and the two rolled and kissed while wrapped in the tightest hug they'd at that point ever shared or known at all.

When they reemerged from the dark tangles of the forest's grasp, the clouds and rain had scattered and the sun had pulled up all the little hidden details from the day and started everything over with the renewal of its promise. They crossed over Agate Pass, onto San Piedro Island, took a left and two rights, and drove an airy single-lane stretch to where the bend hit the westernmost point, and through the dew-covered windshield together they gleaned the damp wooden sign that read CLOVIS LYNCH, CREMATOR.

CHAPTER 19

DEB CALETTI

"ARE WE HERE?" LINDA SAID.

"I guess. Clovis Lynch is our man."

"There's a *chimney*."

"OK, that's creepy. I guess we're in the right place, then."

"Smoke is coming out of the chimney," Linda said.

"Jesus."

The sign read CREMATORIUM. The place wasn't what Alexis was expecting. She'd somehow envisioned big, rolling golf-course lawns and funeral-place men in dark suits wearing grim expressions. One of those cemetery buildings that looks like a faux colonial house, a plantation house—the kind you'd see in Virginia, where some guy would come out and show you how they made horseshoes in the old days. Definitely somber someone-just-died-and-we're-respectful-about-it music. "Wind Beneath My Wings" played by a church lady on an organ. Piped-in religious elevator music, if there were such things as religious elevators.

But not this. Not this creepy brick building down this damp path. Not in this wet place, with muddy leaves on the ground, sticking to the bottom of your shoes.

"All right. Let's do it." Linda was suddenly cheerful. Alexis didn't know if it was the promise of finally ditching the dead body in the back of the car, or if it was that caramel macchiato she'd just had at the drive-thru espresso place. Her straw was at the bottom of the cup. It was making that slurping sound.

Linda put the car in park. They sat there for a moment, staring down that brick. They looked for a long time at that chimney with the smoke pouring from it. Shit. It was too *real*.

"Do we carry her in?" Alexis asked.

"I don't know! She's your dead mother, not mine."

There were things to like about Linda, for sure, but sensitivity was not one of them.

"Let's carry her in," Alexis said.

They struggled getting the box out the back. Alexis grabbed the handles, and they scooched Edith out, sliding and wiggling until the casket was free.

"It weighs a ton," Linda said.

"Let's go fast."

"More than a ton."

"Just . . . hurry." Alexis took a big breath and lifted. They headed for the door. They were stumbling and knocking around, and the wood was hitting hard against Alexis's thighs.

"Wait, wait, wait," Linda panted. "I've got to set my end down."

Goddammit! "No, no! we're almost there."

"I can't. Heavy, heavy! I've got to rest." Linda plunked down her end before Alexis was ready. There was a disturbing slide-clunk.

Linda shook out her shoulders. "OK." She exhaled. "Ready." She picked her end back up again, and they wrestled the casket inside, holding the door open with their elbows, and with Linda's hip.

"Set her down easy," Linda said. Like she was talking about an appliance. Like she'd all at once become some refrigerator-delivery guy.

This was not what Alexis pictured at all. *At all.* Inside, the building looked a little like the vet's office where they'd brought Habib after LJ found him. Or else, the Sears Outlet store on Aurora, where she went with LJ once to return some defective band saw he'd bought on super discount. Yeah. This place—it had that same speckled linoleum, the tired fluorescent lights, a row of vinyl chairs with distressing splits and cracks from years of too-weighty asses.

"Do you have a quarter?" Linda asked.

"What? Oh for Christ's sake," Alexis said. There was one of those machines in the corner of the room, filled with those plastic globes with the various toys inside.

"I want to try for a tattoo."

"Come on. Focus. I need you, here."

The place was empty. There was a counter with a bell on it—one of those silver ones you see in the hotel lobbies in the movies. A lucite tray, too, holding some stupid pamphlets about the grief process. Five stages of grieving, whatever. The words on the cover read LOST SOMEONE? which reminded Alexis of those GOT MILK? ads. Grieving, grief. Had she even had the chance to grieve?

"Look," Linda said. She pointed up toward the wall. It was a sign. No Smoking. "Heh, heh," Linda chuckled.

"Hilarious." Alexis stared at the bell, wondering if she should use it. Those things always seemed so rude, but they didn't exactly have time for good manners. Before she could decide, though, a man appeared. A thin, ancient man—it had to be him. That had to be Clovis Lynch. Ancient, but wearing old cowboy jeans and a cowboy shirt with pearly buttons and one of those string ties, whatever they were called, Alexis couldn't think of it. Bowl? Ball? Started with a B.

"St. Bernard?" the man said.

"Excuse me?"

"You got a St. Bernard in there? Damn big box."

Alexis thought this was a rude way to treat the grieving. Maybe he needed to read one of those pamphlets.

"Clovis Lynch?" Alexis asked.

"Who else?"

"I'm . . . Alexis Austin? My mother. Edith? Edith Austin? You knew each other."

Clovis looked at her blankly. He found a toothpick on the counter and began chewing on its end. "Don't put much faith in the past. The past . . . *poof*." He gestured with one hand, wove it in the air like a column of smoke.

"You were friends."

"Don't know," he said.

Alexis wasn't sure what to do now. She'd thought they were friends. Good friends. And this was the first cremation discussion of her life. "We need . . . your services?"

"What kind of animal you got in there?"

"Animal?"

"Pet? Dog? Gotta be a dog, by the size of that thing."

"Maybe we got this wrong," Linda whispered.

"Pets?" Alexis said.

"Pet cremation? That's what we do, that's what we always done. Beloved Fido? Rover? Binky? Who you got?" The man chewed.

Alexis thought. "My mother. My mother, Edith."

Clovis Lynch blinked once. "We can do mothers."

Alexis exhaled.

"For a little extra."

OK. She'd have to figure out that part later. Take up a collection at the Angeline? Focus. First things first. "Fine," she said.

"Edith Austin, you say?" Clovis pulled out a pen and a soiled notebook.

"Um. Yes."

"Paperwork?" Clovis's eye twitched.

"I'm not sure what you mean."

Linda kicked the side of Alexis's shoe. They'd missed something important, here.

"You think you can just go light people on fire? Burn any old person right up? That could be anyone in there. That could be the mayor for all I know. Paperwork. Death certificate. I don't do humans without one."

"We . . ."

"Left it at home," Linda said. "We can get it. No problemo."

Alexis shot her a look. A death certificate? How were they going to manage *that*? What *was* that even?

Alexis felt desperate. The linoleum, the toothpick, her mother in that casket down there on the floor . . . And, Jesus, God, what did she hear in the back there? What was that sound? A television. *Wheel! Of! Fortune!* She heard an audience cheer.

It was surreal. But maybe it was a sign. Was it possible? Her mother had loved that show. She was good at it, too. She always seemed to know the phrase, even after a few letters. She would shout advice to the players. And her mom loved when they spun that big wheel. It represented hope and possibilities, maybe, the kind of chances that her mom never had. That show was glittering dresses and people clapping and new Buicks.

Wait. A smell. Could you smell a body burning? All at once, Alexis felt sick. Probably it was her imagination. In this place, an imagination could run away with you. There it was, though. Charcoal and flesh . . .

"Meatball sub," the old man said.

"What?"

"I saw your face. I know what you're thinking. Meatball sub. My lunch. It had the foil on when I put it in the microwave."

"OK."

"I always forget about the foil. You think I don't know what you're thinking? I've been doing this job for most of my goddamned life."

"The death certificate . . . ," Linda said. She wanted to get out of there.

"No shirt, no shoes, no service," the old guy said. "What, I want to get sued? I want to lose my license?"

"Pets," Alexis said. "Have you *done* people before?"

"I've done people. You get me the paper, I do people."

Alexis's mind was tumbling, racing. How to get a death certificate? Could you Photoshop those things? Could you find one online somewhere? Some legal service you pay $19.95 for?

"I'll keep her for forty-eight hours. This isn't some kind of hotel," Clovis said. The end of his toothpick was wet and frayed now.

"All right. We got it," Linda said. "Come on, girl. We better get a move on."

Clovis Lynch's jaws kept working as he watched them. His eyes narrowed suspiciously. "You sure you don't have someone important in there? A political figure, maybe? Governmental official? Celebrity? I don't want to end up on the news. I don't want big stories written up about me. Books. Movies. Clint Eastwood playing me. I'd have to go to some Hollywood premiere."

"Just my mother," Alexis said. She felt her throat close up, suddenly. She might cry.

"Fine. Get what you need, then, and come back," Clovis said.

Alexis paused. "Can I have a moment alone here?" Alexis asked.

"Got no issue with that." Clovis gave them a last look, disappeared through a doorway. His old cowboy jeans were slumping in the back. His creepy old watery eyes were probably still watching her.

For the first time, Alexis realized something. It hit her hard, a surprise. How can it be that she'd never thought about this before? That this moment would even come? This would be the last time she would be with her mother. Clovis would carry her to that back room and she'd be gone forever. She waited for her mother's voice to say something, anything, but Edith had gone silent. No advice came Alexis's way now.

Alexis could hear the tick-tick-tick of the wheel on the television in the back room, the muffled voices buying vowels and taking guesses at half-finished phrases.

So much felt half finished. Still, it was time to go.

Alexis wished she had some of that sherry her mom used to drink every day at four o'clock. A proper toast, or something. Ashes to ashes. Everybody dies, right? "The existential response," her mother had said.

Alexis wasn't sure how to do this. She knelt down, right there on the floor of the Sears Outlet Crematorium. She laid her hand on the smooth wood. She felt Linda's hand on her shoulder. She felt the heat of Linda's palm through her shirt.

"I might love you," Linda whispered into her hair, but her timing was off. This didn't have anything to do with her. Other things, but not this.

Alexis brushed Linda away. After Linda stepped aside, Alexis closed her eyes. Maybe it was a prayer. It was stupid, probably. Definitely. The box was wood, and her hand was only flesh, and it was too much to ask of either. But Alexis hoped her mother could feel her love, from here to wherever she was.

"Ready?" Linda asked.

It wasn't much of a good-bye.

But, then again, when is a good-bye ever good enough?

CHAPTER 20

KEVIN EMERSON

DESPITE ALL THE FLOTSAM SWIRLING around her, like she was the central whorl of that garbage patch out in the middle of the Pacific, Alexis always considered herself a prepared person. Of the many—far too many—pieces of advice that her mom had repeated, seemingly over and over, the one that went something like, *never get caught with anything around your ankles*, was one that Alexis actually subscribed to. Not that she'd told her mother that. That would have been like the time when she was nine and she'd clicked Yes on that Disney DVD Club e-mail and suddenly princess after princess had started arriving at her door on a monthly basis. Stopping that had been a nightmare. It would have been the same with the advice. But still . . .

I could use a few of those old tips now, Mom, she thought, and for a moment, listened into that space in the top right corner of her head, where her mother had seemed to reply from.

They were pulling up to the hotel. Alexis had been thinking that maybe her mother was still here, the ghost having taken up residence— that would have explained the recent silence— but there was only silence in her head.

"You want me to come in?" Linda asked.

Alexis didn't. They had taken the ferry home, a long and mostly silent drift through a gloomy late afternoon of misty rain, with the droplets that seemed too small for wipers to corral, the kind that made everyone drive like idiots and so everything took forever. Alexis supposed not everyone was trying to beat a search warrant home.

"'Cause I've probably got a little longer," Linda continued, "you know, to hang out, or"—she reached over and ran her index and middle finger up Alexis's forearm—"if you need some coffin time."

Alexis snatched her arm away, thinking, *Jesus, no! How much of the EVERYTHING that's happened have you missed?* But she held it back, had to hold so much back lately, and instead just pretended that her sudden retreat had been to check her watch. "Nah, I . . . I should just get back in. Everyone's going to need me."

"OK, fine," Linda said, the end of each word nosediving with disappointment. "I just want to make you feel better."

"Yeah, well, me feeling better is a lost cause at this point. Why don't you check back in when I'm out of jail? I'll see you later."

Alexis popped open the door and dropped out of the Escalade. She was suddenly glad to be out of the car, glad to be out of Linda's reach. Linda, who thought that Alexis's last moment with her mother was a good time to drop the L-word, like she sensed a dramatic stage and just assumed that she had the right to step on in, like every goddamn spotlight was hers to occupy.

"Fine," Linda snapped. "Hey, Linda," she said, "thanks for driving my ass all the way to San Piedro Island with a cadaver, and on that note, here's some cold shoulder."

"No," Alexis said with a sigh. "Come on. I am thankful, just . . . come by later. Get the car back before you get busted."

"See ya." Linda reached over and closed the door. The car lurched away, tires grinding the pavement.

Alexis watched her go for a moment, feeling a hundred things, or nothing; the two sensations had become similar at this point. She didn't need to be hard on Linda, but maybe she did because Linda didn't get it, did she? Because what were the current standings? Linda plus parents 3, Alexis 0. She hadn't been through something like this. Not even close.

Alexis turned toward the hotel. She surveyed its damp and sagging exterior, the windows grimy, each old inhabitant's belongings pressed against them. It occurred to her that this would be the first time she stepped inside on her own. Sure, she'd been on her own for weeks now, but at least her mother had still been there. It had still been their place. What was it for her anymore? Memory, logistics, pain.

An urge struck her: *Run*. Just turn and start across the park and maybe take a bus or just keep moving over the hill and down to Amtrak. In Portland by midnight, sleep in the terminal, Sacramento by midday Sunday—Mexico, Alabama, wherever. Just disappear. Because if she stepped back inside this place now, she was inviting it back into her life, making it part of her future.

Last chance, she thought.

Then her eye fell on a pirate's flag flying from the far corner of the third-floor balcony. Ursula's. It hadn't been there before. What would become of them if she left? Who was left for these people?

Something dropped away inside her, a heaviness falling from the underside of her diaphragm, down into unknown depths. She started up the stairs.

The door was locked. She fished out her key, turned the lock, but the door wouldn't move. Was it blocked?

She knocked, calling, "Hey!"

There was a commotion inside—a long, squealing sound of furniture moving. Alexis pictured the burgundy chair in the sitting room—that was how well she knew this damned place—and the door creaked slightly open.

"Who calls?"

"Duh, Kenji, it's me." Alexis leaned in toward the door, only to jump back as something darted out toward her.

It was Pluto, gazing at her and flicking his tongue curiously.

"No one gets in without the password!"

"Roberta, let me in!"

"She doesn't know the password," Mr. Kenji whispered.

"We said that everyone had to know the p—"

Alexis huffed to herself. Half a day she'd been gone, and already things had gone to hell. She grabbed Pluto just behind its jaws and yanked. There was a thud against the door. Alexis leaned in again. "It's me, Alexis, and I don't know the password and you are going to open this door. Right. Now."

"She doesn't know the—"

"Shut up!"

The door finally opened a foot, and Alexis squeezed in, tossing the python back at Roberta. "Jesus, what's with you two?"

Mr. Kenji and Roberta looked away sheepishly. "Sorry," said Kenji, "we—"

"What's going on down there?" Otto tottered down the stairs, leaning over the railing. Alexis saw that he was in some kind of costume, wearing a hat and a military uniform. "This bunker is on lockdown!"

"Bunker?" asked Alexis.

"Last stand! Nobody gets in! Nobody gets out!"

"Otto, it's me," Alexis muttered.

"He may think we're in Berlin," whispered Mr. Kenji, "but everyone's on edge since the break-in."

"Break-in?"

"Spies! Infidels!" Otto called.

"Curse you, Otto, get back up here!" Ursula called from somewhere upstairs.

"Have the police been back?" asked Alexis.

"No," said Mr. Kenji.

"Then who was here?"

Deaf Donald passed them, brandishing Ursula's pirate broadsword and wearing what was possibly a pair of women's leggings as a headband.

"Ursula's been advising us on defensive attire," said Roberta.

"OK," Alexis muttered, now noticing that Roberta had various kitchen utensils stuffed into the wide elastic waistband of her jersey skirt, "You are going to tell me what is happening here. Now. And I don't want to hear about Berlin, or anything else. *Tell* me."

"We'll show you," said Mr. Kenji. He dragged the chair back in front of the door and then headed upstairs. Roberta followed, then Alexis.

"Watch out for the trip wire," Kenji advised as they neared the top step. Alexis saw a line of pink knitting yarn stretched across the staircase. It wrapped around the banister and led up to the ceiling, where hung the tiny silver creamer.

"Hey," said Alexis.

"Brilliant, right?" said Roberta.

"Ready to pour a point-five percent solution of sulfuric acid on any intruder," added Mr. Kenji.

"I don't even want to ask," said Alexis.

"When the koi die, I can't bear to flush them. Dissolution is better for the environment."

Alexis looked at him, and decided, quickly, to let whatever that meant go.

"Ow, dammit, hurry up!" Ursula called.

They stepped over the trip wire and turned the corner to find the old pirate hanging upside down from the ceiling, her peg leg poking through the retracted attic staircase, which hung partially open.

"Who would have thought those springs were strong enough to suspend a person," mused Mr. Kenji.

Otto and Deaf Donald stood to either side of Ursula, yanking on her thighs.

"How did this happen?" asked Alexis.

"We were all watching the news downstairs," said Ursula, her voice strained from her blood-filled head. "If it wasn't for Deaf Donald hearing the intruder, we probably never would have known."

"Deaf Donald," Alexis repeated.

"He felt the vibrations in the floor—footsteps, coming up from the basement. We figure he got in through a basement window."

Alexis looked at Donald. "Nice work."

He smiled.

"We mustered arms and headed upstairs, where we found him trying to break into LJ's room."

"I tried to drop the attic door on him," said Otto, still yanking at Ursula's impaled leg, "but it missed."

"And my roundhouse missed, too," said Ursula. Though upside

down, she reached and massaged her lower back. "It's been a long time since those jujitsu classes."

"Three decades," said Roberta disapprovingly.

"OK, but so he didn't get in?" Alexis was already moving past the residents.

"No, but he got out the front door before we could catch him. That's why we're on lockdown."

"I ordered them to raise the flag so all would know the danger of entry!" Ursula gasped, her face a bloated beet.

"Never!" Otto cried, simultaneously yanking viciously on Ursula's leg.

There was a splintering crack and Ursula toppled to the floor.

"Did you get a good look at him?" Alexis asked.

"Well, not a good one," said Mr. Kenji.

"He was a man," said Roberta, "Pluto always twitches around men, and he was sure twitchy."

"Anything else?" asked Alexis.

The residents looked at one another.

"He was damn fast," said Ursula.

"Or maybe your kick was slow as Log Cabin maple syrup," chided Roberta.

"You—"

"OK, great," said Alexis. Her mind was spinning. So, it wasn't just the police now. Someone else was after LJ's information. Her mom's body was safely out of the hotel; now she had to figure out what LJ had left for her on the disc. Maybe it would make her world make sense again.

Or you could just run, she thought again, remembering that urge, thinking about Mexico . . . but as she looked from one odd face to the next, she realized that wasn't, and had never been, an option. These residents were trying to defend what was theirs, and what was hers, too.

"Listen, you guys did great," said Alexis, and she watched as these words ignited smiles around the group. "I want you to keep it up. I will be right back. But if the police do come, let them in. Nobody else. Defend the bunker."

"*Achtung!*" Otto exclaimed.

"Mr. Kenji, I need to borrow your Discman."

Mr. Kenji's face lit up. "Do you need any of my mix CDs? Polynesian Disco Funk? It's great for self-reflection. I invented the genre—"

"No, thanks. Another time. I just need the player."

Alexis ran upstairs to her room and grabbed the *Gone With the Wind* movie case before Mr. Kenji was back with the Discman. She left out the back door, the CD and the player in her bag. She needed to find somewhere safe to listen to the disc, and until she knew what LJ had left her, she couldn't have any run-ins with the police.

The undersides of the evening clouds were gathering twilight, but the sun had lowered below that ceiling, orange beams splaying across the tops of buildings. As Alexis headed away from the hotel, one such beam lit the tower atop a nearby landmark—Saint Ignatius chapel at Seattle University. Her mother had taken her there often, to sit in the calming silence.

There was no longer a voice in her head, but she wondered at those sunbeams, guiding her, and wondered if her mother's spirit, now a part of the oceans and the universe beyond, were reaching out to subtly guide her. Probably not, but it was a nice thing to believe.

She'd go with it.

CHAPTER 21

KIT BAKKE

AS ALEXIS SAT IN THE gloaming light, LJ shouted in a stagy, hysterical voice from the spinning disc: "Good people of the world, if there are any of you left, which I am beginning to doubt, *unite*! Please! You have *nothing* to lose but your infantile fantasies. There is no Man Upstairs who will make everything come out right. It *won't* happen! God has left the building. The Fascists have taken over and will see you rot in Hell. Fight back! Confront the Truth! Reality will set you *freeeeee*."

LJ went on like this for way too long. Alexis couldn't quite follow the thread of his argument, if that's what it was. He clearly was giving a speech, as if to fire up millions of misguided masses. *What a crock he is*, she thought, *but what a sweetie, too*. Then she remembered her last sight of him, lying all bloody and burned on the Fremont curb, and her tears came more freely than his stream-of-consciousness conspiracy theories ever had.

She blew her nose and tuned back to his words, now turned down a couple decibels.

"I gotta tell you something, kiddo. This is about your dad. He was the best man, the best. Well, Mao was really the best, but he was in China. Busy freeing a billion Chinese from the running-dog reactionaries. Mao was a poet, too. A poet and a genius. God I wish I'd gotten to China in the old days. What a rush! Red flags everywhere. My Little Red Book's still around here somewhere." Alexis heard some rustling and then some screechy sounds. "Damn, wish I knew how to play this!" Then more silence and then she heard LJ clearing his throat.

"Poem by LJ. Title: The Revolution Cometh.

Red Sun Rises

Orange Flames Lick the Sky

Stormy Waters Raging Below

Feed the People's Righteous Wrath!

Victory Is Ours! *Venceramos!*"

Alexis felt the tears start again, but worked to keep her attention on LJ's voice. It was a shaky lifeline, but it was all she had. "Come on, LJ, pull it together. What about my dad?"

More screechy sounds, then LJ intoned, "Which came first, the omelet or the egg? Shit, it's time for the Truth. People, get ready. A Journey of a Thousand Miles begins with the Sweep of a Single Broom. I loved your dad, Alexis, and your mom made me promise never to tell you about him. But now's the time. Break an egg, break a promise. The Revolutionary Life is never easy. It ain't over till the fat lady gives her cake to the Starving Serfs."

Alexis heard him take a deep breath, some more rustling sounds, a short silence, and then a crash. "Never get that tree pose right!"

"Come on, LJ!" Alexis was getting exasperated, but immediately felt guilty. How bad is it to be exasperated at a dead person? She was even feeling a tiny bit angry at her mom. All this breaking news was over-whelming. She felt a little sick to her stomach.

"OK, kiddo, here it is. The Truth, man, and nothing but. Maybe the only time in the History of Man, I mean . . . People. Truth ain't as easy as it sounds. Your dad and me, we were comrades. He was always better than me, but we were a team. I learned a lot from him, but not enough, not enough. You, Alexis, you are so like him, it knocks me out. All the good parts of him are right there, in you. And you're a girl, too. It's spooky sometimes. Like I'm here to protect your back—the way I didn't protect your dad's.

"We were into a very big action. Stun the Man, that was the plan. We were the fifth column, working from inside. We were going to bring down all the evil forces of Imperialism. TKO. Out in one. Buried so far in the heap of History that nothing could revive it. Capitalism dead! Exploitation a faint memory! We were saving the world!

"Your dad took a lot of the risk on himself. I can't tell you the whole scoop, 'cause then I'd have to kill you." Alexis heard him cough and cackle—his version of a laugh. "But imagine the most devastating blow to the Capitalist, Imperialist running dogs and their lackeys you can possibly conceive of, and that's exactly what we were doing. Ten times over. It was totally cool.

"So there's your dad, leading the way. We were in the prep phase, doing dry runs, weapons practice, collecting fake IDs, safe houses, getaway cars, learning the routes. Partying, too. That was always in the mix. Drugs, sex—FBI, CIA, they trained themselves to tolerate rock 'n' roll, but never the drugs or sex. Against their stupid rules, but it worked in our favor. They couldn't infiltrate us. Brilliant, if I do say so myself. By the way, kiddo, watch out for that J. Edgar Hoover—people think he's dead, but he's not. He's a Cylon.

"Anyway, I'm avoiding the hard part, chica. Don't want to tell you about this. Where I let him down. Big-time. But I can do this. . . . So he had a weapons run to make. Stolen car. Car full of shit. The plan was to make the drop-off and then ditch the car. Done it a hundred times before. Well, maybe not a hundred. Gotta stick to the truth, promises . . ." His voice faded off a little and Alexis had to strain to hear.

"The drop-off went fine, but the ditching, oh God, the ditching was the big fuck-up. The plan was for him to drive the car onto the ferry and go right off the other end, into the water. I'd pick him up in the Duck Boat. I had a part-time job driving the tourists around in a Duck Boat. But I screwed up. Oh man, I screwed up big-time." Alexis heard him take a big gulping breath. "I forgot if he was going off the Bainbridge or the Bremerton ferry and ended up driving the damn Duck Boat around between both docks. It was dark. I . . . I don't know, kiddo, I don't know." Alexis could hear him sobbing. "I think I ran over him."

Now Alexis was sobbing, too. For about five minutes she'd had a dad, and now she didn't again. And he was a good guy, too, cool and brave. Damn LJ—damn him for being an idiot and damn him for telling her. Damn the whole fucking world. God, life was unfair. Hers in particular. What a mess.

"So now you've heard the worst," LJ was whispering now. "I've spent the rest of my life trying to make up for it. The worst mistake of my life. My best bud. My comrade in arms. I'm nothing like him. Not even close, Alexis. I've tried. Mao knows I've tried. I've spent years on this bridge project. Trying to make up. Trying to keep the revolutionary fires burning. In your dad's name and the names of all the oppressed and fighting peoples of the world."

LJ sounded as if he were trying to wind himself back up. He went on muttering about selfless communism, the interests of the masses and the evils of capitalism, but all the capital letters and exclamation points were gone from his voice. Then Alexis heard the screeching sounds again.

"Damn. Wish I'd learned to play this. The least I could have done."

The screeching stopped and she heard some plucking sounds and LJ's voice, for the last time, "maybe I can make it work like a guitar."

CHAPTER 22

JULIA QUINN

ALEXIS DIDN'T MOVE. THE DISCMAN clicked off, and she didn't move. She just sat there, trying to digest what she'd just heard.

LJ had killed her dad. Not on purpose, but still. And the crazy thing was, she wasn't even mad at him. How could you not be mad at someone who killed your father?

Maybe because that person had spent years trying to *be* a father to her. It all made sense now. Well, maybe not sense. Nothing LJ did made sense. It was kind of what made him LJ. But he had always been there for her. Even just the other night, when he'd helped her to find clothes to wear to see her uncle at the Sorrento. He'd been there for her.

Alexis pulled the headphones off and rubbed her ears. She looked up at the tree. There was a tree in the middle of the chapel. What was up with that? It was totally in the wrong place. She supposed some thoughtful New Age yoga-type person thought it would be cool to stick a tree in the middle of a chapel, but to Alexis it was just wrong. It should be outside. How was a tree supposed to live on its own?

She stood up, making her way slowly back outside. She was just like that tree. She needed help.

Linda's stepdad. He hated her. No, he more than hated her, but she had nowhere else to turn. He was the only lawyer she knew, and she had a pretty good feeling she needed a lawyer.

She started walking toward the bus stop, then stopped. The papers. The ones she'd found in her mom's room about the hotel. She needed to go get them. If Linda's stepdad was going to help her save the hotel (and that was a big if) she was going to need those papers.

When she got back to the hotel, everyone was still up in the hallway. Ursula was waving a plunger at Mr. Kenji, and Otto was sitting on the floor, his back to the wall, with Habib on his head.

No one seemed to find any of this the least bit odd. Alexis had to stop and smile, because she didn't either.

"What are you doing back?" Donald yelled. He was trying to wrestle the plunger from Ursula before she accidentally took out Mr. Kenji's eye.

"I forgot something," Alexis said. "Forget you saw me."

"Forgotten!" Otto said with a salute. "I can keep secrets, you know."

Alexis gave him a thumbs-up and ran to her room, where she'd stashed the papers. She took one look at them, as if she needed reminding that lawyers did not write in English, and shoved them in her bag.

Then she ran back out, barely pausing to say good-bye. She needed to get to Linda's apartment. Fast.

"Alexis?" Linda gasped. "What are you doing here?"

Alexis tried to smile. Well, maybe not smile, but some kind of expression that conveyed something other than panic. Linda did not look happy to see her. Alexis once again gave silent thanks to the random person who'd held the front door open for her when she'd arrived at Linda's apartment building. She had a feeling that if she'd buzzed up, Linda would not have let her in.

"I need to talk to your stepdad," Alexis said.

"Are you crazy? He hates you."

"I know that. But I need a lawyer."

Linda just stared at her.

"What about your mom? She likes me, kind of."

"She's out of town."

Alexis lost it. "I witnessed an explosion, I just found out that my dad was run over by a duck, someone broke into LJ's room, and my uncle is trying to steal the hotel. Oh, and I un-faked my mom's death and enlisted your help to hide the body."

"You un—"

"Whatever the hell you call the opposite of faking your death. Please, Linda, I need help."

"OK." Linda swallowed and slowly opened the door to Alexis. She looked younger all of a sudden, and Alexis wondered how much of her tough-guy personality was an act. Linda looked furtively over her shoulder. "Just don't tell him—"

"Don't worry," Alexis assured her impatiently. "I won't say a word."

Linda gave a jerky nod and finally opened the door all the way. "Kenneth!" she called out, then cleared her throat. She said it louder. "Kenneth!"

"I'm in the living room! What is it?"

"Uhh . . . you know my friend Alexis?"

There was a long silence. "Yes?"

Linda grabbed her by the wrist and pulled her down the hall to the living room. When they could see the back of Kenneth's head, she said, "She's here."

Still Kenneth didn't turn around. He just stared at the TV, which was flickering some cop show Alexis didn't know. "Why?" he finally asked.

Alexis thought maybe it was time she spoke for herself. "I need help."

Slowly, Kenneth twisted around. Alexis could see that he was holding a drink in his hand. "What do you need?" he asked, but he didn't really sound like he cared.

Alexis took a deep breath. People like Kenneth Whatever-the-Hell-His-Last-Name-Was-Because-It-Wasn't-the-Same-As-Linda's always made her nervous. Maybe it was the suit. Or the way his dark hair was so neatly trimmed and combed. He was too polished. He was the Man.

Alexis fought an extremely ill-timed giggle. What would LJ say?

"Alexis," Kenneth said in that über-calm voice of his. "Why are you here?"

"I . . . uh . . . ." Where the hell was she supposed to begin? She didn't know how to talk to lawyers. Hell, she didn't know how to talk to any adult who wasn't at least a little bit insane.

"Her mom is dead," Linda blurted out.

Alexis choked against the grief lumping in throat. She knew it was true, but it was so much harder when someone said it out loud. "My uncle . . . he uh . . ." She opened her messenger bag and dug around for the legal papers, grateful for the excuse to look away. She didn't want him to see her face, not if she was going to cry.

"Here," she said, thrusting the documents at him. "I found these in my mom's stuff. I think my uncle is trying to steal the hotel."

Kenneth took the papers and looked down at them. After a few seconds he flicked off the TV and asked Linda to turn on the light for him. Alexis waited nervously as he slowly made his way through the document, licking his finger before using it to flip each page. When he was about halfway through, he looked up and used his head to motion to a chair across the room. "Sit down," he said.

Alexis moved awkwardly across the room. The furniture was modern and spotless, and the chair Kenneth had directed her to looked ruthlessly uncomfortable. She perched at the edge, watching him as he reached the final page of the papers.

"Can you help me?" she asked.

Kenneth set the papers down on the coffee table in front of him. "Did you read these?" he asked.

"I tried. I couldn't understand them."

Kenneth gave her a wry smile. "I'm afraid lawyers aren't known for their clarity."

"Well, what does it say?"

"Your uncle wasn't trying to steal the hotel," he said gently.

"Well, no," Alexis said, starting to feel a little more at ease now that he was actually being nice to her. "But he was going to force my mom to sell it. They own it together, and I know that one of them can't sell it unless the other agrees."

"That's true," Kenneth said, "but your uncle wasn't the one who wanted to sell the hotel. It was your mother."

Alexis shook her head. "No. No, you've got it wrong. She would never do that. She loved the hotel."

"I'm sure that's true," Kenneth said carefully, "but for whatever reason, she was suing your uncle to force a sale."

"No," Alexis said again. Awkwardly, she came to her feet, bumping her thigh against the arm of the chair as she rose. "You're wrong." She looked over at Linda, desperate for someone to back her up. "Linda," she said, hating the desperation in her voice. "Tell him."

Linda looked back and forth between Alexis and her stepfather. "I . . . uh . . . um, I don't think Edith would have sold the hotel. She really seemed to like it."

"A building that size takes a lot of money to maintain," Kenneth said.

"But we were doing OK," Alexis said belligerently. It was two steps to the coffee table and then she snatched up the papers. "Forget I said anything. Forget I asked for your help." She turned to Linda. "I'll go."

"No," Kenneth said. He stood and put his hand on Alexis's arm. "We can help you."

Alexis looked down at his hand suspiciously.

"Who is staying with you?" he asked. "You're a minor. You can't stay in the hotel by yourself."

"I'm not by myself."

"Your tenants don't count."

Alexis thought about Ursula and Mr. Kenji, Deaf Donald and Otto. And LJ. She especially thought of LJ. Maybe they weren't the kind of people Kenneth would ever deign to talk to, but they counted. They all counted.

"I'm leaving," she muttered, yanking her arm free. "I'll figure something out."

"Alexis, you can't go back and live at the hotel," Linda said. "Maybe if LJ was still there, but he's dead, too, and—"

"Wait a minute," Kenneth said, his head snapping back and forth between the two girls. "Who the hell is LJ?"

Alexis glared at Linda. This was not about LJ, and she should have known better than to bring him up.

"Linda, who is LJ?" Kenneth demanded, when it became apparent that Alexis was not going to answer.

"He lived over at the hotel. He was—"

"Linda!" Alexis practically snarled the word. The little traitor. She couldn't believe it.

"I'm sorry, Alexis," Linda said, "but this is too big. You can't handle it yourself."

"Who is LJ?" Kenneth demanded again.

"He lived at the hotel," Linda said quickly, before Alexis could interrupt again. "He died in that explosion last night."

"*What?*" Kenneth swore under his breath. "Please tell me you didn't have anything to do with that."

"Of course not," Alexis snapped. "But—"

"But what?"

"Nothing." She hugged her messenger bag closer to her body. There was no way she was going to let him listen to the disc. He would think LJ was completely whacked out. He'd use it to—OK, she had no idea what Kenneth would do with the disc. But she didn't want him to hear it. She owed LJ that much.

Kenneth let out a long breath. "OK, this is what we're going to do. Alexis, you'll stay here tonight."

"No," Alexis said automatically. She wasn't staying anywhere with this guy.

"Look," Kenneth said sharply, "I ought to call Child Protective Services right this minute."

"Oh my God." Panicked, Alexis shot a glance toward the door, trying to gauge how long it would take to get there.

"Listen to me," Kenneth said, grabbing her arm again.

"No!" Alexis yelled. "I knew I shouldn't have come over here. You're just going to put me in some foster care so you never have to see me again, and—"

"Just stay here until I can figure out what to do," he said. "What I was trying to say is that I *should* call CPS on you, but I won't. Not yet. Let me look into this first. There might be some other solution."

Alexis eyed him warily.

"I'm trying to help you, Alexis," he said.

Maybe he thought he was. But what he thought was right and good would never be what was right for Alexis. Still, she knew that if she left right now, he'd call the police in a heartbeat. Better to let him think she had given up.

"OK," she said. "I'll stay here for now."

"Good," he said, giving her arm a reassuring squeeze. "You're doing the right thing."

"I know." She nodded, trying to look like a good girl, whatever that was.

He seemed to buy it. "I'm going to go look into this." He turned to Linda. "I'll be in my office. Why don't you two get something to eat?"

"Sure," Linda said. Alexis nodded again. More of that good-girl thing.

But she wasn't a good girl. She never had been. And there was no way she was spending the night there.

CHAPTER 23

MARY GUTERSON

ALEXIS WAS STARVING. GOD, WHEN was the last time she'd had anything to eat? She couldn't remember. That morning? The day before? She remembered throwing up. *That* she remembered.

"So, what do you feel like eating?" Linda asked. "We've got everything you can think of. Steak? Macaroni and cheese? Tuna sandwich?"

"I don't care. Anything. All of a sudden I feel like I'm going to pass out. This has been the longest day of my life."

"Just go sit on the sofa. Let Linda take care of you."

Alexis sank down into the deep cushions. Man, did rich people have nice sofas. And chairs to match. And nice coffee tables with framed photos. And paintings everywhere. Alexis wished she knew more about art. One of these paintings could be by somebody famous and she wouldn't even know it.

What was wrong with her? Why couldn't she be like other people? Other people would know who did these paintings. Other people lived in normal houses with normal families. Other people got up in the morning and ate pancakes and eggs instead of serving booze and tea to old people at four in the afternoon.

And college. Other people went to college. Alexis had never even considered going to college. What would she study, anyway? She had no idea what she wanted to be in life.

What a loser.

Alexis closed her eyes, remembering middle school and they way the other girls treated her—like she was poisonous or something. And they'd called her names. Lesbo. Ha! Well, what do you know? Turned out they were right! She was a lesbo! How about that!

She set her hands over her belly and tried to calm its growling. She was going to fall asleep. She could feel it coming over her, the urge to simply let sleep overtake her. No, she mustn't let that happen. She had to stay awake. She had to get back to the Hotel Angeline.

"Here you go," Linda said.

On the platter that Linda held in front of her sat a big bowl of tomato soup and a fat, doughy-looking roll. Alexis could almost cry, it smelled so good—like the smell of home, of the soups Edith used to make and serve with white toast, slathered with butter.

"Thanks," Alexis said.

Linda sat down next to her. She lifted a hand to Alexis's cheek and stroked it softly.

"I'm sorry, " Linda said. "I'm sorry about everything. I'm sorry your mom had to die and that maybe you'll lose the hotel and that LJ is gone and all of that. But you know, I honestly think something good is going to come of all of this. I really do. I know you wish everything could just go back to the way it was before. But you know as well as I do that isn't going to happen. It sucks, I know."

Alexis took a big spoonful of hot soup. If only she could give in right now. Be done with it. Fess up to the police. She was tired of being so responsible.

"You look like you're conking out," Linda said.

"Yeah."

"Do you just want to go to sleep here on the sofa? You can, you know. I can bring you a comforter and you can just fall asleep whenever you want. In the morning, all of this will be over. And it will all be OK, I promise."

Alexis nodded, but inside she'd already begun to plan.

"A comforter would be great," she said.

Moments later, Linda had tucked the comforter around her on the sofa and tiptoed out of the room, switching off the lights as she went. Alexis waited five full minutes, then opened her eyes and sat up. She was going to have to get back to the hotel. She'd come this far; she wasn't going to let anything stop her now.

She switched on the lamp next to the sofa, stood, and listened carefully. Silence. No one.

As quietly as she could, she walked to the front door in the foyer and placed a hand on the door handle. Suddenly, a voice behind her made her jump.

"What do you think you're doing, young lady?"

Alexis turned around. It was Kenneth, staring at her. He didn't look happy.

"Oh. I. Well. I. I just wanted to get a little fresh air is all," Alexis said. "That's all I was doing. Just stepping outside for a moment."

"How about we open a window in the guest room for you?" Kenneth said. He took Alexis by the arm and led her away from the door and down the hallway. Halfway down, he opened a door.

"In here, my dear," he said.

Alexis looked inside the room. A bed. A bedside table. A dresser. A lamp.

"I'm sure you'll find it quite comfortable," Kenneth said. "Now, no more monkey business. We'll see you in the morning."

He shut the door.

"And by the way, I'll be right outside, so don't try anything!" Kenneth yelled through the door. "Sorry, my dear. But extreme measures seem to be in order for you."

An hour went by. Maybe two. Alexis didn't know how long she'd been lying on the bed awake, waiting for morning. She'd been so exhausted, and now she couldn't sleep to save her life. Her head was spinning. First she thought about Edith and the place where she and Linda had left her. There had been something funny about that guy Clovis. Something wrong with the way he talked. Alexis suddenly wondered if it had been a huge mistake, leaving Edith with him. My God, who knew what he might do with her? How could she have trusted him? Oh, God, she was so stupid. And then she thought about Linda. She had thought Linda loved her and would take care of her and it turned out that Linda was a traitor. And then LJ, the only man she had trusted with all of her secrets, and look what had happened to him. Dead. Just like her mother. She couldn't help it. She started to cry. And then she was weeping, the tears streaming down her cheeks. When she was a little girl and cried, her mother had come to pick her up.

Now she had no one.

She had only herself.

Alexis stood and walked over to the window, where she could look out over the viaduct. She opened the window and stuck her head out into the night air. It had rained earlier—poured, really—but it had stopped now and the air felt fresh, almost harsh, inside her nose. She had to think. Think. Think. Think. How was she going to get out of this room when there was only one way out and it was through the window? She looked down. There was a ledge, almost a small deck that ran the length of the building. To the right she could see the living-room windows. And farther down, the windows of the bedroom Linda's mom and stepdad shared. All the lights were on and she could hear the sound of the television. Maybe Kenneth had gone back to the bedroom after all.

Linda would be sleeping soundly by now, in that deep sleep of hers where she couldn't be woken, even by a hurricane. And Linda's mother was out of town, probably a business trip. So it was only Kenneth Alexis had to contend with.

How many floors up was she? She looked down. Eight. That was a lot of flights. She didn't want to fall and kill herself. That would be stupid. Well, she was going to have to try something.

She took a few deep breaths and then put one leg through the open window. So far, so good. She put the other leg up and then she was sitting on the window ledge, eight floors above the street. This was crazy. What was she going to do?

Then she heard something. Something familiar. She sat still as she could, listening as hard as she could. Yes, in the distance. The familiar cawing of a bird. Habib. Was it really Habib?

"Habib!" she said in a loud whisper. "Habib! Over here!"

The cawing grew louder and a moment later, there was the big black bird, swirling around in circles in the sky in front of her. He swooped and swirled and then dove toward where she sat, perching himself on the ledge next to her. Habib. The bird that had always driven her crazy. And now she couldn't believe how happy she was to see him.

"Hey boy," she said to him.

He dipped his head and allowed her to smooth the feathers of his back.

"What are we gonna do, Habib?" she said to him. "It feels like this is the end of the road, boy."

At that, Habib flapped his wings and took off into the night sky.

"So that's it, huh?" Alexis said. "You're abandoning me too, are you?"

She heard the bird caw, and a moment later she heard a second caw and a moment after that came the sound of tens and then dozens of caws, and then a hundred crows suddenly appeared out of nowhere. Habib led them all, his fine black body making swoops and circles while Alexis watched in awe.

"Well, that's all fine, birdy boy," she said to him. "But whatcha gonna do for me now?"

As though he'd only been waiting for her to ask him that very question, Habib suddenly stopped in midair and gave the loudest, most ear-piercing caw she'd ever heard. All at once, the birds came flying—one huge black mass of pure energy, flying full-speed toward the building and then crashing into the windows of the apartment. The noise was deafening. They came in waves, crashing and crashing and cawing and screaming and making enough noise to wake a ghost.

"What the . . . ?" she heard Kenneth call.

Alexis leaned back into the guest room as she heard him lifting one of the windows in his bedroom.

"Get out of here!" he yelled, as several crows flew right past him and into the house.

He slammed the window down, and still the crows came.

"Oh my God!" Alexis heard him yell, and then he was running down the hallway and the caws were everywhere.

"Get the hell out!" he was screaming. "The birds are going crazy! I don't know what's going on, but we gotta get out of here."

She heard a crashing noise and realized that the crows had smashed one of the living-room windows.

"Out!" Kenneth yelled—at her or the crows, she didn't know. But she wasn't going to stop to find out. As he turned toward Linda's room—was she really still sleeping through all this?—Alexis ran out of the guest room and down the hall, now filled with crows. In the living room, Habib was leading dozens of birds in a sort of crazy crow dance, looping and sailing and making big circles right over the three-foot-tall Dale Chihuly vase that sat in the middle of the room on the coffee table. The room began to vibrate, and so did the vase.

"*No!*" Kenneth yelled.

But the crows didn't care. At least two dozen crows converged in flight and dived for the vase. It swayed this way and that, and shuddered and trembled and then all at once it toppled onto the glass coffee table and broke into a million pieces.

"My Chihuly!" Kenneth yelled. "Oh. My. God! The world is going crazy."

No *shit*, Alexis thought. Nothing had been right for weeks.

Kenneth began to leap around the room, grabbing vases and photographs and then trying his best to pull a huge painting off the wall. But each thing he tried to save only seemed to make the crows angrier. They swarmed the paintings, the vases, the tables, the sofa. They were everywhere.

Suddenly, Habib was on Alexis's shoulder, and he was prodding her chin with his beak.

"Right, little fellow," she said. "Let's make some tracks."

She ran for the foyer, opened the front door, and ran down the hallway to the staircase. Then she took all eight flights seemingly at once, ending up at a door that led into an alley.

Freedom.

The door slammed behind her and she stopped for a moment to lean against the alley wall, her hands on her knees, to catch her breath. She could hardly breathe. Habib nudged her.

"I know. I know. Just give me a second, would you?"

She took one big gulp of air, blew it out, and then said, "OK. Ready."

But how was she going to get back to the Angeline? She was miles away in Pioneer Square, and the Angeline was up on Capitol Hill. Habib was making little noises and then he lifted off of her shoulder and flew away.

"You go home," she called after him. "I owe you big-time."

She ran down the alley, past a junkie nodding off in a back doorway, and past a couple of homeless people sleeping on top of cardboard boxes covered with black garbage bags. The world was a harsh place. She stopped, dug into her pocket, and came up with a dollar bill. Then, she ran back to set it down in front of the sleeping homeless people, placing a beer bottle on top so that it wouldn't fly away. It wasn't much, she knew. But she couldn't just pass a homeless person without doing something.

She'd reached the street, and it was empty. All the shops were closed, and the street was lit by only one dim streetlamp. She looked around. A coffee shop, the mission, the place where the bookstore used to be. The rug shop, the bread shop. And outside the bread shop, a pedicab. Just sitting there. She looked left and then right and then left again. No one. She thought for a moment. It would be very bad karma to steal somebody's pedicab, but really what choice did she have in the matter? She'd bring it back as soon as possible, she really would, and she'd leave some money tucked in an envelope and taped to the bike when she returned it.

She hopped aboard and began to pedal. It had been years since she was on a bike, but this was easy—really a glorified tricycle. Piece of cake. She cruised along in the middle of the street in the darkness. There was the Hammering Man at the art museum, still hammering away, with no one watching. And then she reached Pike and looked left at the Pike Place Market, where she had spent so many Saturdays, buying cherry candies and comic books and drinking coffee inside the Athenian restaurant. She hung a right and headed straight, past the Paramount Theatre and the convention center, where there seemed to be some sort of costume event going on. Adults in silly-looking superhero costumes were wandering the sidewalk. Comic-Con? She had no idea and she didn't have time to find out. Outside of Gameworks, several packs of kids stood smoking and laughing and punching at one another. A few couples were making out in the doorway while others pretended not to notice. She rode on. Up the hill. Past the taverns and the shops and the coffee bars. Past the old REI, where there was now a huge bookstore, and then a left and one more block and finally . . . home.

She didn't realize how fast she'd been pedaling until she stopped, but now she felt her heart beating crazily. And her throat—it had dried out so that she found herself coughing and choking on the night air. She got off the pedicab and walked it around to the back of the hotel, where she could stash it in the darkness of the alley. Then she came around to the front of the house and stared up at it. So much trouble for one little piece of real estate. It almost didn't seem worth it. And to think that maybe her mother had been planning to sell it all along. No, that was crazy talk. Why had Kenneth told her that anyway? She couldn't believe it. Wouldn't believe it. Her mother would never sell the Angeline, not if her life depended on it. The Angeline was her mother's life, and now it was Alexis's life. It didn't matter what that stupid Kenneth said or what anybody thought or what anybody did. The Angeline was hers now, and she would make the decisions about it. She would save the hotel. And if she wasn't saving it for her mother, or for LJ, like she thought she'd been doing before, well, then, she'd save it for herself, and for the others who still lived there and who called it home. *Life is for the living*, she said to herself. *And I'm staying here.*

She walked up the steps to the front door and opened it. The smell of the place—so familiar in its damp coolness—brought a smile to her face. It was all going to be worth it in the end, no matter how hard it was to do the right thing.

"Hello?" she said softly.

She didn't want to wake anyone, but the residents of the building kept all kinds of crazy hours. Someone might be up.

"That you, Alexis?"

It was Mr. Kenji, sitting on the sofa and drinking tea, the violin by his side. Alexis realized that she had never heard another word from Mia on the subject of the concert. So Linda had been right—Mia was all talk. Well, Alexis would find another way.

"Yeah, it's me," she said. "Hi, Mr. Kenji. Are you having a nice evening?"

"Oh, fine, fine. And you, my dear?"

"Well," she said, "I've had better, but at least I'm home now."

"That's right, little girl. You're home. Now, come sit on down and have some tea. You look like you could use a drink."

Alexis sat down on the sofa while Mr. Kenji poured some tea into a tiny cup for her. He added a teaspoonful of sugar and a touch of milk.

"It's not the Japanese way," he said. "But I kinda thought you'd like it better with a little cream and sugar."

"Thank you," she said.

"Now, you just sit back and tell Mr. Kenji what's going on. You look like you've been to hell and back. No offense or anything."

"No offense taken."

Alexis thought for a moment. She wanted more than anything to share her life story with someone, and Mr. Kenji seemed like he'd be the right person. But she stopped herself. It wasn't fair to include anyone else. Besides, if she told him the truth about her mother, he would be like all the rest and want to call the authorities, and the next thing you know she'd be in a foster home, miserable and alone. She might not even be in Seattle anymore, and she certainly wouldn't be able to see Ursula and Roberta and the rest. And she would never, ever let that happen.

"What's goin' on down here?" a voice said. "Somebody having a tea party and didn't invite old Ursula?"

"Sit on down," Mr. Kenji said as the older woman came into the room. "Take a load off that foot of yours."

Ursula sat down across from the two of them and Mr. Kenji poured her tea.

"'Fore I forget," she said as she sipped the tea. Then Ursula fell silent.

"Yes?" Alexis said.

"Hmm?"

"You just said, 'Before I forget . . .'"

"Forget what?"

"I don't know. You were the one not forgetting it."

"Hmm. Well, can't remember now. Tell me if you think of it."

"Sure thing, Ursula," Alexis said. Who was going to take care of these people if not her? Who would have the patience to listen to Ursula's crazy pirate stories or to watch while Mr. Kenji pruned his little trees, and who would watch Roberta's python for her when she went to the grocery store?

"I remembered," Ursula said.

"What?" Alexis said.

"I remembered the thing I forgot."

"Great. What? What is it?"

"Phone message."

"Phone message?"

"For you. Some guy named . . . Clover? Clever? Cleon?"

"Clovis?"

"That's it."

"Clovis called?"

"Yes, yes he did. Clovis. He called."

"What did he *say*?"

"No need to shout, young lady. I kin hear ya just fine."

Alexis sighed.

"He said, hmm. Something about things not being right."

"What do you mean, things not being right?"

"That's what he said. Things don't seem right, something about your mom and certificates and then he said something about the authorities."

"What authorities?"

"Well, how should I know? I was simply taking the message. I'm no snoop, you know, like some people." She looked meaningfully at Mr. Kenji.

"Now, Ursula," Mr. Kenji said. "For someone who can't remember a thing, you sure have a long memory for the one time in my entire life that I read someone else's postcard."

"Didn't like it."

"I apologized."

"Don't matter."

"I apologize again."

"Stop!" Alexis yelled. "God, you two! Ursula! Focus! What did he say about the authorities?"

"I told you not to yell."

"Clovis," Alexis said quietly.

"He said . . . let me see, how did he put it? He said, 'Tell that girl that something's fishy in Denmark and I'm calling the authorities.'"

"So he called them. Already. He called the authorities."

"I don't know how many more times you want me to tell you."

"That's fine. That's good. I got it. Clovis called the authorities . . . shit . . . excuse my French." Alexis stood.

"Aren't you going to finish your tea?" Mr. Kenji said.

"Thank you, but no thank you," she said. "Now, if you'll excuse me. Good night."

"Good night, dear," Mr. Kenji said.

"Good riddance," Ursula said. "I mean, good night, dear."

Alexis took the stairs very slowly. She had used up all of her energy getting home, thinking she'd be safe, but now everything was ruined. The authorities. They'd probably be there in the morning, if not in the next five minutes. First there were the cops asking about LJ. Then there was her uncle, wanting to buy the hotel, or the other way around. Then, there was Kenneth. And now Clovis. Could anything else go wrong?

She didn't let herself think about it, for surely the moment she did, something else *would* go wrong.

She stood at the top of the stairs and rested a moment, one hand on the banister. There was nothing left to do. She didn't know what she'd been thinking. There was no saving everything now. It was over. It was good and over and she'd lost and now she may as well just go to bed and wait for the men in blue to come and take her away. For good.

She wished Linda would show up and crawl into bed with her and hold her all night long. There was no one to do that. She'd have to go to sleep by herself. Sleep and dream and in the morning it would all be over.

She walked past her own bedroom and headed for LJ's. She didn't really know why. Maybe because she was pretty sure she would never get a chance to be in his room again. She opened his door and stepped in. The sound of a crow's caw hit her ears.

"Habib!" she said. "Came in through the window, did you? Hey, boy. You're a good boy. A good, good boy."

The crow sat on her shoulder and nuzzled at her cheek, and the feel of the sweet creature brought tears to her eyes again. Habib had lost his owner. Alexis had lost her mother. They were both of them orphans. A pair of orphans with no one to talk to.

"You wanna lie down with me, boy?" she said.

She plunked herself down on LJ's bed, the muscles in her body suddenly giving way. It felt as though she'd never be able to stand again, even if she wanted to. Habib hopped around the bed a bit and then settled himself down next to her. She set a hand on his warm body.

"This is it, boy," she said. "Our last night in this place. Thanks for being here with me. And thanks for saving me earlier tonight."

Habib poked at her shoulder with his beak and Alexis patted his head.

"OK, good night then," she said.

She shut her eyes and thought of her mother, and a scene came back to her. A time when she was a little girl, sick in bed, coughing and unable to sleep. And in the middle of the night, her mother must have come and swept her up and carried her to her own bed, because that was where she awoke in the morning, in the arms of her mother, Edith's soft breath against the nape of her neck. Safe and sound.

She imagined that her mother was holding her now, and with that image in her mind she let sleep overtake her, the darkness wrapping her in its spell and dreams of crows and coffins spinning around her tired brain.

CHAPTER 24

ERIK LARSON

THE DAY BROKE COLD AND wet, with a light drizzle, a typical bullshit fall day in Seattle. Dark. Probably the same latitude as Svalbard, for all she knew. Everywhere else in the world at that hour there was light, or so Alexis imagined. One thing was certain. Someday, somehow, she'd find a place with sun and a beach.

It didn't help that she'd spent a restless night. Crows. Coffins. LJ's body arched against the tangerine blast. She needed a walk. She eased down the stairs and put on a sweater she found in the parlor—she didn't know whose. Possibly Roberta's, possibly Ursula's. Roberta's, she decided. It had just the faintest scent of dead mouse, Pluto's favorite meal.

Otto, God bless him, was asleep by the front door, back in uniform. Somewhere he'd found a pistol—old, boxy—which he cradled in his lap. She lifted it gently. The police would surely be back, and the last thing she needed now was to have Otto get hurt, too. She hid the gun under the radiator, then slipped outside.

She walked. Large droplets of accumulated drizzle slipped from the giant red cedar at the corner and fell with a startling pop. She lengthened her stride and raised her face to the cold. So, OK, that was one thing about Seattle she liked—the tingly Christmassy feel.

The coffee shop at the corner was just opening. She knew the owner—Mr. Mack—and knew that if she walked in now he'd offer her a coffee on the house, just for the company. She considered it, but kept walking, watching the walk below and pretending not to see Mr. Mack's beckoning wave.

She walked miles, it seemed. A slash of light across the eastern horizon suggested the day might not be so bleak after all. But then the smoldering remnants of a homeless person's trash-can fire brought back to her the scent of burned wood and incinerated perfume.

She stopped, turned, and headed back toward home. There was nothing for her here—not anymore. LJ was dead. Her father was dead, killed in some crazy spasm of revolutionary zeal. She didn't even know his name. And her mother lay on a gurney in a crematorium on San Piedro Island. What Alexis needed now was for the crows to come back and just take her the hell away.

As she neared the Angeline, she stopped. A car was parked in the red zone out front. Plain. A Ford. At first she thought it might be an unmarked police car, but she knew enough to look for the telltale antennae and the usual giveaway—the plain hubcaps that the cheapskate cops always selected. But this car didn't fit the pattern. And yet it was too boring to be anyone's personal car. Which meant it had to be a rental. A rental at nine a.m. in front of the Hotel Angeline.

She walked slowly. The front door flew open and a tall, slender man stumbled down the front walk, followed by Otto, waving his pistol. Leave it to him to know to look under the damn radiator.

The tall man turned and laughed. "Jesus Christ, old man, what in the hell—that's a Walther, correct?"

Otto stopped short. "How would you know?"

The man shrugged. "One of those little things you pick up along the way. Nice weapon. Clean slide, medium pull. And it looks like you take good care of it."

Otto let the pistol drop to his side. "OK," he said.

"OK."

"OK. You can come inside."

The tall man walked up the steps and held out his hand. Otto shook it. Both men went inside. The door closed behind them.

It was a small moment, but oddly powerful. Her eyes filled. Somehow it seemed to encapsulate all that had occurred. She was alone, outside the

Hotel Angeline. It reminded her of the moment when she first closed the lid of the basement coffin, with her mother inside.

The front door opened. Otto stepped out and waved to Alexis.

She stopped and shook her head. Otto waved again, angrily. She pulled her sweater close and walked to the entrance.

The tall man came outside and down the stairs. He smiled. Lots of teeth, but a nice smile. Sandy hair. Age hard to determine, but maybe in his forties. Possibly even fifties, but very fit. Brown eyes. He held out a hand. "You must be Alexis," he said.

No. I'm the fucking man in the moon, she wanted to scream. I'm the man in the moon, for all anyone cares.

She nodded but did not take his hand. She took a closer look. He had a certain style, unusual in men that age. All the guys at the Angeline wore Costco jeans with the flabby butts and old, worn oxford shirts. This guy wore jeans with just the right wash, and a trim-looking shirt, untucked, and meant to be untucked. His jacket looked to be a mix of linen and silk. What most drew her attention were his shoes. Unless she was mistaken, these were Prada. She knew the look from the secondhand place, Take Two, on Fifteenth where she always shopped. Only these were cobalt blue. Alligator, or something like it. Was everyone in the world rich except her? Uncle Burr and his fucking steaks, and Linda's dad? And now this guy with the smile.

"Otto was just telling me about our mutual friend," he said.

She didn't understand at first.

The man smiled again. Not such a nice smile this time. Speculative, as if gauging how she would respond. "I think you knew him as LJ. I knew him as Lynn. Lucky Lynn—that's how everyone knew him."

"He's not our 'mutual friend,'" she said.

"All right, then, your friend, my—interest?"

"You *are* a cop." She stepped away.

"Look, let's start over. Let me say first that I'm sorry for your loss. But can I also say that LJ was not exactly a harmless guy. You know that, don't you?"

She glared, then turned and began to walk.

"I knew Dr. Ramos as well."

The name meant nothing to her.

"Dr. Ricardo S. Ramos. Good-looking guy. Funny. Passionate. I wrote about him once a long time ago. And Mr. Lynn Johnson Robinson. The Seattle Seven was quite a big deal not so long ago. If not for that Patty Hearst thing, the Sea-Seven, as we knew them, would have been right up there with the Snick."

"Snick?"

"S-N-C-C—Student Nonviolent Coordinating Committee."

"Why should I care about some Dr. Ramos?"

The man shrugged. "People I interviewed said he had a big smile. The thing that always got to him, though, made him flip, was when people called him Ricky Ricardo. Anyone who knew him learned very quickly not to do it. Bad temper, or so I hear."

"I don't understand. Who—"

"My name's Frank Neff." He pulled his wallet out of his back pocket and removed a card. He passed it to her.

At first she refused to touch it, but she was curious.

R. FRANKLIN NEFF, it read. CONTRIBUTING WRITER. ROLLING STONE.

"Right," she said. She turned away again. He fell into step with her.

"Can I buy you a coffee or something? That place on the corner looks open."

She stopped. "Anybody can flash a business card. You reach in one of those jars in a restaurant and you can be anyone you want."

"Need proof? Come on, let's fire up your computer. You have a computer, don't you?" That smile again.

Instantly she went on red alert. The disc. He knew about it somehow. That had to be it.

"Magazines are dead," she said.

"Most are. Not ours. Didn't you follow that whole McChrystal dust-up? Not only did we get the guy fired, we upped our circulation by ten percent. We did good for the world and for us."

"I don't have a computer."

"Right," he said, "and I suppose you don't have a cell phone, and you've never sent a text message in your life."

She glared. "What's a text message?"

"Ms. Austin, please, give me some credit. I have a sixteen-year-old daughter."

And that sixteen-year-old has a family, Alexis thought. Her anger spiked. "Get away from me, please, or I'll call the police."

"Right," he said. "Why do I think the last thing you want right now is for a cop to appear at your side?"

She watched him.

He pulled out a photograph of a man. It was the same man Alexis had a photograph of—the one she took from LJ's room. He said, "Dr. Ramos was your father." This time he did not smile. "I guess you never knew."

"I never had a father."

He threw his head back and laughed. "I'm sorry," he said. "You don't have a computer. You never had a father. You just appeared on the earth. Last piece I did was about the Brethren in North Carolina. You'd fit right in."

"Very funny."

He said, "I've already spoken with the police. I interviewed Detective Francolini yesterday. The one with the woman's first name? I believe you've met him. As I understand it, he's a little annoyed with you. I also spoke with an old friend, Detective Lou Rivers, of the Seattle Police Department's intel unit. I knew him from something else a few years back. We had some friends in common. He's the country's leading expert on the Seattle Seven. He's going to have a big part in this piece I'm doing."

Alexis shook her head. "You don't get it. I couldn't care less about any of this. All of it. It's just—dead. It's all dead."

"Look, I know about the disc. The police know about the disc. And they're going to find it, unless you give it to me first. I promise to keep it safe. I'm a reporter, you—"

"Oh fuck you, I can *trust* you, right? Just leave me alone."

He watched her a moment. "I'll be in town for quite a while. We'll talk, I'm sure. In the meantime I want you to think about something.

Your friend LJ had four pounds of plastique in his warehouse. According to wiretaps, he was planning to blow up the restaurant in the Space Needle. At least, that's what Detective Rivers thinks. He was ready to move against your friend, but something happened. Think about it, Alexis. Then please call me. You've got my card."

She walked away, into the hotel. She watched through the window until the guy's car disappeared around the corner.

Trust him. Right. Trust him, and next thing you know I'd have to trust Fox News.

She ran up the stairs to her room and found the disc. How strange—the past resided on that shiny piece of high-tech modernity. Her past. All of it. And now she would have to destroy it.

She found the disc. She moved it so that the light that played around its edges broke into hues of blue and green. This was the past. Her reality. And yet there was nothing real about it. Nothing was as she had thought. Her mother had wanted to sell the hotel. LJ was not the warm, loving man she had imagined, but a deranged burned-out revolutionary who had planned to kill countless others. And her father, Dr. Ramos—Dr. Ricardo Fucking Ramos, was a gun runner and probably a killer.

The past resided in invisible digital dust. It was time, she realized. This past no longer mattered.

She ran down to the kitchen. She had seen this trick done once on a television show. She took the twist-tie off a bag of bread and shaped it into a loop, then twisted the ends together. She put the disc on a plate and put the loop on top, then put both into the microwave oven in the kitchen.

She turned the cook time to one minute and set the power on High.

Thirty seconds later the microwave filled with the same tangerine light as the blast that took LJ away. A sound like a dragging chain. Smoke. The oven shut down.

There was little left of the disc. She took the remains to the basement and hid them in one of the coffins, then shut the lid.

CHAPTER 25

GARTH STEIN

THERE IS NOTHING MORE REASSURING to Alexis than a moon in the daytime. Something about the palest white shard pinned up against the blue. Something about the swipe of the Sea of Tranquility. And now with the disc gone, with all the garbage gone, what is left? Nothing but Alexis and the moon, making quite a couple in the late morning.

Exhaustion seems to have seeped into her very bones, right to the marrow. Oh, she slept a few hours the night before, but the psychic toll has made her tired to her soul. It will be lifetimes until she recovers.

Downstairs, Otto is still being Otto. Ursula, Ursula. Nothing has changed. And yet the seismic rift in Alexis's life is nothing short of catastrophic.

She pours herself half a glass of orange juice and fills the rest with mostly flat TalkingRain from a two-liter bottle that's been lurking at the back on the refrigerator for who knows how long. But before she can put the glass to her lips and drink, the doorbell rings. The residents come to order. The house is alive again.

Otto looks at her from the front door, where he is standing guard by the peephole.

"Coppers," he says. "A bunch of them."

Alexis laughs and drops her shoulders.

"Let them in, Otto, I give up. Game over."

Of course the game is over. All those things, those secrets about her father, about LJ and the accidental killing, are now hidden forever. All the players are dead, and she'll be long dead before they can beat the information out of her, that's for sure. "Let them in," she says. "Tell them they can find me in the sea of tranquility with the man in the moon."

She turns and goes upstairs, marches up the steps she knows so well with the worn carpeting that should have been replaced years ago, holding the banister that was not up to fire code—no, thank you very much—but always seemed to pass code when Edith offered up a little sherry to the inspector (don't tell on him, please, he was a nice guy). She retreats to her apartment and waits for the knock that will signal the end of the end for Alexis. Foster care. Adoption. Who knows?

In the disgusting apartment, which has really gone to hell since her mother died, she turns on the bath. That's what she wants. A hot bath. With little bath toys like she had as a kid. She wants a mom to wash her and dry her and tousle her hair, dress her up in her pajamas and snuggle her in bed. She can't have all of that. But a bath. That she can have.

The knock comes. She opens the door without even asking who's there. She knows.

"Detective Francolini," she says. "So good to see you."

Her mock smile vanishes as she opens the door. Hillary Francolini is there. And the other dude with the sandy hair—that must be Lou Rivers. But who are the other two? The Men in Black. Who are they?

"Are you dating?" she asks Francolini. "Or multiplying? What's with the clones?"

But they are not clones. While SPD has its "look," so do the feds. These guys look just a little sharper. Like they spend their slightly bigger paycheck exclusively at Brooks Brothers.

"Detectives," one of the other guys says to Francolini, "I think this is ours. You run along now."

"Fuck you, Chuck," Francolini says.

"Hillary!" Alexis says, shocked. "Such language in front of a minor!"

"You're not a minor," Francolini says. "You're a thirty-eight-year-old stuffed into a midget's body."

The other cops laugh.

"That's derogatory," one of the nameless ones says. "A 'little person's' body."

Francolini glares at him.

"Who's got jurisdiction here, Chuck?"

"May we?" the guy supposedly named Chuck asks, and Alexis invites them in.

Well, Francolini and Rivers are actual real cops, and Chuck Dalaklis and the other guy, Lindquist, are feds, it turns out, once all the IDs are thrown on the table like guys showing their hands at a Friday poker game.

Alexis sits back on the ratty sofa. *How quickly we adjust to our new circumstances,* she thinks. A federal penitentiary or a state prison or a correctional facility for women out near Gig Harbor . . . does it matter what hell looks like when you finally get there? I mean, sixth level or seventh level or all the way down. Head facing backwards or being stabbed by demons. Dante was cool.

"Who first?" she asks.

Lindquist clears his throat. "We have no claim to your fate, Ms. Austin," he says. "So in that sense, us second. But our local friends here with SPD—you know, we like to work with the locals. It fosters a degree of, well, work-togetherness . . ."

"Work-togetherness?" Alexis asks. "Um. School much?"

"Collaboration," Chuck, the other fed, says. "Reciprocation. Back-scratching. You know."

"We're friends."

Alexis snorts. "That would explain the mutual verbal abuse."

"Bottom line," Chuck says, "we get to chat with you a bit, and then we'll turn you over to our compatriots, and they'll take you into custody."

And flush me into the toilet, Alexis thinks. Flotsam and jetsam (where's Jim Lynch when you need him?).

"We need to talk about Robinson," Chuck says. "He has information that we could use to clear up about . . . well, about twenty-four unsolved cases over the past forty years. If we could get to Robinson's files, we're pretty sure we could lock up about, well, twenty-five of them."

"You said twenty-four," Alexis says.

"The Fremont Inferno," Lindquist says quickly. "And counting."

"Well, officers, or, if you're federal agents, I guess I should address you as . . . what? Your Highnesses?"

"Special Agents will suffice."

"Right. LJ left me a computer disc. But it was a personal message for me. And if you can figure out how to suck my brain out of my ear, paint it onto a CD, and play it on your computer, you can have access to that information. Otherwise, the four of you can bugger off."

The men look at each other.

"Feisty," Chuck says to Hillary.

"I told you, Chuck. You know who her dad was."

Chuck nods and frowns.

"I'm sorry to hear that, Ms. Austin. So, look, we'll get the ram and take down LJ's door and go get it ourselves. How's that sound?"

"Get what?" Alexis asks.

"The laptop."

The laptop. Right. On LJ's desk. But what good would that do them? It was locked up and shut down with some self-destruct mechanism LJ had the clarity of mind to install.

"His laptop is garbage," she tells them. "I tried it. He erased the whole thing. Done. Doesn't work."

Chuck and Lindquist laugh heartily. Rivers and Hillary chuckle like dopes, trying to be in on the in-joke. But these losers have never been in on an in-joke in their lives. Sycophants. Sidney Suck-butts.

"Here's the thing," Lindquist says, leaning in. He's a leering one. Thin, bladelike skull, likely squashed into that shape by a horrible obstetrician yanking him into the world with a clumsy pair of forceps back in the day. Blue eyes that are too big for his head. And a dimple in his chin that looks absolutely horrible to have to try to shave inside of.

"Computers are like people," he says, continuing his leer, head tilted ten degrees starboard and a little dot of spittle in the corner of his mouth. "Just because it's been erased, scrubbed of data, wiped clean and killed, that doesn't mean that traces of it aren't floating around in the ether, you know? Like, a person dies. Sure, that person is dead, but there's the soul, right? The spirit? Most people can't see that stuff. But if you find the right *talent . . .* You think ghost movies came out of nowhere? Plato said we can't conceive of something that truly doesn't exist. So . . ."

"So?" Alexis asks, really not getting it. "Is this a history lecture or an interrogation or what?"

"So, just because a computer hard drive has been erased, doesn't mean the right 'talent' can't see what is on that disc."

He sits back and nods at his comrades. Compatriots. The Man.

And Alexis has to admit to herself that it took her too long to really put the pieces into place. The puzzle was a tough one, because she had been working from the middle. If you want to solve a puzzle, you have to find the corners, then the edges, then you go for the belly.

The laptop. All of LJ's information. All incriminating. All of it. They could pin twenty-four or twenty-five criminal acts on him, postmortem.

She's brought back to attention by the sound of running water. Shit. The tub.

"Left the tub running, boys!" she shouts. "I'll be right back!"

She bolts into the bathroom and locks the door behind her. Oh, shit. She was so where she was, and suddenly she isn't there anymore. *LJ. Laptop. Camera. Think. Think. Think.*

She doesn't turn off the water. She lets it overflow. Running over the rounded tub and onto the cool, old-style hex tiles Edith liked but probably didn't really like; she realized how expensive it would have been to replace. And why replace them when the house would be torn down in a matter of months. Alexis opens the bathroom window.

Ha! Fire Code Man with the sherry! Ha! You are my new "The Man"!

The Fire Code Man at the time had required the installation of a fire escape on the outside of the building when it was converted from a funeral home to a hotel. So Edith's parents had bolted an iron stair on the outside of the building, along the bathroom line, because all apartments had bathrooms and it was the cheapest way to go.

Alexis climbs out onto the fire escape and starts up.

Immediately, Habib arrives.

"I'm cool, bird," she says. "Got steps. Humans use those. No need to go ballistic again. All is good."

The crow caws at her. She starts down the steps and makes the top floor landing. LJ's apartment. Ha. She pulls at the window. It's locked.

"Crud," she says. She looks around for a tool, but nothing is obvious. Now what?

She hears a strained caw and looks over the edge of the fire escape, and there he is—Habib, trying as hard as he can to get to her while carrying a footlong piece of iron pipe in his claws.

Oh, how he works!

"You can do it, kid!" she shouts. And that bird does do it. He brings her the pipe, which she promptly uses to smash LJ's bathroom window.

Inside. What's to get? Laptop. Camera.

Laptops are like people. They have souls. They have a lasting life. They have to be destroyed in the most incredible fashion, or they will live forever, a ghost stuck between the living and the dead. They will carry echoes through the dimensions.

She grabs them quick, stuffs them into a purple shopping bag from the PCC and makes for the window. Down the fire escape, she hits the latch, drops the ladder and is in the back alley and lands . . . well, when you're on a roll, you're on a roll. When things are going good, they're going good. She lands right next to that damn pedicab she hijacked the night before.

I mean, if you could have seen this scene, you would have laughed. A fourteen-year-old girl busting out from an alley behind a decrepit old hotel on Capitol Hill riding a pedicab to beat all hell, and four dark-suited gumshoes running down the street after her waving guns and shouting and calling on their cell phones.

And she turns a corner onto Pine, and she is gone.

She takes out her cell phone and dials as she rides. The ride down Pine is fast when you don't use your brakes, and she calls Linda.

"Honey, baby, sweetheart," she says when Linda answers, "I need you."

There is silence, but not discontent, she knows, because she doesn't hear that beep-beep-beep of the phone being disconnected.

"I need you bad."

"Physically, metaphysically, socially, or what?" Linda says. "Because Papa Bear has me on lockdown over here because *you* fucked up by running. Again. Pattern recognition will come in handy when you start your standardized testing for college."

"I need you and I need your Bug. Cops are on me. One last time. I promise," Alexis says.

"Yeah," Linda snorts. "*Thelma and Louise,* Part Seven."

"One more," Alexis says. "One more and I'm done."

There's a long pause. "You know what my dad said to me this morning? He said to me, 'That friend of yours, Alexis, is worth keeping.' Do you know he said that?"

Alexis could hear the emotional edge in Linda's voice, even though she was on a cell phone going nearly thirty miles per hour down Pine and about to make a screeching turn onto Third.

"LJ once said something to me," Alexis shouted into her phone. "He said, 'We can't control the past, and we can't control the future. But we *can* control the *now*!'"

Another long pause. Then, "I'll be downstairs at the entrance to our parking garage in three."

And Alexis: "I'll be there in two."

She's got the Bug and is ready to go. Alexis parks the pedicab—ironically, not far from where she'd hijacked it. Return to sender. She gets in the Bug.

"Where to?" Linda asks.

"Tacoma," Alexis replies.

"Tacoma? Why? Let me guess, you have an old family friend down there who's a taxidermist and you want to have your mother's body stuffed so she can forever live in the lobby of the Hotel Angeline."

"Um. No. Just Tacoma."

"Just Tacoma," Linda mutters. She gets on I-5 South and they head down.

A black vintage Bug in the carpool lane is not hard to see. Not from freeway cameras. Helicopters. Cop cars. State patrol. It's not easy to hide from other drivers who are seeing the Amber Alerts flashing on the overhead signs from Seattle to Tacoma. And it was never hard for the feds and SPD to identify when they saw Linda drive Alexis around in the past couple of days. The days of planting tracking devices in cars is over. The Man is truly everywhere.

These are the thoughts Alexis has as they drive sixty-eight miles an hour down to Tacoma, well within the "window" of radar guns. Oh, they're good. They're careful. But Alexis sees the Man everywhere. In cell phones. In Internet tracking. In digital TV boxes. Freeway cameras. The Man is everywhere.

Just like LJ said. Be afraid. Be very afraid.

We all live our lives, giving up our liberties at every possible moment out of convenience, never reading the fine print, never checking our credit card statements for trumped-up charges. The Man isn't as insidious as LJ thought, but The Man has tentacles. The Man has reach.

She remembers Habib and his tribe going all *The Birds* on Linda's stepdad. That was cool. And she remembers what they went after. The Chihuly vase was their first target.

Sure, makes sense. Crows. Shiny objects. Sure.

But don't take that at face value. Don't take anything at face value, LJ said. Jam your fingernails into the crevices and pry, even if it hurts. Even if your fingers start to bleed. Rip off that artifice.

They went after the Chihuly.

They went after the Man of the art world.

Think about it. LJ had been so mad when they took away those rides in the Seattle Center. The Fun Forest. "What kind of fun forest is it if there aren't any rides?" he shouted at the newspaper.

"Do you see what they're doing?" he raged at Edith and Alexis. "They're starting earlier and earlier. They're trying to crush our spirit when we're younger and younger. Now little kids? Crush their souls to smithereens? Break their little-kid hearts? Smash their little-kid dreams and desires? What kind of bullshit is this?"

He was out of breath when he finished, and Edith had tried to calm him, but he was not to be dissuaded.

"It's the goddamn Man!" he shouted. "They want us from birth! They want our spirit and creativity and joy. They want to strangle it!"

Alexis had been on the verge of tears at the table as he went on, as angry as he was at the *Seattle Times* article that talked about the bad Seattle City Council that was to take away the rides from the poor kids . . .

"And for what?" LJ demanded. "For a *fucking Dale Chihuly museum? You've got to be fucking me!*"

"Calm," Edith said.

But LJ would not be calmed.

"It hasn't even been decided," Edith had said. "They haven't even voted."

"Oh, it's been decided," LJ muttered, exhausted after his rant. "You just haven't woken up to the truth of it yet."

So. Get in a Bug with an angel. Because that's what Linda has been. There is no control of the past and none of the future. But there is control of the now.

So get in the Bug and go down to Tacoma and get it done.

They get off the freeway, do the weird circular thing you have to do to get down to Dock Street and find the Museum of Glass.

Linda parks in the garage and Alexis gets out with the PCC bag she's been carrying. Digital camera and laptop and all their soul material in there, too.

"End of the road, girlfriend," she says to Linda over the top of the 1969 perfect little Bug that clearly was too perfect for a regular Garfield girl, but Alexis never saw that. *A man hears what he wants to hear and disregards the rest.*

"What are you doing?" Linda asks. "How will you get home?"

"Home's done."

"I don't get it."

"Hey," Alexis said. "You said it yourself: This ain't no *Thelma and Louise.* I'm going to do something bad now. You should probably get along. I'll catch you on the flip side."

Linda laughed loudly. "You sound like so many bad quotes from so many bad movies, I don't know if I'd rather punch you or kiss you."

"That's from a movie, too!" Alexis said.

"No!"

"*Rocky III*. Mr. T and Rocky!"

"I hate you," Linda said. "For real. What do you need?"

"For real," Alexis said. "You've given me everything I could ever deserve. Go home. Come visit me in the pen."

Linda reached her hand across the top of the car, and Alexis, a bit shorter, stood up on the rocker panel and touched Linda's fingers.

"I'll get a ride home with the cops. You'd better get out of here," Alexis said. She closed her car door, turned, and ran off into the garage toward the elevator.

The Glass Museum has a Hot Shop with two furnaces, both of which run twenty-four hours a day at 2,400 degrees Fahrenheit. (If you have the pleasure of using one of their glory holes, you can get it up to three thousand degrees!)

Every day, all day, glass workers do their thing in the pit, using their long staves and crimper tools and blowing tubes to create works of art, masterpieces—shiny, colorful glass balls that are worth thousands. Tens of thousands. Hundreds of thousands.

Glass. Which isn't even a solid object, LJ had told Alexis once. It's a liquid. They determined this when studying the famous stained-glass work of fifteenth-century Italy. The glass drips—albeit very slowly—and pools near the bottom of the panes. So if you measure the thickness of the glass near the top of a pane, it is significantly thinner than at the bottom of the pane.

She sits in the gallery of the Hot Shop and watches them work. And you know, it isn't all bad. These artists have talent, she knows. But there is still something she has to do.

Her final homage to LJ.

He was crazy. He was wacko. But he was her LJ. She owes him one last protest. One last acting out. The one where he ended up with a shard of glass in his throat doesn't count. He gets credit for that. He gets a redo.

She hopes it will be a gesture, and nothing more. She hopes it won't blow anything up or break anything, or make anyone's life impossible. But she has to do it.

When the show is over, when the crowds have filed out, she makes her way to the doors that lead to the floor of the Hot Shop. Fortunately for her, the guard they have on duty is a kid only a bit older than she is, swimming in a shirt made for a man.

"I'm going to meet Dale," she says to him, pushing for the door.

"Dale isn't here," he says. "That's Preston."

"Preston?" Alexis asks. She looks around and sees a poster on the wall with a notice about Preston Singletary doing his glasswork that day.

"I'm going to meet Preston, I said," she said with a nervous laugh. "What did you think?"

"You know him?"

She leaned in. "I'm his niece!"

"Oh!" he recoiled. "He's a great guy. Nice to meet you. He's really great. Tell him I said I'm a big fan!"

Crap, she thought, heading out onto the Hot Shop floor, *the thing with boys is they're so easy to manipulate. It's almost no fun.*

The heat on the floor is intense. The fires are raging. Workers are hustling about, this way and that, finishing things, putting away tools, cleaning up after the public display. It's easy for her to get lost in the bustle. She makes her way to the fiery opening of one of the furnaces. She reaches into her bag.

"Who are you with?" comes a voice from behind her.

She turns quickly. A carbuncular young man holding a long pole approaches.

"Preston," she says.

"You know Preston?"

"Niece."

"Ah," the boy says. "He's right over there."

He points, and a dude looks up from his work, heavy gloves on, safety glasses, gray hair swept back. "Hey!" he says.

"Hey, Uncle Preston!" Alexis calls out, and when the young man near her turns to look, to see whether or not there is recognition, she snatches the laptop and the camera from the PCC bag and tosses them into the fiery furnace.

"Oh, shit," the young man with the pole says, seeing what she has done, seeing the fire, the rage of the furnace, the colors, the sparks, the death and consummation of a computerized soul.

"Fire in the hole!" he shouts, and suddenly levers are pulled, fire alarms go off, and the entire giant auditorium of the Hot Shop is engulfed in a Halon fog—white dust everywhere—and they are lost, so none of them can see each other. None of them can see their own hands.

Minutes, seconds, how long? How do we measure? But Alexis is running. She is running out of the building and they are chasing. Shouting at her. Boys with long metal spears. Guards with hands at their hips as if they had guns when they really have only pepper spray. They are all chasing her as she bolts out of the museum doors and across the plaza and onto the Bridge of Glass.

It's late afternoon and the sun hits the colorful glass just so and the fragments of light dance before her. She sees them like a rainbow. If only to find the end.

But there is no prize at the end of the rainbow. There never is.

There is a squad car at the end of the rainbow.

She stops mid-bridge. Two flashing Pierce County police cars blocking her egress. She looks back and sees them coming. Security guards with their bellies flopping over their belts. Young artists with their spears of glass. Interested onlookers. They are all there. So she stops and waits for them.

This ain't no Thelma and Louise, she thinks, looking over the side of yet another bridge and pondering the ramifications of a daring leap. But the bridge is only high enough to break her ankles if she jumped.

They meet her. Rivers, and Hillary and Lindquist and the other one who kind of scared her. Dalaklis.

She has nothing more. But LJ's soul has certainly been released. There is no trace of it now. No one can read the shadows of his life on that hard drive.

She holds out her hands to Chuck. He smiles and shakes his head sadly.

"Feisty," he says, and he cuffs her.

"You're a troubled little girl," someone says behind her.

She turns and looks. Dale Chihuly? Crazy curly hair and eye patch and all? For real?

"Do you have anything to say for yourself?" he demands.

She smiles.

"Blow me, Dale Chihuly," she says.

They lead her to the awaiting squad cars and take her away.

CHAPTER 26

FRANCES McCUE

FROM THE BACK OF THE squad car, Alexis could see the streets blur with rain. She couldn't move her hands to smudge the mist off of the windows. The handcuffs were plastic and they bent a little when she strained. But they wouldn't give. Detectives Francolini and Rivers had made sure of that.

After passing the gates to Seattle U, she glimpsed the pink lift of the lights from the chapel. Down Twelfth, they drove. She knew every part of the street: where the noodle shop had replaced the hipster coffeehouse, where the expansion of the campus had scooped out the old Ethiopian place where they used to give her the leftover injera after the men had finished their lunches.

Then the place she hadn't been inside but had always known about: Denny Juvie. The place where the kids went after the police yanked them from Cal Anderson Park. The Hotel Angeline gone wrong.

They pulled in, past the barbed wire that sat on top of the gates. Funny how the places you see all the time hold the weirdest stuff. There was a play field surrounded by Dumpsters, but no sign of life. Alexis knew that they kept kids here. The narrow windows were the size of baby coffins.

"Out," said Francolini. He pulled the car door until it groaned.

The other cop, Rivers, came up behind him, reached around, and pulled Alexis out by her elbow. She ducked her head as she stood up.

At the front of the building, the doors buzzed as they slid open. Then, the second set. They clicked shut. Alexis and the two cops stood in a lobby. In front of them was a Plexiglas wall. A woman sat behind it. Far off, doors slammed. No music, no chatter.

"They're at dinner," the woman said through a hive of holes in the glass.

"Intake room?" said Rivers.

The woman pointed to a door next to her booth.

To Alexis, "intake room" sounded like a place set aside for people to breathe. Like a no-smoking room. She could have an intake room at the Hotel Angeline. She'd like to fill it with smoke and watch people breathe it in and out until the air cleared up.

Rivers, Francolini, and Alexis sat in the room and waited for the juvie people to come. Orange carpet, brown chairs, a whiteboard—it was like a barely furnished, carpeted corner of a parking garage.

An hour passed. Maybe more. Alexis couldn't look at the walls or at her own shoes anymore. She had moved around the room with her eyes, over and over, and finally she looked at the cops. Both of them had lumps and seams under their shirts. Bulletproof vests, Alexis thought. She looked at Francolini's padding. Where was he underneath that puffy stuff? It reminded her of the explosion. It made her think of the bumps she felt when she stumbled out the window at the Hotel Angeline, and all of the nicks and scrapes of her life over the past weeks. If she could have a vest like that, she'd be bigger than she was. She could take on more. She could have a vest that would melt into her insides and protect her from the image she kept seeing of her mother scraping money together, sitting at a table where the embalming equipment once was. Or in the coffin.

A vest could make her into an avatar instead of a real girl. She could bounce around and it would be OK. Someone else could move her around and it would be OK, no matter how much she got hit by things.

While Rivers shuffled a newspaper on the table, a man came into the room. He looked at Alexis. She wished, at that moment, that he would be someone who carried a vest for her. A guy who wouldn't blow shit up, but who would, instead, bring her something with a little padding to protect her from the fall.

"You can go," the man said to the two cops. He didn't look friendly, but he didn't look cruel, either. Sometimes Alexis couldn't tell the difference. But she did know that she never had wanted to get out of somewhere more than she did right then. She needed to slip from that room, out of Denny Juvie. Imagine how her Skechers would flop along the cement halls and how her fingers would flick through combination pads on doors and over buttons that would open gates.

She had no curiosity left. "What will happen to me?" became "Who will help me now?"

When you are fourteen, your sense of bureaucracy is pretty clear. People make up papers to get other people to sign. Then, those people take those papers and they make more papers and get new people to sign those and it goes around in a circle until the music stops and there aren't any chairs left.

Who would be left standing when her papers were finished and the stamping and notarizing and signatures dried up? It was like craving something and the thing you wanted didn't exist. It would be like printing money and then you couldn't spend it because it looked so fake. That's what procedures felt like to Alexis.

Someone needed to say something.

As if he could read her mind, the man said, "We're going to talk. I'm going to ask you some things. You are going to answer them and then we are going to give you a medical exam, a psychological exam, and then we are going to make a plan for your stay with us." He took out a stick of gum and unwrapped it. "Want one?"

"Uh, OK."

"Do you have someone who can be here with you?" the man asked. He was beige. He had no tone.

"What's an exam?" Alexis asked. Were her clothes coming off? Was she scratching in bubbles with a pencil?

"Let's start with the simple things," he said.

She wanted to say the thing that would be the simple thing. Then she wanted to say simple thing after simple thing, beading them together until they were so fucking simple that they were rocks across the stream.

They would be the things she would put under her and skip across, out the sliding doors.

"Do I have to take my clothes off?"

"No," the man said. "There will be a woman, later, for the exam." The slab of gum slithered into his mouth.

"What simple things?" she asked.

"Tell us what happened to the laptop. Tell us what happened to your mother. Tell us about the explosion in Fremont."

"Tell me about how I get to go home."

"Home?"

"Hotel Angeline." When she said it, she thought of her mouth shaping the word "angel." The dim hallways, the nicked-up doors, the thuds that the gutters made in the wind. Her mattress.

"Look, let's be clear. Remember, we are going for simple. Simple, Alexis." The man looked like he was doing math.

"Simple is I go home. I haven't done anything." She tried to imagine the person who would come into the room, tip over the man's chair, and pull her by the hand, back to the Angeline. All she could see was Linda. Not all of Linda, just Linda's hand and her face.

"Tell me about the laptop."

"Gone," said Alexis.

"Things are never gone. They just move around," said the man.

"They are gone when they are burned. And the laptop is burned."

Finally, the man had two packages of orange cheese crackers brought in. And a juice box. Kids had to be fed, the man knew. Food got results, and this was tiring.

Her fate was easy to see: He'd bring the information back to the detectives; they'd send it off to the feds, and that would be that. They'd get the kid put in one of the locked sections of the building and she'd scream and holler for a few days until she gave up and they could locate an adult who might take her on.

Foster care—you could call it that. But you'd be wrong. That's what the man knew as he looked at Alexis.

For the girl, what seemed simple had become a word game. It was like reaching for one of the orange crackers, only she had no arms and she wasn't hungry.

Nothing came in order. The man made it sound like an ordered thing, but it wasn't. But she pretended it was.

"Linda," she said. "Let me call my friend."

"OK, let's play a game. You get to call Linda after you tell me what happened to your mother, the laptop, and what went down at the Fremont explosion."

And so she did. From the glimpse she got of the keys popping off of the keyboard as the computer seethed and sank into the kiln, from the basement of the warehouse along the canal where the final call from LJ came in, from the sight of her mother as the casket lid slowly narrowed shut—she told the man. And she told him again. She could feel the language draining from her, verb by verb, scrunched under his heel.

"Well," he said. "Not so simple."

But for Alexis, the telling wasn't simple but what happened was. It was clear inside her and she tried to empty it out of her until he could see it.

Adults, she knew, had more and more questions. They wanted you to keep giving details until it felt like you were ornamenting a drawing that was already OK as a sketch. Coloring it in. Coloring it in more.

But if you kept at it, the descriptions would start to make the original statements seem murky.

Simple, Alexis thought, *simple*. She would call Linda and Linda would figure something out and Alexis would be back home, flopping down on the mattress and looking at the latest installments of *Ranma* or *Inuyasha*. She'd look up when Ursula clicked down the hall or when Otto gave her the all-clear sign from the doorway.

But the here-to-there of it looked murky. She needed other people who knew more to tell her what would happen in between

"One call," she said. "Like in the movies. I've seen it in the movies."

"OK," he said. "You can use my cell phone."

Was that what triggered her crying? The man leaning over to her, putting the Samsung in the air between them?

Or was it the way that the word "Linda" and the smell of Linda's clothes were tied together? The way that the request was granted too simply? A few feet closer to the doors, she thought.

And so she dialed the number. She did not know how this would save her, this reaching out. She did not see, yet, how Linda would tell her stepfather, how Linda's stepfather would take the rectangle of his iPhone and poke numbers at it. Alexis couldn't see all this, and the folks at "Intake" wouldn't know how their processes would be derailed by a man in a suit more expensive than the whole prison's monthly meal budget. They couldn't see. Alexis couldn't see. She could simply take the phone, her only detonator for now.

CHAPTER 27

ERICA BAUERMEISTER

ALEXIS SAT IN THE HOLDING cell, waiting like she was told.

Linda's voice on the phone had been ragged, scared. "Where are you? What's going on? I heard something on the news about a meltdown at the Museum of Glass? Jesus, Al, what did you do?"

"I don't have time to go into it. I'm in juvie. Can you come get me?"

There was a pause. Alexis had sat in the room with the not-cop, or whatever the hell he was. The guy who wanted everything simple. Ha. She had waited on the phone, listening to Linda breathing.

"Look," said Linda finally, "I'm going to do something. I don't know what. Just wait for me."

Like I'm going anywhere, Alexis thought.

The not-cop had taken her out of the intake room and down a hall. Cold. Gray. Didn't anybody study psychology around here? Didn't they know the effect of color on the psyche? Even Alexis had heard about it in middle school. Or maybe the juvie people did know. Maybe they were trying to freak the poor delinquents out. Make them depressed, ready to give up information. It was working.

The hallway was long and led to a series of holding cells. Alexis could hear the kids in the cells as they passed. One of them was crying; one shouted at the not-cop as they passed. So much anger and emotion bouncing off the walls around her. She had thought it was all inside her— maybe she had let it out and it had infected all of them.

Oh for Christ's sake, Alexis, she said to herself. *Stop being so self-centered.*

And there she was, in this little cell of a room, listening to the people down the hall. Nowhere to go. No one to talk to. No questions to answer.

She took a breath in, let it out. She leaned her back against the concrete wall and felt its cold filter through the fabric of her sweatshirt. She wanted to sleep—what day was it anyway? Sunday?

How long had she been going like this? She counted back. Ten, eleven days since her mother had died? Two since they had left her at the crematorium? It was all moving so fast. She felt like she had been dropped into the leading role in *Crank 3*.

Except she wasn't Jason fucking Statham. She was a fourteen-year-old girl and she was tired of acting like everything but her age.

She remembered when she was younger, her mother always used to bring her books from the library. They would read together, when Alexis was small, and then once Alexis was able to read for herself, her mother would simply leave a stack on her bed and let Alexis find the ones she wanted, or they'd go to the library together.

One day Alexis had asked her mom why all the young heroes and heroines never seemed to have any parents. She wondered if the book choices were maybe her mother's way of making her feel better about not having a father, but no, even the books they read in school were that way. *The Boxcar Children. The Secret Garden. Harry Potter*—of course, *Harry Potter*. It had turned into a joke after a while, trying to find a book with parents, or at least one.

"I think it's so the hero has room to grow," her mom said. "You know, turn into an adult, take on big responsibilities."

They made it look exciting in the books. All that swashbuckling. All those kids being smarter than the villains.

Well, thought Alexis, it wasn't exciting. It sucked. And what sucked were the parts they didn't write about. The stupid, mundane parts of life that grown-ups had to deal with and now she just wished she could give back to her mother. Because these days, as soon as she was sitting still by herself, for just a moment, they all came flooding in. Even now, when she should be worried about whether they were going to put some sick creep in that cell with her, there was a part of her mind that was wondering if anybody had gone to the store and bought more Fig Newmans, or sherry. If Ursula's peg leg was OK after being stuck in the attic door like that. Because from the moment she closed the lid on her mother's coffin, it had started, as if her mother had simply handed the to-do list to her daughter with her last breath. And now, the list was there in the back of her mind anytime she slowed down enough to breathe.

Alexis loved the hotel. She loved the tenants. But sitting there in that holding cell, all she wanted to do was go back to the Angeline, grab a hold of that rotten plumbing and yank it off the wall and send water flooding through the floors, washing it all away.

She thought about her mom. Lists had ruled her mother's life. Alexis had always thought her mother was so boring, particularly the past year or so, when hormones had accentuated the crests and troughs of Alexis's life. Life was out there to be lived, but her mother ran her day one item at a time. Alexis thought her mother had always been like that. So organized. So tired.

On her mother's dresser, there was a photo of Edith, taken before Alexis was born. The first time Alexis had seen it, she didn't even recognize her mother. She looked like a teenager, her eyes open and excited, her grin flying toward the camera. Alexis never knew what to make of the disconnect between the woman in the photo and her mother; it was easier to see them simply as two different people.

But now Alexis wondered, how had her mother gotten from that girl in the picture to the woman in the coffin the basement? How many to-do lists did it take?

She retraced the history in her head. Alexis had been born at the Angeline, her mother had grown up there and taken over the place when her parents died; how, Alexis didn't even know. She'd never thought to ask. Alexis's father had been gone before her birth. Her dad—the man who would rather blow things up than stick around and be her father, or her mother's husband. Just like LJ.

Her mother had always called the Angeline her safe harbor. Maybe it really had been—the place she had gone to when everything else was falling apart. The walls that held her up when family was gone.

Except that wasn't completely true, was it? Her mother had owned the Angeline with her brother, Alexis's uncle. There had been family, somehow. Alexis thought about the man who had sat across the table from her at the Sorrento, who had bought her dinner and given her an envelope for her mother. She had thought he was evil, but Linda's stepfather said he was trying to help.

It hadn't made sense when Linda's stepdad had told her about the legal documents, that it was her mother who had been trying to sell the hotel. But sitting there, unable to do anything but think, all the pieces that didn't make sense started to fall into new patterns, new pictures she hadn't imagined before.

She saw her mother, that ever-present list in her hand, piles of bills and unfolded towels around her. Grabbing the screwdriver and going up to put a door back on its hinges after Otto had taken it off to use as a barricade. Pulling up the linoleum in Roberta's bathroom floor after it had gotten flooded from one of Pluto's baths. It could make you tired, really it could.

Maybe it had. And maybe, Alexis thought for the first time, that made a kind of sense. People did get tired.

She closed her eyes and leaned her head against the wall, feeling the waves of fatigue roll across her, shivering their way down her arms and legs. She could feel her heart beating hard in her chest; it hadn't really slowed since she had realized her mother was dead, as if it had to beat double-time for the two of them.

What she wouldn't give for someone to take care of her—other than a crow, wonderful as Habib had been. What she wanted was human hands, on her shoulders. Human hands taking that list out of her mind.

When was the last time she had relaxed? And then, oddly, it came to her. The dinner at the Sorrento. The tarte tartin, the slices of apple warm across her tongue, the caramel sauce making her feel both grown up and young at the same time. The way the waiter took care of her, picking up the plate just when she was finished and not a moment before.

And her uncle, sitting there quietly eating. Not controlling her, she realized now, waiting for her to relax.

Oh, she really hadn't had anything right, had she? Her uncle had been trying to save the hotel that night. LJ had been trying to kill things, maybe even people. If he had planted a bomb under the Troll that sat like a great gray blob under the Aurora Bridge, he would have taken out more people than had ever voluntarily jumped off its long expanse. And her mother—well, her mother was human, that was the bitch and the beauty of it, wasn't it?

It was more than she wanted to handle. She kept her eyes shut, let sleep come. Her body relaxed, the muscles ceasing their shivering, her heart slowing to a normal beat. Her teeth unclenching, a bit at a time. Like falling into water.

She dreamed she was at Moonlight Phở. She could feel the red plastic chair beneath her, hear the animated chatter of the women in the kitchen, feel the steam heat come across the room. She could smell the phở, the broth rising up toward her nose, the soothing scent of chicken and cooked onions, the sharp green zing of cilantro, even the Sriracha hot sauce that was her favorite, the way its bright red changed the color of the soup. The dream was astonishingly real.

"Alexis." She could hear Linda's voice. It sounded so near and warm.

"Alexis, I brought you soup."

Alexis opened her eyes to a vision of Linda and a huge Styrofoam container of phở.

"I thought you might need this."

Alexis could only nod and take the spoon. The first slurp went down her throat, soothing, as a hand cradled against her check. She thought she might cry, it tasted so good. She picked up a sprig of cilantro with her fingers and crunched the leaves between her teeth, tasting the flavors— sharp, strong, everything she wasn't. But might be, maybe, if she kept eating.

"How did you get here?" she asked Linda.

"My stepdad brought me. I told him everything."

Alexis's eyes grew large. "*Everything?* What did he say?"

Linda smiled. "Well, ever since the crow invasion, he's been doing this End of Days thing. He's been talking about locusts and plagues and making donations to Habitat for Humanity all day. Apparently, in comparison to the coming apocalypse, having your stepdaughter come out of the closet is no big deal."

"Seriously?"

"Well, I'm sure there will be fallout. I'm thinking boarding school. But you never know; he was pretty shook up. We had to take a taxi to get here. When we went down to the garage, he took one look at our shiny black cars and freaked out. He kept muttering about crows."

"So, where is he?"

"He's doing his lawyer magic. Don't worry, that part of him still works."

"Does he think I have a shot at getting out of here? Can I go home?" Even as she said the words, the other part of Alexis, the grown-up Alexis who had spent the past two hours in a holding cell, the one who had put her mother in a coffin and escaped out of windows and melted computers and microwaved CDs and kept the Angeline in cookies and sherry, knew the answer to that one.

"Never mind," Alexis said.

"Linda?" she said after a moment.

"Yep." Linda smiled at her, long and slow.

"Yeah."

"Drink your soup."

There was movement in the hallway, the sound of heavy feet in heavy shoes. More than one pair. Alexis and Linda looked up and saw the not-cop and Linda's stepdad. Their faces were serious.

"Alexis," the not-cop said, "we're ready for you."

CHAPTER 28

SEAN BEAUDOIN

ALEXIS ROSE, THINKING SHE WOULD have to follow Not-Cop to a questioning cell of some kind, but he ducked out of the room instead. After a few minutes he popped his head back in and curled a finger at Linda.

"I want you out here with your stepfather. Now."

Linda looked at Alexis, her geriatric pace a protest all the way out the door.

"And there's someone else here to see *you*."

"Johnnie Cochran?"

Not-Cop gave a not-smile. His not-head disappeared as Uncle Burr walked in. The door slammed. Twice. Uncle Burr's beard seemed whiter, posture less erect, hair more Unabomber-esque than it had been at the Sorrento.

"I'm afraid, Alexis, that we left things on a sour note."

"Don't be afraid. I can live with sour."

Uncle Burr made a face, a senator refusing to be goaded by the press. "I flew in as quickly as I could. Kenneth and I have somehow managed to work out a deal with the CPS people. If you come with me, right now, there will be no charges filed."

"Why would they agree to that?"

"We're very persuasive."

"No one's that persuasive."

Uncle Burr held out his palms, a card trick with no cards. Alexis looked around the holding cell.

"So, then you'd be my legal guardian. Or whatever?"

"Yes."

"And we'd live where? Your pad above Neumos?"

Burr cleared his throat. "Sedona, Arizona."

"No freaking way."

"Hey, if you're not interested, there's always staying here. I under-stand the cafeteria serves a hearty sloppy joe."

Alexis said nothing. There was only one way out she could see, and it wasn't going to the desert to wear a sun hat and collect wrinkles.

Uncle Burr sat down at the interrogation table, the spot where Sipowitz usually glowered for a while before he jumped up in his short-sleeve shirt and beat a perp half to death with the Yellow Pages.

It occurred to Alexis that maybe she'd been watching too much TNT with Mr. Kenji.

"I imagine you have many questions," Uncle Burr said.

"Uh, yeah."

"So, shoot."

Alexis considered, scatological or non sequitur? She went with the red herring.

"Are you named after Aaron Burr?"

"No, it was my great-aunt's first name."

"Her name was Burr Burr?"

"Yes."

Alexis wanted to laugh, but didn't, needing to concentrate. "Well, *Aaron* Burr is my hero. You know why?"

"I'm afraid not."

"He shot Alexander Hamilton in a duel. Like, muskets at twelve paces. Step, step, turn, fire. Ended that *Federalist Papers* nonsense cold. And he did it in Weehawken. That's in New Jersey. Which really doesn't matter much, except it's a cool name. Don't you wish you were taking me to a place called Weehawken, instead of Sedona?"

"No, I don't."

Clutch, gas, second gear.

"Also, though? When Jefferson screwed Burr on his promise to let

Burr be vice prez? Because back in those days they let the Senate decide by votes? Well, my man Burr got an army of freaks and perverts and mercenary Hessians and went down to Mexico and declared himself emperor! Isn't that awesome? How can you *not* love that guy?"

Burr stared at his niece. "I don't really think that's true. Not to mention completely beside the point."

"It *is* true. Read some books. Wiki that action."

"I will look into it."

"Hey, but if you're not named after Aaron, I'm not calling you Burr. That's, like, sacrilege."

"You can call me whatever you—"

"How about 'The Man From'?"

"I'm sorry, I don't understand."

"U.N.C.L.E."

"Still drawing a blank."

"United Network Command for Law and Enforcement. What, you don't get TV Land in Arizona? Robert Vaughn? You know, Napoleon Solo running around with that tiny phallus-gun? Saving the world from whoever the world needed saving from? Which, go figure, at that time was always the Russians. Or, pretty much anyone with a turtleneck and a mustache."

"I don't watch much television. I prefer to sit by the fire and read the classics."

"Are you for real?"

Uncle Burr pinched his arm. "I think so."

Speed shift, third gear.

"I have another question."

"Please."

"What exactly does 'the classics' mean?"

"Oh, you know. Tolstoy. *Wuthering Heights*."

Alexis shook her head. "But back in *Anna Karenina*-land, people like you were sitting there over a glass of absinthe in some drawing room going, 'Oh, yes, well, I don't really read *Tolstoy*. I prefer the classics.' I mean, to them, your classics were like their *Dukes of Hazzard*. And

Vronsky was Boss Hogg. If you weren't reading *Canterbury Tales* and slagging Leo, you were some sort of knuckle-dragger."

Burr stared at his hands, wearing a look of imminent dyspepsia. "I see your point," he said finally.

"Do you? Do you really?"

"Frankly, no. But let me ask you, have you ever been to Arizona?"

"That's a negative."

"I think if you came, you'd find it to be quite a—"

"Don't say 'learning experience.' Just don't."

"I was going to say quite a trip."

"Literally or lysergically?" Alexis asked, channeling the spirit of LJ.

Burr's face darkened. He stood and walked to the tiny, mesh-reinforced window. After a long silence, he turned and said, "I know what you're doing."

"You do?"

"Yes. And it's very clever. If a bit juvenile."

"Thanks. And *ouch*. But what is it I'm supposed to be doing?"

"You're trying to dissuade me from taking you under my wing. You're purposely making a bad impression. Fouling the water, if you will."

Nailed.

"I don't think so," Alexis said, suddenly without much conviction. "Even Habib doesn't take me under his wing."

"You are your mother's daughter, without question. Edith was never . . . demure as a child. And her intelligence was obvious from a very early age. But I feel quite certain you are not always this obnoxious. Either way, I've committed to bringing you into my home. I've signed the papers. I've taken on power of attorney. And I do not frighten so easily."

"You don't?"

"No."

Alexis took her boot off the table. The game was over. Almost.

"I'm gay."

Burr blanched. He tasted eggs, forced them back down, failed, got it on the second try.

"You're—"

"A dyke. One hundred percent flannel. How's that flag fly in Sedona?"

"Excuse me a minute," Burr said, getting up and leaving the room.

Alexis closed her eyes. The performance had been unpleasant, but it had to be done. Or did it? She considered her choices. They seemed to be: (1) accompany Burr to a picket fence in the desert, or (2) bust out like a Soledad Brother. A Soledad sister. Make a quick shiv out of a sharpened toothbrush and hold it to Not-Cop's neck, hostage her way through the doors, demand a helicopter and a half million in Krugerrands. Of course, that was insanely stupid. There were no options. What, cry? *Boring.* Besides, it really didn't matter what happened to her anymore. She still had one tiny piece of leverage.

When Burr came back in, he wore a stern look he'd probably just spent the last ten minutes assembling in the men's-room mirror.

"We've had enough verbal sparring, don't you think?"

Alexis nodded. "You're right. I'm sorry."

"You are?"

"Yes. I've made up my mind, I'll do whatever you want. Go wherever you want. But on one condition."

Burr chuckled. "Renegotiating your contract? Already?"

"My condition is that you don't sell the Angeline. Not only do you not sell it, you don't kick the residents out. Ever."

The chuckling stopped. "I'm sorry, even if I wanted to, I'm not in a position to do that."

"Why not?"

"The fact is that every single resident of the Angeline is behind on their rent. Some stopped paying entirely a long time ago. The hotel loses a substantial sum on a yearly basis. I am not in a position to carry that sum as a matter of sentiment."

It occured to Alexis that maybe she hadn't been watching enough TNT with Mr. Kenji.

"So, what you're really saying is the Angeline needs a good manager. That could be me! I know it inside and out, the rooms, the plumbing, even the mortuary equipment. *Please?* We can work out a deal with the tenants. Garnish their SSI checks. Collect a little at a time. Bake sales or whatever."

"Bake sales?"

"Listen, the point is, we could make it work. I could. Ursula can't just go out into the street. Kato and Kevin can't fend for themselves. Mr. Kenji needs room and the right light to create his art!"

"I'm afraid that really isn't an option."

"It's not? Then is this the point where Nurse Ratched comes in and sticks a big hypo of lithium in my neck and I wake up in a room somewhere, all nice and sunny with a pretty bedspread and I sit up and my arms and legs are in leather restraints?"

"Your imagination, Alexis, is truly a thing of wonder. Have you ever considered writing?"

Alexis blushed more than she wanted to, trying not to smile. "Well, I do write poetry sometimes. But as I understand it, being a writer sucks. It's all about self-promotion. It's all about schmoozing and meeting other writers and pretending to care about their books long enough so that you can talk about yours. Plus, you're always doing readings no one shows up to, and these endless charity events."

"You have a point there," he said with a knowing laugh.

"Listen, *Uncle*, the bottom line is that I am not going to abandon the people at the Angeline. So you need to find a way to make that not happen, or I guarantee you will not want me under your roof. I will resent you forever. You'll never be able to turn your back. You'll never have a pot on the stove without wondering if the pet rabbit's in it."

"Is that, perhaps, an allusion to *Fatal Attraction?* I actually did see that. Ghastly film."

"Yeah, so you get my point. Make it work, *Uncle*, or I will so make this not work."

Burr stood with his hands behind his back, again looking out the tiny window. Birds congregated in the tree below him, dozens of them, almost if they were flying in a coordinated arrangement.

"Are all teenage girls this . . . challenging to negotiate with?"

"I don't know about all of them. But yeah. Probably. Get twenty of us in a room, throw in a gift card and a copy of *Twilight*, turn off the light, lock the door. Come back in an hour and see what happens."

"Well," Burr said, getting up and knocking on the door—*shave and a haircut, tap-tap*. "I can't promise anything. Except that I promise to consider it. I will pore over the financials one more time. But this isn't a movie, Alexis. Richard Gere doesn't just show up out of nowhere with a bouquet of roses, leaning out the sunroof of a limo, about to take Julia Roberts away from a life of Spandex."

Not-Cop came into the room with a stack of papers. Burr took a Mont Blanc from his inside pocket and signed them all, twice. Not-Cop led Alexis to the discharge desk, where Linda was waiting. She broke away from her stepfather's grip, ran over and took Alexis in her arms, kissing her at first gently, and then with increasing need. Tears ran down Linda's cheeks.

"Kenneth says this guy's taking you to Arizona."

Alexis, barely able to keep from crying herself, nodded.

"And you're *OK* with that?"

"I don't have a choice."

"Shit, chica. You always have a choice!"

"You don't understand."

"You're right. I don't. At all."

Two plainclothes cops brought a boy through the steel door. He was handcuffed, kicking, and wrestling. One of his sneakers had come off, a big hole in his sock. The police muscled him over to the desk, slamming him against it.

"Don't!" Alexis yelled, but the police ignored her.

"Yeah, that's right," Linda snapped. "Get involved in what's happening to someone else. That kid, the freaks at the Angeline, bums in the park. Look at everything except what matters. Everything except what's standing right in front of you."

"Linda."

"So go!" Linda said, and pushed out the front doors. Kenneth nodded and followed his daughter.

Burr and Alexis took a cab back to the hotel.

"I can't believe we actually found a cab in Seattle," he marveled.

"I can't believe you're actually letting us stay here tonight."

"Our flight for Arizona isn't until tomorrow. I thought you might want a chance to see your friends."

Alexis reappraised Burr, giving him a sincere nod. "Thank you."

He held the door for her. She stepped onto the filthy sidewalk in front of the Angeline, looking upward.

While Uncle Burr paid the driver, Alexis spread her arms, Jesus at Corcovado, soaking all four floors in.

CHAPTER 29

DAVE BOLING

ALEXIS OPENED HER EYES AND viewed the Hotel Angeline anew.

Jesus, what a fleabag, she thought. So much work needs to be done. But it would be someone else's problem now. A leaky gutter leaned off a gable like a tilted brow, allowing grime to seep down on the decaying hotel sign. A growth of moss had taken over the right side of the sign, leaving only the letters on the left side visible. It read:

HO

ANGEL

She'd never noticed the way the forces of nature and neglect altered the sign. Is this the range of options for women? Ho or Angel? Was the sign an advertisement for the women inside? Where did she fit in?

"Are you all right?" Uncle Burr asked.

"Just looking at the old place," she said. "What a mess."

Alexis leaned into the front door. It jammed where it usually did, leaving her just enough room to squeeze through. She wondered if the house had been trying to keep her out, or forever trying to trap her inside.

She'd only been away from the hotel for a couple days, but the smell struck her as vile. It was far worse than the detention center. It smelled of mushrooms and mold and crow shit and decay, with a hint of embalming fluid. The last scent reminded her of Linda. Linda. Linda on top of her in the coffin. She flushed, remembering the feel of the velvet lining on her bare back, and the silky quilt of Linda's skin against her bare front. She tasted Linda's strawberry-tipped tongue. She shivered, and wondered if she would be forever aroused by the scent of formaldehyde or the sight of a funeral procession.

Uncle Burr had shoved through the front door and was standing at her shoulder.

"Do you want help packing?"

"No—could I have some time, please?" Alexis reached out and touched the sleeve of his jacket. She held it there for a moment and looked in his eyes. He froze in place. She had reached out.

By the time she summited the stairs, she was out of breath. She had no idea how drained she'd been by the shitstorm she'd waded through the past few days. Light-headed, she leaned her forehead against the door. She didn't know what to expect inside—what had the police taken? What had they done to her things?

She eased into the door, and was surprised that it swung open without the usual blockage of dirty clothes. Yes, the police had gone through everything. She wondered if hers was the first room in history that police have "tossed" in a search that finished being more tidy than when they started. She thought to double-check her underthings to see if the perverts had pocketed any of her panties.

On her bed was her Garfield sweatshirt. "Go Bulldogs!" she said in a mock cheer. Shouldn't she be getting ready for some kind of game? Doing things with other fourteen-year-olds? She pulled on her sweatshirt, but stopped when it covered her face. She broke down again, crying beneath the soft veil of fabric. In that darkness, she recognized a fear that she was losing her mind.

Images of fantasy flashed like snapshots. How much of this was real? Her mind fixed on the image of a crow carrying a length of pipe. Crows can't carry pipe, can they? And the swarming birds, as if on a mission? Were those birds or fragments of the black October night fluttering down from a sky suddenly torn apart? She flashed again on LJ with the giant wedge of glass in his throat. Dear God. She saw it in vivid colors. Backlit by the building ablaze, the bloody glass shone red and orange like one of those Chihuly works.

And LJ? Should she even call him LJ? His last name was Robinson.

Nothing was true. Nothing in this entire fucking building. No one was who he seemed. Halloween was coming, but it turns out that everyone had been wearing masks all along. Halloween, she thought. Goddammit, I should be carving a fucking pumpkin or something now instead of wading through all this mental shit.

Could she believe anything LJ had ever said? Ever? The horror of the explosion had pushed from the front of her mind some of the things that LJ had said on that final recording. She tried to remember them now, but they were in broken shards, too. Was any of that real or just the mind fugues that overtook him so often? And her father drove a car off a ferry? Did they find the car? Did they find her father's body? Did they find his fucking body? What if he swam away? Goddamn LJ for saying these things on the CD and then getting himself blown across half of Fremont.

She tried piecing it all together, to find logic in the absurd. Could her father have been a criminal? She had just learned that the man played the violin for Christ's sake. What was it like when LJ and her father were together? Did "Dad" work on his pizzicato fingering techniques while LJ fiddled with high explosives?

No wonder she struggled with her identity; her father was a sociopath violinist. *Fine, nobody is all one thing*, she thought. *We're all bits of things that fit together—or sometimes don't, or sometimes fit and then come apart.*

She wiped her eyes on the sweatshirt again. "Go Bulldogs," she whispered. She saw nothing she wanted to take with her from that room, from that box, from this house of deceit. She had enough baggage. She turned her back to the room and pulled the door closed.

As she walked down the hall, she passed LJ's room. She knew it would be a mess from the police search, but maybe she could find something— even a hint or two about her father—something that hadn't spun wildly from LJ's delusional mind. She was hoping to find some evidence that her father hadn't been as wrong or as violent in his protests as LJ had been.

The pictures were torn from the wall, bureaus gutted of their drawers. She dug into the strata of LJ's clothes as if on an archeological dig through the 1960s. Jesus, did he never do laundry? Soiled jeans, crusty bandanas, flannels and cowboy shirts—and a small doll.

"Holy shit."

LJ had taken her monkey, the doll that had perched on her shelf and watched over her—the sentry against bad things that might come to harm her in the night. It had been gone for years. She was certain it wasn't coincidental that her life had gone in the crapper in the monkey's absence. She petted it. It felt worn and old and looked frayed.

But here it was. Without thinking, she brought it to her cheek. It was cool and smooth, and felt like Linda's cheek on hers. But those two thoughts collided in her mind. Her doll and her girlfriend. Don't they trap her in time? She hugged the doll harder, and felt so much a child. And she thought of her times in the basement with Linda. On the top floor a child, in the basement, something different. The child, the woman. The ho, the angel. Where was she headed? Forever on the stairs between the two?

She would not leave the guardian monkey. If she took nothing else, she would keep the monkey. But she wanted no one else to see it, and jammed it deep in her jacket pocket.

"Alexis—do you need help?" Uncle Burr called.

Do I need help? Do I need help? she asked herself. *What kind of question is that? God damned right I need help.* But not with carrying anything beyond bad memories and this heavy cargo of lies and questions.

She closed the door to LJ's room, but before heading down the stairs, she turned back. Where was Habib? She opened the door again. All she saw was crow crap everywhere. But no black bird. She hadn't seen him downstairs. The window to LJ's room had been closed. Wait—had anybody fed the python lately?

Somebody else's problem, she thought. Somebody else can worry about the leaky gutters, the mold-covered sign, the faulty pipes, the peg-legged pirate. But could she just walk away from it all the next day? It had been her home, her only home . . . such as it was. She was surprised to feel that, yes, she could leave. The future, in fact, felt like an open door. Open to her, that is, once she managed to squeeze out of the Hotel Angeline the next morning, for the last time.

CHAPTER 30

PETER MOUNTFORD

AN OFFICIOUS REAL ESTATE AGENT, whose gender fluctuated but who was always toothy, sparkly eyed, with an eerily orangeish tan, led Alexis and Linda around an old mansion. In the capacious kitchen, a dozen-plus refrigerators lined the walls. The agent opened the first refrigerator and Alexis saw a cadaver inside on the chrome table—an elderly man, his pasty bald head turned to the side. The agent appeared embarrassed and shut the door quickly. Alexis felt sick. She opened the next refrigerator—she was alone in the kitchen now, and found LJ there, cold and dead, his face waxy and alabaster. She opened the next refrigerator and there lay her mother, in repose, milky eyes open unseeingly.

Alexis drew a deep cold breath and awoke in her room at the Angeline.

The heat was off and she could see her ghostly breath. She could hear a pigeon cooing outside the foggy windows, scratching at its nest. Beside her in the bed she saw the silk monkey. She stepped out of bed onto the same creaking board that had been there beside her bed forever. It was, she knew, her last morning awakening in that bed. She rubbed a peephole in the foggy window, still hoping to see Habib, but outside it was just the pigeons.

She padded to the bathroom to brush her teeth. The hotel was freezing and she shivered in front of the mirror. Then she heard something. Something odd . . . a tapping, or a squeaking . . . a squeaking and a tapping. She spat out the toothpaste, rinsed, and headed out to the hallway. The sound had been coming from Ursula's room. Maybe Ursula was in distress? She knocked.

"*Mffff—alla*," came the muffled voice from within. Then a scary silence.

Alexis pushed the door open and, lo, standing buck naked beside Ursula's bed stood Deaf Donald, holding a Scrabble board and Ursula's peg leg.

"Oh. My. God." Alexis's face went red and she stared on in shock, paralyzed with wonder and fascination and horror. Ursula pulled the sheets over herself, shouting, "Aarrrggh!" and Alexis backed out of the room, muttering apologies.

Wearing a coat and scarf and woolen gloves, Alexis headed downstairs. No one else was up yet. She continued down to the basement, for one last visit with the phantoms. When she was younger, the creaking in the Hotel Angeline had always seemed, to her, like the unintelligible murmuring of those ghosts. Down there that morning, she ran her fingers along the dusty lid of a grand old teak coffin, its top half open, revealing a zebra-print fur interior.

"Mom?" she said.

No one answered. Alexis shivered and headed upstairs again.

Deaf Donald and Ursula, now dressed and composed, though his silvery hair was still quite askew, were in the sitting room. Ursula was hunched over the fireplace lighting the season's first fire.

Donald turned to Alexis and smiled apologetically.

"Sorry!" he yelled, apparently thinking he was whispering.

"It's OK," she said, although the image of his pasty pale torso, the dark brown nipples (three of them!) would be forever scalded onto her memory.

"Heating's off!" Ursula yelped, her head still in the fireplace. "Damn cold in this place, you know!" she continued.

Alexis settled down with a cup of tea and some soggy, stale Ritz. Over the next twenty minutes the rest of the motley residents shuffled down the stairs. They all cast sideways looks at Alexis, smiled with their lips pressed together furtively, but no one mentioned her pending exodus. Uncle Burr seemed far less dignified than Alexis was used to, sitting,

disheveled, on the same couch he'd slept on. He still had paisley uphol-
stery lines imprinted on his cheeks.

Once they were all there, Otto Kenzler produced the sherry, saying,
"Well, if we're going to be freezing our asses off, we might as well get
drunk, too! Ah? Ah? *Scheisse!*"

Roberta, wearing a silk bathrobe over her plaid pantsuit, had Pluto
draped over her shoulders and wrapped around her waist like a belt. She
stood by the mantel, keeping Pluto warm.

Mr. Kenji was the last one down, and he had a bonsai in his hands. He
walked right up to Alexis and held out the bonsai toward her. He grinned
and blinked at her.

"Thank you. It's . . . it's beautiful." She wasn't going to cry, she'd
determined that, but already it was starting to be hard. She felt like Frodo
at the end of *Lord of the Rings,* weepily bidding farewell—in gauzy, soft-
focus, unnecessary slow-motion—to the other Hobbits and to all of his
pointy-eared friends.

Kato and Kevin, clad in matching houndstooth greatcoats, entered
from the cold outside, a shopping bag between them, each brother holding one of the handles. The bag was obese with Fig Newmans—dozens
of packages of them. The twins set them down on the table.

They pulled Alexis into a hug and the others gathered around, forming a giant group hug around her.

"We're going to be . . . ," Kato said.

"Sorry . . . ," Kevin added.

"To see you go," Kato finished.

By now Alexis was tearing up.

"What'd they say?!" Deaf Donald bellowed, and everyone laughed.

Back upstairs, Alexis surveyed her room one last time. She heard a tapping at the window. She figured it was just the pigeons, but she rubbed
another peephole in the glass just in case and there, in a pile of lead gray
pigeon feathers, stood Habib, his black beak glinting in the morning
light. He had something in his beak, too. She pushed open the heavy window and Habib hopped over toward her on the ledge and dropped LJ's

cheap silver disk onto the ledge. She picked it up. He squawked loudly and squawked again, then flapped off noisily into the crisp air.

"You ready?" Uncle Burr said.

She turned around and gazed at him, annoyed that he'd broken the spell.

"What do you want?" she said, and gave a loud sigh.

"Can I show you something?"

She shrugged, unsure of what to make of him. She wasn't ready yet to see herself living with him. He was no replacement for her mother, for LJ.

"C'mon." He led her down the hall to LJ's room. He opened the closet and shoved LJ's musty old jackets aside, rapped on the wall behind. "You ever seen this?" he said.

"What are you talking about?" she asked, and crossed her arms.

"This." He banged on the wall harder and a large section, perfectly rectangular, popped out.

She followed him inside and up a set of steep stairs to an attic she'd never seen before. She'd seen the old dormers up on the hotel's steep roof but had not known there was anything up there. But now, here she was in this dusty old place with bird's nests littering the corners and bird shit spackling the floors. The windows were cracked and browned by decades of smog and there was no seeing out. The ceiling was a thin lattice of wood with fleecy, ancient pink-gone-umber insulation bulging out and hanging loose.

"Why didn't anyone . . . ?" she started.

"Use this place?"

"Yeah, it's awesome."

"I came here, all the time, as a kid. Here . . ." He walked over to the far corner, where a mildewed old cardboard box sat. He lifted it up, but the soggy bottom gave way, dropping the contents onto the floor. He kneeled down and smiled ruefully at the objects littering the dirty floor. Alexis saw old, chipped Matchbox cars and old beakers and tubing and Pyrex bottles from the mortuaries.

He picked up a box of matches, "I was a bit of a troublemaker, used to try some amateur chemistry in here. Almost blew up the house more than once."

She laughed involuntarily and then pulled it together again.

"This was our place to come as kids, you know. The hotel was crazier then than it is now, if you can believe it. We had a bearded lady here for a couple years, barked like a dog in her sleep. Helga. She made great gumbo, though. Was sorry to see her go in the end. That's the thing with a residence hotel, as I'm sure you've noticed. It wears on the soul, eventually. Not all that much better than mortuary living, I bet."

"Is that why you left?"

"Anyplace you can't leave eventually feels like a prison. I needed to break out, make my own life."

"So you left my mother here to handle everything alone." Alexis meant to say it matter-of-factly, but the accusatory tone couldn't be hidden.

He bit his lip and shook his head, looking at the floor and, after a moment, said, "Yes, I did." He sighed. "But maybe, near the end, she came to understand, in a way."

"When she decided to sell the Angeline herself."

Uncle Burr met her eyes, looking somewhat startled. "Yes, well, your mother still didn't really want to sell the Angeline, but she had started to think maybe she should—to give you a better future."

Alexis felt a little dizzy. It had never occurred to her before that her mother might have placed her welfare above the Angeline, above her duties to the tenants. For the first time, she could see how maybe her mother wouldn't have wanted her to shoulder all these burdens alone.

She picked up one of the Matchbox cars, a chipped red Mustang. "This is cool," she said.

"It's yours, if you want it."

She looked at Burr askance, slipped the car into her pocket. She picked up another car and put it in her pocket, too. "Thanks," she muttered.

Once they'd dressed in their funeral best, Alexis and Uncle Burr set out for Lakeview Cemetery. It was misty still, Capitol Hill draped in a cold and heavy fog that wouldn't burn away for anything. She kept an eye out for Habib, saw plenty of crows, but none of them were him.

"You know Angeline herself—daughter of Chief Sealth—is buried up there, too."

"Same place? Really?"

"Bruce Lee, too, actually."

"No shit."

"Yes shit. Kung Fu-ing out of his old box, I'll bet, kicking his way to the surface."

She smiled at that, too. Burr confounded her with his charm, that old asshole. Maybe it wouldn't be so bad in Sedona, after all. The weather sounded like hell, though. They fried eggs in the parking lots of their Kmarts. They baked old people to death in their houses. It was hostile to humanity, that kind of weather.

"I'm not going to start wearing shorts," she said.

"Fine with me," he said. "But if we go on a hike . . ."

"A hike?!" she belted. "Hell, no!"

Now it was Burr's turn to laugh. "You'll want to, I promise. It's beautiful. You heard of the Grand Canyon? There's a reason they don't call it the Dumpy Canyon, you know."

They crossed Twelfth and continued up the hill to Fifteenth. They turned and continued on toward the cemetery. As they crossed John Street, Alexis slipped her arm under his and he patted her hand, but said nothing.

CHAPTER 31

STEPHANIE KALLOS

IT BEGAN LIKE THIS, WHEN the girl was smaller and had about her less sadness, less confusion, less heaviness of spirit, and the old man who was like her father but not her father moved with greater ease.

Habib—who should technically be Habibah (but how was the old man to know, and besides, such things as sexual identity have long ceased to matter)—used to see them every day, when she began her long journey home to the rookery at the top of the hill.

A city dweller by choice (for Habib has always found humans endlessly fascinating, and not nearly as stupid as many of her kind believe) she liked to take her time going home, observing the humans along the way—for this was her work then: to observe, to learn, to apprentice herself to the ways of people so that, eventually, she could be of some use.

Habib would fly for a while, then loiter, greedy to learn as much as she could about these flightless, featherless creatures—above on the wires or fences or roofs, or below on the pavement—always making a great deal of noise. (Habib learned early on that humans are irritated by noisy animals, concluding that they are stupid, and thereafter ignoring them. This can be a great advantage for one who is in the business of observing.)

The old man with the ponytail and the girl walked the same way at the same time every day—from a small neatly groomed brick building where there were many young humans to a tall wooden building with the shabby look of a molting bird where there were no young humans, just more old ones like the man. And a woman with sparkling feet! They were an odd pair—the old man and the girl—hardly birds of a feather.

And yet there was between them a rare kind of connection, some-thing sensed, invisible, a bond not comprised of language or gesture but something wordless and unseen and—in that sense—very like the bond between animals.

The girl even hopped like a bird in those days! And spun and skipped and flitted, dashing a few steps forward, but never too far from the man, as if she were tethered to him, and the shadow that shrouded the old man would lift a bit, a loose-fitting garment being teased away from his body by a breeze.

Habib's rookery at that time was in a park at the top of a hill in an old part of the city. She chose this—to reside among humans, and in a big city—but not for the reasons some of her fellows did, which was because of the easy access to an endless variety of food and the plentiful oppor-tunities to annoy, taunt, and humiliate. (Habib has never been proud of these tribal tendencies; just because it is easy for crows to mock humans does not mean that it should be done).

Habib (who has had many names before and will have many more) chose to live in the city because she is intrigued by humans—chiefly by their insatiable craving for suffering.

She chose this park specifically because of the plays.

In this park, each summer, actors put on the plays of Mr. William Shakespeare. Battles and romances, all the dramas and absurdities of human life, played out under the trees where Habib sleeps. And so often in these plays there is talk of birds!

"The crow makes wing to the rooky wood: Good things of day begin to droop and drowse. . . . It is the lark, the herald of the morn, no night-ingale. . . ." Ah, Shakespeare! Now, there was a human who appreciated crows—not only writing about them, but in the very rhythms of crow-speak: *cuh caw cuh caw cuh caw cuh caw cuh caw!*

One evening another time, not as long ago as the first, Habib heard a pounding noise like the hammering of a bachelor thrush trying to attract a mate (although the season was wrong) and looked down and saw a light in a place where there had not been light before: a window, a patch of gold on the dingy roof of the old hotel where the hopping girl lived with the old ones and the one with sparkling toes. (Habib had been long-ing for an excuse to get closer to that one!)

Habib circled, spiraling down.

Standing squarely in the rectangle of light was the old man, the shrouded one; he was the source of the pounding noise. He was doing something that required him to look up and strike against whatever it was that was above his head.

Habib was intrigued. She perched on the nearby chimney, where she could continue to observe.

The old man talked to himself as he worked: a nonstop babble that seemed to serve no purpose other than to make him more and more angry.

And then, from another place in the building came the sound of what Habib had come to understand was human song. It was the voice of the girl, Habib realized.

The old man stopped banging, stopped making himself angry with words, and sat down on the floor. He lit a cigarette. He stared beyond the window, up at the sky. Habib had not seen him like this. She had not seen his face, his blue eyes, his essence: He had the look of a man who was earthbound but longed for freedom. The look of a man who had been staring at his own shadow for too long and didn't know how to stop.

That is the cause of human suffering, in Habib's opinion: Humans are like the Crow of legend, Crow who became obsessed with her shadow, pecking at it, tearing at it, scratching at it, until she woke her shadow up and it ate her so that Crow is now dead and her shadow is alive.

Humans cannot stop staring at their own shadows, at some shape they think is fixed, a shape that they come to believe is real. Everything constricts to that shape; they become only that, nothing more, and then they are dead.

Oh, life for humans on this planet would be so much less fraught with sadness if they could know one thing: that shape is an illusion. The woes and angers, the confusions and pains—all these are born of that narrow vision, that staring into the unchanging shape of one's own shadow.

There are worlds beyond this one. There so many other shapes to fill.

So there he was, the old man, looking up into the sky as it began to darken, wanting to see to something beyond himself—building a window to the stars!—but unable to see anything but his own sad shadow.

When death came to that place where the old man and the girl lived, and Habib heard him crying over the one with sparkling toes (who must have been his mate) she hurled herself against that very same window when she knew the old one was there to hear, and she let herself fall into that dark, dirty, treeless alley, knowing that she was saying good-bye to the park and the broad, open views of water and sunsets and her comrades in the rookery and the actors and the words of William Shakespeare.

But she was happy there, as much as a crow with a broken wing can be happy. She loved the colored glass in the old man's room and the strange lingering smells that they contained, and his cawing, excitable voice, and riding on his shoulder and being so close to other humans.

And she grew strong and she watched and learned and she was of use. She commanded a rescue, shattered glass, witnessed grief, returned what was lost, whispered what wisdom she could to the living and the dead, and now this intervention was over.

Habib knows it is over, because she is looking down at the girl (who is, after all, still a girl) walking through a park with another father who is not her father. An animal bond is forming between them. The girl is learning to fill a new shape.

And that is all Habib can hope for.

CHAPTER 32

JAMIE FORD

ALEXIS STARED UP AT A partially pregnant sky. Typical Seattle, overcast with a hopeful, glowing luminescence. She wished it would rain. She wished the sky would make up its mind, as she had.

Looking down, she regarded the hole in the ground—a resting place for her mother, swiftly dug with a trowel Otto had purloined from an army surplus store. The makeshift grave looked meager, unceremonious compared to the massive granite headstones that dotted the damp, mossy hillside of Lakeview Cemetery.

Milling about the dewy grass was a collective of residents, past and present. In place of flowers, Mr. Kenji had provided assorted greenery from the hotel, potted plants and planted pot.

Alexis dreaded that it had come to this. She wished her mother had been afforded a real funeral instead of this drive-by-shooting version—she and her family from the Angeline, quickly interring . . . *something*.

"I'm not sure we should be doing this," one of the twins said.

"We need *someplace* to visit," the other argued. "Someplace to remember. The Angeline won't always be there. . . ."

Alexis nodded, feeling the weight of the soiled cardboard box in her hands.

Inside were her mother's ashes.

Clovis had relented, preferring to bend the rules of his crematorium rather than store her mother's body indefinitely. In the process, he had removed the pearl necklace Edith wore, not realizing they weren't real. Only paste. But Alexis wore them anyway.

As she handed her mother's ashes to Ursula, she noticed the old Seafair pirate was tearing up behind her ceremonial eye-patch (worn for special occasions such as this). Everyone was. Her mother's death heralded the end of an era.

Mia walked up, glamorous in a long black dress, and late, as usual. Mr. Kenji handed her the violin and she began to play a haunting melody.

Nervously, Alexis touched each pearl, the way a priest might regard a rosary bead, the way she'd seen in movies. Each pearl represented a resident, a member of her extended family—a wayward saint cared for by her mother.

As the wind blew, Alexis closed her eyes. When she opened them, she was at another funeral, the only other funeral she'd ever attended, nearly ten years earlier. A memory that she'd rarely revisited, until now.

Lost in the dusty corners of her childhood, she remembered a similar gathering. Her mother was ever-present, as was Ursula, who had more teeth back then. The rest she didn't recognize, though she knew they were part of her colorful extended family.

As she struggled with the faint images, she realized where she'd been—her father's funeral. He'd knocked up her mother and vanished, but evidently the circumstances of his death brought strangers back together, if only for one surreal afternoon.

"Who was he?" she had asked.

"Just a friend." Her mother answered, fidgeting with the pearls around her neck.

Alexis had never realized it was her father. But now it made sense. The most vivid memory was of LJ, a huddled mass on the periphery, babbling to himself.

"He mixed up his medication this morning," her mother had said.

As Alexis watched the scene again, she realized what LJ had done. She'd seen it once before. He'd dosed himself and was tripping badly, probably on purpose. He wasn't escaping the memory of accidentally killing her father; he was forcing himself to remember every detail. He was punishing himself. The guilt had derailed him, along with the acid, until his murmurings took a detour and he started shouting about how Buddy Holly had been a narc and was killed by J. Edgar Hoover.

Ursula pulled him away, sending him on a mission to clean Jimi Hendrix's grave. That task kept him occupied for some time; Jimi was buried in Renton.

Afterward, they'd had a wake at the Angeline. Alexis had sat on the cracked, coffee-stained linoleum, coloring letters on a scrap of cardboard. The adults milled about, drinking her mother's sherry like sacramental wine.

"She's so creative," Mr. Kenji had remarked. "Practicing her ABCs?"

The conversations drifted in and out. No one realized that her letters formed a sign that read need help. She had learned how to read early and write early, and people were still surprised by it. And in between debates over her father's career choice and whether Jerry Garcia was actually a better guitarist when stoned, she had wandered outside and found a spot on the sidewalk next to the meth kids that was overlooked by members of Seattle's more polite society. She hadn't realized that they were panhandling. But she'd seen the signs soliciting assistance and thought she'd fit in.

Alexis sat there, alone in a crowd of strangers with her cardboard sign, expecting something—she wasn't sure what. Then she felt he mother's hands on her shoulders.

When Alexis opened her eyes again, she was at Lakeview, Ursula was pouring out her mother's ashes. Part of them. The rest would be scattered as she'd wished. She felt hands on her shoulders again.

"You OK, chica?" Linda whispered in her ear. "You were gone there for a while . . ."

She felt Linda's hands wrap around her waist and leaned back as her dry, chapped lips brushed her neck.

"You didn't think I'd stay mad forever, did you?"

Alexis inhaled Linda's scent, reached down and touched her hands. She noticed that Linda's fingernails had been chewed to the quick. She did care.

"Not forever." Alexis said, looking at the rest of the funeral gathering.

"Just until you track me down in Arizona and I have to get a restraining order . . ."

"I don't mean to spoil the moment," Linda said, "but I think this is where—you know—you're supposed to say a few words. You're family and all. . . ."

Family? Alexis glanced at her uncle in the distance. And what about the residents? Her mother had known them for a lifetime longer than hers. They were family as well.

Linda whispered in her other ear, "Awkward . . ."

Alexis leaned back, enjoying the embrace. For once Linda was there for her, not just in it for *coffin time*—unconditional and unexpectant.

It was an interesting change.

Inhaling, Alexis blurted out, "I guess this is the part where I'm supposed to tell you how great my mother was, but most of you know that."

Alexis paused to collect herself, noticing a crow flying overhead, wondering if the black bird might be Habib.

"Edith was a lot of things. A friend, a defender, a protector, a benevolent dictator, a warden, and 'a bull-goose loony,' as LJ once said. But to be honest, she had her struggles as a mother." Alexis swallowed hard. "All of you were her family—she called you heroes. But what was I? Where did I fit in? She kept me here, under wraps. Sometimes it was like she needed to be needed. I needed a mother, not a caretaker. But she did her best . . ."

Alexis paused, staring back at the eyes that watched her struggle to put together a fitting eulogy. She wished LJ were here in more than spirit; he would have been up to the task.

"Last year, for Mother's Day, I went looking for the perfect card, among all the sappy Hallmark offerings. I couldn't find what I was looking for. Because the perfect card for Edith would have read, "Well . . . *you tried*.""

"She did," Roberta chimed in, and the others nodded in agreement.

"And I've tried, too," Alexis answered, "to keep going, to keep the Angeline sailing." As she spoke she winked to Ursula in her pirate garb. "But we've run aground without her, and despite my desperate attempts,

I need to move on."

She couldn't make eye contact with Otto, Mr. Kenji, Roberta, or any of the residents. She knew they were crestfallen.

"Now for the hard part," Alexis said as she knelt down and removed the necklace, placing the pearls in the grave, kicking up a bit of dust from her mother's ashes.

After each resident said a few words, sang a few songs, or recited a few lines of poetry, Alexis walked back toward the black, wrought-iron fence that surrounded the cemetery. Her uncle was waiting for her. Linda trailed behind.

Mia caught up with her, handing out the violin. "I'm sorry I didn't get the concert planned in time."

"Don't worry about it; that wouldn't have changed anything." Alexis took the violin with a weak smile. "Maybe I'll actually learn to play this in Sedona."

"Don't tell me that's it?" Linda said. "You're free now, you can emancipate yourself, go from minor to *major*. You can stay here, in Seattle. My stepdad can help with the lawyerly things, he's good at that."

Alexis paused, nodding, part of her agreeing. "But I can't." she said. "Look at me. I'm the world's oldest fourteen-year-old. I'm not my mother—"

Linda interrupted. "You're more. You're like Edith 2.0. And Edith 2.0 can do what she wants now."

"Even if that means going to Sedona?"

Linda looked crushed. She dropped her head, paused a moment, maybe waiting for a reprieve; it never came. She turned and walked away.

Alexis knew that despite Linda's support, there were strings attached and those cords were binding her here. If she were to have any kind of life, it would have to be away from those closest to her. She would have to leave the Angeline. Like Habib, she would have to fly away.

CHAPTER 33

CLYDE FORD

DEATH.

Alexis looked around, a tiny shaft of sunlight glinting off the shiny surface of a nearby tombstone.

Death.

Sunlight, also off the window of Uncle Burr's sleek black limo.

Death.

The *caw, caw, caw* of a crow. Alexis chuckled to herself. Wasn't it supposed to be a raven and not a crow that heralded and accompanied death?

Death.

She seemed too young to have Death following her so closely for so long. Death felt like to her than the child's blanket she never knew.

Death.

LJ in his drug-induced stupors used to rant about Death . . . And . . . He used to rant about more. What was it? Death and . . . The word, the sense of what he used to mumble escaped her.

"Alexis."

Uncle Burr's voice called her back from the past.

"Dear, I think it's time we made our way to the airport."

His voice blurred in her mind, blurred into LJ's ramblings about Death.

"Alexis." Uncle Burr raised his voice.

She looked in his direction, nodded. Her feet trailed through the grass, each blade festooned with tiny globules of moisture, reminding her of minuscule tombstones, reminding her of . . . What was it that LJ used to say?

She ambled toward the limo. The chauffeur held the door open. Uncle Burr's face was barely visible in the dark recess. Alexis lingered, a part of her not wanting to enter the limo, as though she were being asked to enter her own moving tomb. She looked back at the cemetery with a strange, macabre fondness as though the familiarity of death was also a comfort and this new life she was off to something wonderful, perhaps, yet strange.

She slipped into the passenger's seat beside Uncle Burr. He patted her fondly on her thigh. A part of her stiffened. As appealing as the idea of now having a father figure was, it was also appalling. She'd been alone. She'd tried to make her own way. Tried to meet the world head-on as an adult. Tried . . . and failed. Yet another death—the death of Alexis's attempts to be a grown-up, a young woman.

"Alexis." Uncle Burr's voice, almost hoarse, rumbled from his chest. "You know this is the point in the story where—"

"What story?" Alexis blurted out.

"Any story," Burr said. "This is the point in the story where the characters remaining after a death comfort each other."

"But it's not a story," Alexis said. "It's my life, and anyway how would you know this is that point in the story?"

"Well, because I'm a mystery writer."

Alexis looked at him in disbelief.

"It's true."

"I guess I always assumed you were an accountant or something." She felt off-kilter. "Well, being a writer, even a mystery writer, doesn't make you an expert on a real person's life.

"LJ used to say," Alexis continued, "I mean he used to ramble about how truth was stranger than fiction, and fiction, he'd say, was better than truth."

Uncle Burr chuckled. "Readers read my mystery novels because they want to escape from the truths of their lives."

The limo slunk down the narrow roadway between burial plots.

Alexis's gaze lingered on each passing tombstone "And is that what you're hoping for me? Escape from the truths of my life?"

"No, dear," Uncle Burr said. "I'm hoping that in Sedona you'll find the time and the space to discover the truths of your life."

Death and . . .

LJ's rantings still hovered over her, like the mist hanging over this Seattle day.

The limo passed through a chain-link fence, turned into a small parking lot. Out the windshield, Alexis saw a gleaming, needle-nosed, white plane parked on the asphalt, the whine of its engines barely audible within the car. She chuckled, this wasn't SeaTac.

"That yours?" she asked.

"No," Uncle Burr said. "It's chartered."

"Cost a lot to charter a jet?"

"Enough."

"Not sure I'll get used to living with someone who can charter a jet at his whim."

Uncle Burr laughed. "Oh, I imagine you'll find a way."

Alexis rubbed her hand over her butter-smooth leather seat. The jet's engines whined louder. She watched out the window as the ground passed by faster and faster. Then, just as the plane's wheels left the ground, a flock of crows at the end of the runway scattered as a group, leaving one lone crow to fly its own way.

"Habib," Alexis said to herself. "Habib, what was it that LJ used to say? Death and? . . ."

Uncle Burr's jet pierced through one layer of clouds after another. Finally, bursting through to a sunlight that seemed too brilliant for Alexis. The plane made a sweeping bank to the right and now, out the window, the majestic peak of Mount Rainier awash in golden sunlight protruded above the highest layer of clouds.

LJ had once told her the story of two mountain climbers so anxious to make their ascent that they climbed the wrong peak. She understood what that must have felt like. Hadn't she been climbing the wrong peak for years?

She turned to Uncle Burr. "Why?"

"Why?" he asked.

"Yes, why did you want to keep the Angeline? Why not sell it and let the everything . . . let all of the past die? Wouldn't that be easier, better?"

Uncle Burr leaned back in his seat, rocked slightly, folded his hands, brought them under his bottom lip.

"Easier? Yes. Better? No. In the end, the promises we make to loved ones are the most important gifts we can give."

"Not to my mother. She wanted nothing to do with the place, and stupid me. I thought all along that she did."

"Edith didn't know all of the Angeline's secrets."

"I don't understand."

"Did Edith ever tell you the history of the Angeline?"

"Yes, that it had been a funeral home and it was named after Chief Sealth's daughter, Angeline."

"Yes, but before that, long before that, the ground that the Angeline was constructed on was a sacred Suquamish site. In handing over that site to the founding families of the city, Chief Sealth, as was his actual name, asked that whomever the owner was, whatever use was made of the property, that some aspect of that original sense of that place be retained."

The cockpit door opened, and a tall man wearing a short-sleeved white shirt with military epaulets stepped out. Alexis flinched, her first thought that a captain should never leave the controls of a plane. He must have noticed her surprise. He smiled, pointed back to the cockpit. "There are two of us up there, and the plane's on autopilot. I stepped out to see if there's anything I can get either of you to eat or to drink."

He pushed down on a lever and a table rose from the console between Alexis and Uncle Burr. The captain smoothed out a linen tablecloth over the table. He placed a bowl of phở in front of her.

Uncle Burr smiled. "Heard somewhere that you liked that."

"The Suquamish used that site for a masked ceremony of initiation.

Anyone making a transition could go there. If you were moving from childhood to adulthood, you went to this site. If you were moving from being single to being married, you went to this site. If you were moving from being a woman to having a child and becoming a mother, you went to this site. If you were about to die, you went there. And the ceremony . . . well, I actually wrote about it one of my mystery books.

"The ceremony was a death ceremony. You laid on the ground while other tribal member piled on top of you dirt, and ashes, and small stones, and objects that you had once held important. And then they drummed and danced around you, and sang songs of your death. 'Die you must die,' I have heard the songs said. 'You must die in order to live.'"

Uncle Burr tapped on the table as he spoke. The sound, his rhythm entangled Alexis's thoughts, entrained her mind, seducing her.

An image of her mother lying in a coffin flashed before her; her father, bubbles issuing from his mouth, drowning; LJ bleeding on the sidewalk; her life exploding, imploding, exploding again. The sound of the jet engine now fusing with Uncle Burr's drumming, pushing her deeper into herself, into her life.

Tears came uncontrollably. A few at first, then a gush. Her body shook. She cried, not knowing why, not caring. She cried for all of them, for all of it. For her mother. For her father. For LJ. For Linda. For her life . . . interrupted so many times.

Uncle Burr continued. "When the person lying under this pile of their past started shaking, the drumming, singing, and dancing stopped. Everyone fell silent. Then, *whew. Whew. Whew.* The entire community gathered around this person and began blowing breaths. And one by one the objects were removed. An old woman came forward and reached a hand out to pull the person up from the rubble. She was called the 'Bringer of New Life,' and the person was then considered to have born again. Angeline, Chief Sealth's daughter, was the last Suquamish native who knew this ceremony, she was the last 'Bringer of New Life.' Chief Sealth simply asked that this site always retain some manner of helping those who entered it to find 'new life.'"

Uncle Burr's words mixed with Alexis's tears, with the sounds of the jet engines, then suddenly LJ's voice burst through, not as a mumble now but like a clear bell . . .

"Death," Alexis heard LJ say. "It's all about death and resurrection; about what you have to let go of in order to move on."

"I wanted to keep the Angeline," Uncle Burr whispered, "to keep that promise to the chief."

CHAPTER 34

ELIZABETH GEORGE

THE DAY HAD BEEN ONE long series of firsts for Alexis, and they just kept piling up. First there was the first of saying good-bye to her mother . . . really saying good-bye this time in ways that no fourteen-year-old girl should ever have to experience. The second first was having to say good-bye to the person she had begun to figure was her first true love, more or less. The third first was being in an airplane. But the biggest first was being in a private jet. No matter that the jet was chartered, it was still P-R-I-V-A-T-E, and that said things about Uncle Burr's "cash position," as LJ would have said in the most derisive tone possible, that nothing else ever would.

Alexis spent a lot of the time on the flight in awe, and she didn't much care for this feeling. Awe meant difference. Awe meant entering into a whole new world. Awe meant, more than anything, the unexpected, and she'd had so much of the unexpected lately that she wasn't sure how she was supposed to cope with any more of it. She knew that she should be grateful that she even had an uncle who'd walked into her life and had taken care of many of its problems. And while she *wanted* to feel grateful, part of the problem was what came after being grateful. She knew enough about life to know that what came after generally was someone having an expectation. Like "I'm really grateful," which was answered by "So what're you going to do to show it?" And that was a problem for Alexis. The way she saw it, it would probably be a problem for anyone.

Aside from talking about the Suquamish tribe on the flight, Uncle Burr was pretty much quiet. After they'd had their meal, after they'd chatted about the Suquamish Indians, he'd taken out of a briefcase the tiniest laptop computer that Alexis had ever seen and he'd started to write. She read over his shoulder for a second—just wondering what it was he was writing and more or less figuring it was about her and what the heck he was going to do with her now. She figured it was a letter to his attorney or something, maybe passing her off to someone else. But it turned out to be part of his next novel. Or at least, that's how it seemed, since he began with chapter 134 and the sentence was "The corpse was starting to smell." *No shit,* Alexis thought when she read that. After 133 chapters, there was very little doubt the corpse would be ripe.

She dozed for a while then. She figured Uncle Burr knew what he was doing. Maybe it took him 133 chapters to clear his throat artistically or something. Since he was a jillionaire because of his writing, he didn't need any advice from her.

It was the captain's voice coming over the loudspeaker that awakened her from an uneven slumber. She saw that her uncle had put his laptop away and he was fastening his seat belt as the plane banked to the left. She looked out of the window. What she saw was a real eye-blinker for her.

Alexis had never been out of Washington state. She'd never been south of Olympia, even, so to find herself suddenly in the environment of Arizona was nothing short of astonishing.

They were descending into a vast valley. On either side of it towered huge, flat-topped bluffs. The word for these came to her as the plane evened out from its bank: mesas. She was looking at mesas. They represented enormous tabletop plains surmounting tall cliffs and the cliffs themselves were red. Beneath these cliffs the valley spread out, pimpled with shrubbery but bare of trees.

Another first. To be in a place where there were no trees. How was it going to feel? She didn't know, and she couldn't even begin to imagine.

In the distance, a bridge sketched a silver arc across a wide gulley. It reminded her of pictures she'd seen of Deception Pass Bridge on Whidbey Island, but here again, the difference was what it spanned, going from mesa to mesa where cactus grew, sage green under a true-blue sky that was cloudless but beginning to mark the day with the colors of sunset.

As the plane approached the ground, towering shapes came into view. These were the red of the cliff sides, but they looked carved by someone into fantastic forms. It was, Alexis thought, like being on another planet—one designed by a god who saw colors in a different way, that was for sure. It was big and bold, but seeing it made Alexis wonder if she was big enough and bold enough to be part of it.

The plane landed. One bump and that was it. Uncle Burr unfastened his seat belt and smiled at her. "Ready for it?" he asked, and it was as if he'd been reading her mind all along. He added, "Toto, we ain't in Kansas anymore," and for a moment she hoped that he wasn't giving her some loopy nickname. But then she remembered *The Wizard of Oz*. She said, "Oh, right. That's for sure."

A vehicle was waiting not far from where the jet taxied to stop. Here another surprise greeted Alexis. For a guy who had a limo deposit him here and there, who chartered airplanes, who felt comfortable enough to write 133 chapters of whatever before anyone figured out why the corpse was a corpse, she'd assumed there'd either be another chauffeur waiting at the airport or one hell of an impressive vehicle like . . .who knew? Maybe a Maserati. Maybe a Hummer. Or maybe a Rolls-Royce. Or whatever. But what she didn't expect was to see a worn-down pickup truck with two years of red dust obscuring its color and a windshield whose only bow to being able to be seen through was the fan shapes made by windshield wipers.

But that was their transportation, and after Uncle Burr thanked the captain, the co-captain and the flight attendant, he said to Alexis, "Let's do it to it," by which she figured it was time to go. She followed him down the narrow stairway and over to the truck.

It wasn't locked. *Well, who would want to steal the thing?* was what Alexis thought. This thought was reinforced by the fact that the keys were in the ignition as well. Uncle Burr told her to climb aboard and he said they had to "warm this baby up" to get her to run right. He added "Just like a woman" with a wink, but it turned out that the real reason that they had to wait was because her stuff was being unloaded from the plane and a member of the ground crew at the airport was wheeling it over to the truck. A thump indicated it was all in place, at which point Uncle Burr put the truck into gear and off they went.

Alexis got a clear indication that Sedona was a bit different from the rest of the world the moment they got out onto a highway. A billboard asked her if she wanted to know her life's purpose, which she could find out by having a spiritual reading at Sedona Spring of Hope (call this number and ask for Annapurna). Shortly thereafter, she discovered that at Sedona Spiritual Vortex she could have a customized spiritual experience within the most powerful of the Sedona Vortexes, which was Completely Unknown to the Public. Or she could enjoy a Mystical Head Massage, a Cleansing Foot Massage, or an extended stay in an Authentic Sweat Lodge. This last was something Alexis was familiar with, and it prompted her to ask her uncle a couple of questions.

"How'd you end up here?" was the first of them. For she knew that, like her, he'd been born in Seattle, and she couldn't imagine what had brought him to a place where one could purchase spiritual experiences, customized or otherwise.

"Started out with early arthritis," he said. "Ended up with Namche Waterfall."

Uncle Burr had said it all as if she already would have known what he was talking about, but she didn't. The years, the dissension, and the chasm created by both her mom and this man amounted to a void into which mountains of information needed to be poured. Meantime, she was going to have to play this relationship largely by ear.

"You like it here?" was the second of the questions. She'd counted sixty-seven cacti by that time and one lone sketch of bark and desiccated leaves leaning to the right in an indication of the direction of the wind, when there was wind. "I mean, it must be weird not to have trees . . . I mean, after Washington."

"Well, that's true," Uncle Burr said. "But there's Namche Waterfall, which makes up for a lot."

"Will I get to see Namche Waterfall?" Alexis asked. To give up trees in exchange for a waterfall might be just fine, if the waterfall was spectacular, she figured.

"Oh yeah," he said. "Sooner than you think."

So he lived at the waterfall, she thought. Cool.

They drove through town. This wasn't much, as things turned out. Four lanes of highway and mostly strip malls with lots of advertisements for massages, for spiritual readings, for dawn and sunset hikes into the "spiritual realm of the ancient Anasazi," who turned out to be the Indians who'd lived six hundred years ago in the area. Native Americans, Alexis reminded herself. She had to work her way some distance from years at LJ's side, hearing one diatribe after another on the worthlessness of political correctness. Maybe Sedona was a politically correct place. She'd have to be careful about how she talked.

Through the town, they began to wind along a narrow road flanked by cacti and chaparral. Occasional boulders in the deep red of the distant cliffs broke up the landscape and the minor miracle of a rise in the topography occurred about three miles along. They were well out of town when Uncle Burr made a turn into a gravel driveway. There was no house in sight, and there sure wasn't a waterfall nearby, but he began to slow down near an impressive formation of rocks and towers of sandstone that, as they approached, morphed unexpectedly and almost miraculously into a house.

It was huge. She could see that the place had been constructed to blend into the environment, as if the building were in the Federal Witness Protection Program. He pulled up next to it and said, "Here we are, then," and she looked around for the waterfall. It was probably behind the house, she figured. Or maybe it was within hiking distance. She was about to ask her uncle this question, when the front door opened and a woman came out.

"Namche Waterfall," Uncle Burr said.

"Huh?"

"You can call her Aunt Namche."

Uncle Burr was married? Uncle Burr was married to someone called Namche Waterfall?

As if he heard her last question, he said, "Listen, sweetheart. She has a thing for this waterfall in Nepal. Her real name is Sheila Lou Pronsky, but if that was your name . . . You sort of get the idea. Don't let on that you know." Aunt Namche came clattering down the path from the front door. She wore what looked like six thousand scarves, and her hair was as red as the sandstone. She had on earrings that dropped below her shoulders and so many necklaces that Alexis wondered how she could even walk with her head held upright.

"Here you are! Here you are!" Aunt Namche cried. "Burr, hon, I was worried all day. The omens . . . I can't tell you how bad they were. I cast entrails at five this morning and the way they landed . . . I would have phoned you, but I didn't want to worry you. And this . . . What a sweetie. Alexis, yes? Well, stupid of me. Who else would you be?"

Alexis found herself smothered in the embrace of Namche Waterfall, which was not unlike being enveloped by a human-sized marshmallow. Not because Namche Waterfall was fat. Far from it. But she had bazoombas the size of Volkswagen Beetles—the old kind, not the new kind—and they were the real thing, she figured, because they were soft. Alexis wasn't an expert in this matter, but she remembered LJ going on one time about fake bazoombas. "Ever feel an elbow?" was how he put it. Well, Aunt Namche didn't feel like an elbow.

She went on to Uncle Burr next. "Hon, hon, honeybear, lovekins," she said to him. Uncle Burr blushed, but he allowed himself to be nuzzled thoroughly. He winked at Alexis. He mouthed *Sheila Lou Pronsky* and grinned. And Alexis could understand very well why her uncle had stayed in Sedona, Arizona.

Inside the house was a place of wonder. Namche Waterfall had definite ideas about interior design, and Uncle Burr had—as he said—"given my baby free rein." There were pillows everywhere and lots of draperies and low-slung furniture and colorful rugs. There were also lots of pictures because Namche Waterfall was a photographer, it seemed. And she was good as far as Alexis could tell. She might have been given a bit too much to focusing on people's intimate dental work as her subject, but there was a certain something about the way she went for the cavities that had its own appeal.

Aunt Namche told her that she hoped she liked the bedroom that would be hers. She said, "Burr and I . . . well, you know we don't have kids. We were never blessed. But now we have you, and we want you to have the room of your dreams. A very, very special place for a very, very special girl. That's you," she added, just in case Alexis might think she was referring to someone else. She said, "It's just this way. It's on the other end of the house from me and Burr, because everyone likes privacy and you're part of everyone so you like it, too."

She led the way with a fluttering of scarves and a rattling of necklaces. Uncle Burr went second. Alexis brought up the rear. She wondered—as any girl would—what this very special room was going to be like, and considering Namche Waterfall's taste in decorating, she didn't have real high hopes for the place. At the far end of the house, a door stood closed. Namche Waterfall headed straight for it, threw it open, said "Ta-da!" and clasped her hands over her copious bazoombas to wait for Alexis's response.

Well, it had to be positive. It absolutely had to be. Alexis began rehearsing adjectives as she approached. Fabulous, wonderful, perfect, delicious, excellent, mind-bending, serene, outstanding, fabulous . . . no she'd used that already.

There was nothing for it but to walk inside.

Two steps and she stopped. Two steps and her world altered on its precarious axis. Two steps and her eyes filled with tears. The room was fourteen-year-old-girl-come-home. In its middle stood a four-poster bed. Not a canopy bed, which would have been too dumb for words, but an antique four-poster with a comforter created not to resemble anything remotely Arizona, but to remind her of the Pacific Northwest. It was fashioned to be a quilted landscape, its colors forming trees, water, and sky. A single Orca spyhopped from the water, a single girl stood watching from the shore.

There was a dresser in the room, a rocking chair by a window, a desk on which a laptop computer sat. Next to the desk was a pile of schoolbooks. On top of these was a folder with WELCOME TO RED ROCK HIGH printed on it.

"Got you all enrolled," Aunt Namche said. "I figured that would be better than making you sit there and go through it all on your own. Only thing to be added is the electives you want, but we can do that tomorrow. Either Burr or I will take you. Oh, look at this, too."

She moved to the closet and pulled open its door. There wasn't a plethora of clothes hanging there, although for a moment that was halfway what Alexis expected to see. Instead, there were just three articles that Aunt Namche brought out: a purple school sweatshirt, a pair of black jeans, and silver tennies.

She said, "Looks sort of dumb, but purple, silver, and black are the school colors. Seems dumb to wear them to school, I know, *but* tomorrow's a pep rally. You know pep rallies, right? Well, here they always wear the school colors on pep-rally days, so I figured you'd probably want to fit in."

Fit in, Alexis thought. Fit in, fit in. When in her life had she ever fit in? And, more important, could she fit in here, could she fit in now? Could she mold her frame and figure into what would work in this time and this place after such a long period of being the one who held the rest of life together for so many people? She wasn't sure. But she sure as hell wanted to give it a try.

She realized that Aunt Namche was waiting for her answer and on her face was a look of worry. At her side, Uncle Burr was waiting, too. And he was either worried that she wasn't happy with what Aunt Namche had done or he was thinking about how to move that corpse from chapter 134 to where it belonged, a heck of a lot earlier in the book.

Alexis said, "You guys . . ." And then she could hardly say more. Because she felt real tears coming, not tears because she was afraid or she was lonely or she wanted someone to love her and be there for her for the rest of her life, but tears that meant she was filling up . . . and up and up . . . till soon there would be no empty space in her that needed filling anymore.

* * *

School was scary. But the first day at a new school was always scary, especially in a place where most of the kids knew one another and had known one another since they were in kindergarten. But after what Alexis had been through in the previous weeks, being the new girl at school was no big deal. You don't drive around in an SUV with your mother in a coffin in the back to then be scared because thirty-two kids are staring at you when you walk into geometry. You don't watch a guy get killed by his own bomb and you don't end up in a police cell trying to figure out how you got there in the first place, only to worry that someone's going to think you're a fatso in PE class. This was nothing compared to what she'd been through. She could, at this point, pretty much survive anything.

Which was largely why she was able to survive her phone call to Linda. She made it at lunchtime. She found a private place near the gym, under an overhang and out of the sun. She made a note to herself to get used to the sun. It was hot and it blasted down like something being rayed from an alien spacecraft. Linda answered. No voice mail, but that was a good thing because voice mail would have been chicken.

"Shit in half, Alex," were Linda's first words. "Why the hell haven't you called before now? Didn't you get my voice mails? Didn't you get my texts?"

Truth was, Alexis hadn't looked. She went with that. "I got caught up in getting organized here," she told Linda. "I haven't checked my phone."

There was a silence. Well, one thing Linda wasn't was a dumb-shit. She never had been, which was part of why Alexis loved her. And she did love her. True and through. It was just . . . she wasn't sure *how* she loved her.

That was, essentially, the message for Linda. I'm fourteen years old. I know you knew at fourteen who you were and what you wanted and where you were heading. But here's the deal: I don't know yet. I want to know. I would really, really love to know. But I don't. And I need to figure that out. See, the way I look at it, my life's been crazy for a long time. I mean, life at the Angeline was pretty weird. There were cool things about it, but there were also . . . I mean, look. How many kids live with a snake lady and a python? How many kids have a pirate lady with a peg leg for a neighbor? And how many kids . . . And here there were tears, for there were going to be tears for some time to come about how her mom had died and what she'd had to do because of that death. But it all boiled down to a single piece of information that she had to give Linda, that she had to make Linda understand.

"I think I need to be a kid for a while," she said. "I think I've found a place where I can do it."

CHAPTER 35

SUSAN WIGGS

FOUR YEARS LATER ... THE HOTEL ANGELINE, SEATTLE

She walks up the hill from the train station, feeling the freshness of the autumn air on her face for the first time in four years. In one hand, she drags an oversized suitcase. The other cradles Mr. Kenji's bonsai plant, badly in need of the moist air of the Pacific Northwest.

The coffee smells, the reek of exhaust, the distant snorts of ferry horns surround her, and her heart expands with a feeling of anticipation. She passes a guy selling *Real Change* and pauses to hand him a dollar. Another panhandler rattles a cup at her; she finds some oyster crackers from the train in her pocket and hands them over.

Already, Seattle is taking hold of her. She still holds Sedona in the dry tan of her skin and in her hair, but the fine mist of the Northwest is making its way to places she didn't know were parched. In her heart she carries the love and care of Uncle Burr and Namche Waterfall, who let her spend the last of her childhood being a *child*.

The next step is up to her. She didn't really debate with herself much about her future. She knew she wanted to return. There is a program at the University of Washington that is perfect for her. Tomorrow she will move into student housing and into a new life surrounded, for the first time ever, by her actual peers.

First, though, there is a little unfinished business to take care of.

She considers flagging a taxi—the hill is a challenge with the giant suitcase—but decides against it. She trudges past her old landmarks and haunts, past the parks and public buildings, making her way up Pine Street.

A youth soccer game is going on in the ball field across the street, and just as Alexis turns the corner, a cheer goes up. She smiles briefly, feeling encouraged.

The sight of the Hotel Angeline freezes her on the sidewalk. She stands staring up at the old building. The front walkway is flanked by still-blooming *Ligustrum*. Sunset-colored leaves litter the damp sidewalk. There is a heaviness in the air, the weight of remembrance. Stuffing her hands into the pockets of her coat, she gazes up at the mullioned windows and odd, angular gables and dormers.

As if it were yesterday, she knows which resident occupies each room.

In Roberta's window is the dreamcatcher Alexis sent her from Sedona, and in Ursula's, a crystal on a nylon string. Deaf Donald's window is plastered with "Save the Whales" stickers and yellow happy faces. Mr. Kenji's window, off to the side, is serenely empty.

And then there is Otto. . . .

Alexis takes a deep breath, filling her lungs with piney, damp air, and hoists her big suitcase, bumping its wheels up the front steps. Her old key still works—no surprise. When she steps into the foyer, she is transported back to the past. The faint afternoon sunlight splashes through the front windows, painting the floor with bars of light and dark.

She is about to call out, but stops herself. She needs a moment. Did all that really happen? To her? It seems so distant, yet she can remember everything as though it had just happened. The memories are as crisp and well defined as old rose petals pressed between the pages of a girl's diary.

She reflects on the girl she had been in this place, and the things she had to do in order to survive. For a long time, she'd had to live her childhood backward, forced to step up and take charge of things that were thrust into her hands.

It isn't fair, but maybe that's the whole point. Fairness has no part in real life, and she took that lesson away from the Hotel Angeline with her. The time in Sedona had been her refuge and her reward, but now she was ready to come back and face the things that had happened here.

The creak of old wood signals the arrival of Deaf Donald, tottering down the stairs. She rushes to him and slips her arms around him, feeling the nubby warmth of his sweater, the same one he has worn every year when the weather turns. His hearing is gone entirely now; Roberta had written to her about it. Alexis steps back and signs, "I've missed you."

His face lights up with surprise. "You're signing now."

"I learned it in school, down in Arizona."

The uneven thump of Ursula's gait alerts her.

"Christ on a crutch, look what the cat dragged in," Ursula says, holding out her arms. "Welcome back."

The others join them, one by one, and they sit together in the parlor with furniture arranged just as it had always been, the overstuffed chairs, the settee, the bookcases crammed with bestsellers by her uncle Burr.

"You look wonderful," Roberta says, beaming.

"I'm sorry I had to go," Alexis says, looking around at their dear faces. "But I had to."

They give her a plate of Fig Newmans and some organic green tea, and she feels their love surrounding her. Yet her pleasure at being among them again dims.

"It's not the same without Otto, is it?" she asks.

There's a beat of silence. Mr. Kenji says, "We miss him every day. It was a good death, though. No sickness or pain. Just . . . sleep. After a very good life."

She gets up and fetches the bonsai tree, handing it to Mr. Kenji. "I kept this in my room the whole time I was away. I'm bringing it back in memory of Otto. Will you tend to it for me?"

Mr. Kenji's hands are tender and reverent as he takes it from her. "Of course. It is in good hands."

They sit together for a while in companionable silence. Alexis pretends she's not tense about the upcoming meeting, but it's not working.

"Nervous about seein' Linda, are ye?" Ursula asks bluntly.

"Is it that obvious?"

"Alexis," Roberta says. "We see you. We know you. Even though you've been away, we'll always be family."

She braces her hands on her knees and stands up. "I need to go down to the basement."

It is about closure, coming here to remember some things, and to lay other things to rest. She opens the door to the basement and the damp, fecund smell makes her catch her breath. She recoils a little, then forces herself to go on, step by step, descending to a place that has haunted her dreams.

"Let me get the light for you," Roberta calls, and flips a switch.

Alexis catches her breath again, this time with surprise and pleasure. "What did you do?" she asks, feeling a lightness in her chest.

"We didn't see the point of storing coffins down here," Ursula says.

"Bad karma," adds Mr. Kenji.

She studies the warm, friendly glow of green-shaded desk lamps, listens to the faint hum of computers. Seven of them.

A couple of the people working at the computers look up, nod, and smile slightly. "Come on in," says a woman in sweats and fuzzy slippers. "Everyone's welcome here."

"We had a brainstorm," Roberta explains. "This is a big, beautiful space now, isn't it? We've rented it out."

"So . . . who are they?" Alexis drops her voice to a whisper.

"They're a bit quirky," says Roberta.

"On account of them being writers, you know?"

"They're writers?"

"All seven of them. They needed a space to meet and to work. It's perfect."

"You have seven writers in your basement?"

Donald nods, signing, "They like it here. There's a poet, a couple of novelists, an opera librettist, an essay writer . . . . They don't usually make much trouble."

She stands back and takes it all in—the nicely designed workspaces, the lighting, the sounds of Rush and Neil Young drifting from various speakers. The lumber used to construct the desks and bookcases looks vaguely familiar.

"Is that? . . ." She turns to Mr. Kenji.

He offers a solemn nod. "We used the lumber from the coffins. No need to let it go to waste."

"It's brilliant," she says quietly, then smiles at the writers. "I'm glad you're here."

"Thanks," says a guy hunched over a Mac. "Drop by anytime."

She heads back up the stairs with her friends. Her family. The writers in the basement have no idea what used to fill the space, and that's probably a good thing. Now it's filled with the ideas from their imagination, with laughter and conversation.

Her mother would have liked that. Her words, spoken so long ago, drift back to Alexis's mind: *The Hotel Angeline is the place where your family lives. You have to take care of your family.*

She'd done her best. At fourteen, she'd given it everything she could, for as long as she could. And then she'd been given an opportunity to dive back into her childhood—a refuge, a welcome respite. The world had stopped, and Alexis had willingly stepped off.

The time is right to return now. She checks her watch. It's the same Xena Warrior Princess watch Linda had sent her that first Christmas in Sedona. Coming from Linda, it had been a peace offering. At least, Alexis chose to construe it that way.

She feels a pinch of tension in her chest. "I'm going to head outside," she tells the others.

They don't object; they know this meeting is going to be difficult.

Sunlight slants across the front garden. Alexis sits on the stoop, watching families head home after the soccer match. She sees a young couple pushing a stroller, a small soccer player bouncing along beside them. There are a lot of ways a family can look, she reflects. As many ways as there are people.

A wave of gratitude sweeps over her. She used to yearn for a different life, for comfort and ease and tradition, but finally she understands that the life she has is the one that's meant to be. Rather than fighting to stuff herself into a role, she has discovered that letting go and letting things be as they are bring the richest rewards.

Or so she hopes.

The streets grow quiet; evening is coming on. It occurs to her that she doesn't even know what kind of car Linda drives these days. Each passing

VW Bug or Subaru or SUV makes her tense up.

Finally a shiny pink Vespa whines to a stop in front of the Angeline. The matching pink helmet comes off, revealing a mane of hair dyed purple.

Alexis stands up, studies the young woman she hasn't seen in four years.

"Hey," she says.

"Hey yourself." Linda offers a flicker of a smile. "Long time no see."

Alexis hesitates. She studies the pretty face, the dark skin, the eyes that still sparkle with mischief. She doesn't feel that revved-up youthful excitement that used to fill her when Linda was around.

"You've changed," Linda remarks.

"Four years will do that to a kid."

"How are you doing?" Linda really seems to want to know.

"Getting ready to start school at UW," Alexis says. "I'm a little nervous, but excited." She's curious about her own emotions. When she looks at Linda now, she sees someone who once meant the world to her, like a child's beloved toy that now sits on a shelf in a room she doesn't visit anymore.

"I'm sorry about that phone call," she says.

"It's OK," Linda assures her. "I understood then, and I still do." She pauses. "You staying here tonight?"

Alexis nods. "They've got my old room waiting for me. Just for one night."

"Got any other plans?"

"Not really. You?"

Linda twists around on the Vespa. "I'm going downtown to meet some friends. Want to come?"

Alexis pauses. She looks at her friend, feels nothing but a warm sense of nostalgia. Then she turns back and looks at the Hotel Angeline. Its windows glow in the lowering twilight, and she thinks of the people inside—her family.

"Maybe another time," she tells Linda.

"Sure, whenever." Linda looks at her for an extra moment, then pushes off. The motor crescendos as she heads downtown, leaving a brief puff of exhaust in her wake.

Alexis stands very still, listening to the murmur of conversation coming from somewhere inside. In the distance, she can see the lights on the water, glittering like diamonds along the shores of Puget Sound. The stars are coming out.

It's going to be a beautiful night.

ACKNOWLEDGMENTS

NEVER IN 36 MILLION YEARS could we have accomplished the writing of a thirty-six-author novel in six days without the participation, sponsorship, and fellowship of so many wonderful people and organizations from Seattle to New York to India and Australia.

We thank everyone from the bottom of our hearts, including Sam Read and Hollis Palmer of ArtsCrush (www.artscrush.org), Jon Fine of Amazon.com (www.amazon.com), everyone at Richard Hugo House (www.hugohouse.org), and the good people at our fiscal arts management agency, Shunpike (www.shunpike.org).

It takes a village to write a novel, and we're grateful to our village of Seattle for incredible backup. Many fine dining establishments fed our authors; local businesses provided parking, raffle prizes, and equipment. They are listed on the acknowledgments page of our website (www.thenovellive.org/acknowledgements).

In addition to our authors, who all gave up good honest writing time on their own projects to participate, we thank our generous volunteers and staff, also listed on our website (www.thenovellive.org/acknowledgements). And we thank Marilyn Dahl at Shelf Awareness (www.shelf-awareness.com) and so many other bloggers and supporters for bringing the live event to the public.

Without a publisher, our thirty-six voices would have gone silent after the event, but thanks to the clear vision of the people at Open Road Integrated Media, *Hotel Angeline* can now light up the ereaders of our devoted fans and new readers. Many thanks to Brendan Cahill, Jane

Friedman, Rachel Packman Chou, Luke Parker Bowles, Danny Monico, Andrea Colvin, Lauren Naefe, and our fine editor, Julie Doughty.

And probably most especially, we thank the thousands who came and watched the process, whether in person or online from around the globe, urging our authors on, encouraging us when we grew weary during the six-day marathon, and always, always, eager to read the story as it unfolded and morphed and cohered. And now, we thank you, for joining their ranks.

Long live Hotel Angeline!

Jennie Shortridge and Garth Stein
Co-founders
Seattle7Writers

Seattle7Writers (www.seattle7writers.org) is a nonprofit collective of Northwest authors whose mission is to create connections between readers, writers, booksellers, librarians, and all of those who believe in the power of the written word. All funds raised by Seattle7Writers, including from the sales of this book, are donated to literacy.

Hotel Angeline: A Novel in 36 Voices is the result of The Novel: Live! project, which is one of a diverse range of not-for-profit programs that has received support from Amazon.com for its commitment to fostering the creation, discussion, and publication of new works and new authors. Other recipients include Lambda Literary Foundation, 826 Seattle, Poets & Writers, Ledig House, Macondo Foundation, Teachers & Writers Collaborative, Hedgebrook, The Moth, Seattle Arts & Lectures, Open Letter, Council of Literary Magazines and Presses, The Loft, Archipelago Books, Pen American Center, Copper Canyon Press, Milkweed Editions, Richard Hugo House, Words Without Borders, the Association of Writers & Writing Programs, Asian American Writers Workshop, New York Writers Coalition, and the Alliance for Young Artists & Writers.

CONTRIBUTORS

KATHLEEN ALCALÁ is the author of *Spirits of the Ordinary* and four other award-winning books. She teaches creative writing at the Northwest Institute of Literary Arts on Whidbey Island.

MATTHEW AMSTER-BURTON is a personal finance columnist for Mint.com and co-host of the hit food-and-comedy podcast "Spilled Milk." He is the author of *Hungry Monkey: A Food-Loving Father's Quest to Raise an Adventurous Eater*, and has been repeatedly featured in the *Best Food Writing* anthology.

KIT BAKKE spent the twentieth century as an anti-war street fighter, a pediatric nurse and a business consultant (though not at the same time). In the twenty-first, she turned to writing, which she also thinks is fun. Her books, so far, are *Miss Alcott's E-mail* and *Dot to Dot*.

ERICA BAUERMEISTER is the author of the bestselling novels *The School of Essential Ingredients* and *Joy For Beginners*. She is also the co-author of *500 Great Books by Women: A Reader's Guide* and *Let's Hear It For the Girls: 375 Great Books for Readers 2–14*.

SEAN BEAUDOIN is the author of the novels *Going Nowhere Faster, Fade to Blue*, and *You Killed Wesley Payne*. His stories and articles have appeared in numerous publications including *Narrative, The Onion*, the

New Orleans Review, Glimmer Train, The Rumpus, the *San Francisco Chronicle,* and *Spirit,* the in-flight magazine of Southwest Airlines.

DAVE BOLING is a Northwest journalist. His first novel, *Guernica,* won a Pacific Northwest Booksellers Association award for fiction in 2009, and was a Barnes & Noble "Discover Great New Writers" selection. Published in fifteen languages, it made several international bestseller lists.

DEB CALETTI is an award-winning young adult author and National Book Award finalist. Her many books include *The Nature of Jade, Stay,* and *Honey, Baby, Sweetheart,* winner of the Washington State Book Award, the Pacific Northwest Booksellers Association Best Book Award, and a finalist for the PEN USA Award.

CAROL CASSELLA is a practicing anesthesiologist, the mother of two sets of twins, and author of two nationally bestselling novels, *Healer* and *Oxygen.*

WILLIAM DIETRICH is the author of ten novels, four non-fiction books, and was a longtime Northwest journalist who shared a Pulitzer at the *Seattle Times.* He has taught environmental journalism at Western Washington University, and his fiction has sold into thirty-one languages. His newest novel is *Blood of the Reich.*

ROBERT DUGONI is the *New York Times* bestselling author of the David Sloane Series: *The Jury Master, Wrongful Death, Bodily Harm,* and *Murder One.* His books have been translated into twenty-three languages.

KEVIN EMERSON has published six novels for middle-grade readers: *Carlos Is Gonna Get It* and the *Oliver Nocturne* series #1–5. His next novels, *The Fellowship for Alien Detection* for middle grade, and *The Siren and the Skull* (book 1 of a YA trilogy), will be published in 2012. A former elementary school science teacher, Kevin teaches writing to teens in Seattle, and sings in two bands.

KAREN FINNEYFROCK is a poet and novelist. Her second book of poems, *Ceremony for the Choking Ghost*, was released in 2010. Her young adult novel, *Celia, the Dark and Weird*, is due in 2012.

CLYDE FORD is the author of many works of fiction and nonfiction, and is a Zora Neale Hurston/Richard Wright Legacy award winner.

JAMIE FORD is the *New York Times* bestselling author of *Hotel on the Corner of Bitter and Sweet*, which was an IndieBound NEXT selection, a Borders Original Voices selection, and a Barnes & Noble Book Club selection. It has been translated into twenty-five languages, though Jamie is still holding out for Klingon (because that's when you know you've made it).

ELIZABETH GEORGE is the awarding-winning and internationally bestselling author of many mystery novels, including the popular Inspector Lynley series. Most of her books have been filmed for television for the BBC and broadcast in the U.S. on PBS's "MYSTERY!".

MARY GUTERSON is the author of the novels *We Are All Fine Here* and *Gone to the Dogs*. She has written for public radio, print magazines, and blogs, and her fiction and poetry has appeared in a variety of literary journals and anthologies.

MARIA DAHVANA HEADLEY is the author of the novel *Queen of Kings*, and the memoir *The Year of Yes*.

TERI HEIN is the Founding Executive Director of 826 Seattle, a youth writing center. Her memoir *Atomic Farmgirl* was a Booksense pick. She has had stories and essays published in a number of other books and magazines.

STEPHANIE KALLOS spent twenty years in the theater before turning her full attention to writing. Her first novel, *Broken for You*, was selected for "The Today Show" book club by Sue Monk Kidd. Her second novel, *Sing Them Home*, was chosen by *Entertainment Weekly* as one of the 10 Best Books of 2009. Stephanie is currently working on her third novel.

ERIK LARSON's most recent book is *In the Garden of Beasts*. His international bestseller, *The Devil in the White City*, won an Edgar Award for best fact-crime writing.

DAVID LASKY is a comic artist who created the series *Boom Boom* and *Urban Hipster* (in collaboration with Greg Stump). He has drawn comics for numerous anthologies (*Kramers Ergot*, *Hotwire*) and is currently at work (with collaborator Frank Young) on a graphic novel biography of country music's legendary Carter Family, which will debut in 2012.

STACEY LEVINE is the author of four books, including *The Girl with Brown: Fur-Tales and Stories*. Her fiction has appeared in *Fence*, *Tin House*, *The Fairy Tale Review*, *Yeti*, and other venues. A Pushcart Prize nominee, she has also received the PEN/West Fiction Award, the Stranger Genius Award for Literature, and other honors.

FRANCES MCCUE is a poet and prose writer. From 1996–2006, she was the Founding Director of Richard Hugo House in Seattle, WA. Currently, she is the Writer in Residence at the Undergraduate Honors Program at the University of Washington.

JARRET MIDDLETON is the author of *An Dantomine Eerly* and other surrealist fiction. He is the editor and co-founder of Dark Coast Press, an independent literary publisher in Seattle.

PETER MOUNTFORD is the author of the novel *A Young Man's Guide to Late Capitalism*. His short fiction has recently appeared in *Best New*

American Voices 2008, Michigan Quarterly Review, Conjunctions, Phoebe, and *Boston Review.*

KEVIN O'BRIEN was a railroad inspector traveling throughout the Pacific Northwest before his thrillers landed him on the *New York Times* bestseller list. He worked all the live long day and wrote at night. Now he writes full time. His latest thriller is *Disturbed.*

NANCY PEARL is a librarian and reader. She's written four books in her acclaimed *Book Lust* series: *Book Lust: Recommended Reading for Every Mood, Moment, and Reason*; *More Book Lust: 1,000 New Reading Recommendations for Every Mood, Moment, and Reason*; *Book Crush: For Kids and Teens: Recommended Reading for Every Mood, Moment, and Interest*; and *Book Lust To Go: Recommended Reading for Travelers, Vagabonds, and Dreamers.*

JULIA QUINN is the #1 *New York Times* bestselling author of over twenty novels of historical romance.

NANCY RAWLES is the author of *My Jim*, the 2009 selection of the Seattle Public Library's popular program "Seattle Reads," and a realistic picture of the bereaved family of Huck Finn's famous companion.

SUZANNE SELFORS began her first novel a few moments after the school bus whisked away her youngest child for full-time school, and she hasn't stopped since. She writes middle grade for Little, Brown and teen novels for Walker/Bloomsbury. She's been published in a dozen countries with more on the way.

JENNIE SHORTRIDGE is the author of four bestselling novels, including her latest, *When She Flew*. Her nonfiction work has appeared in numerous magazines and newspapers. A co-founder of Seattle7Writers and an active volunteer in the community, she is currently at work on her next novel.

ED SKOOG is the author of a collection of poems, *Mister Skylight,* and the forthcoming collection *migratory restlessness*. His poems have appeared in *Paris Review, American Poetry Review, The New Republic, Slate,* and *The New Republic.*

GARTH STEIN is the author of three novels, including the *New York Times* and international bestseller *The Art of Racing in the Rain.* He has also worked as a playwright and documentary filmmaker, and is a co-founder of Seattle7Writers.

GREG STUMP is a teacher and artist. He is a longtime contributor to *The Stranger,* the co-creator of the acclaimed comic book series *Urban Hipster,* and a former critic and journalist for *The Comics Journal.* His most recent work is the graphic novel *Disillusioned Illusions.*

INDU SUNDARESAN is an internationally bestselling author of five books, including the three novels of the Taj Mahal Trilogy. Her work has been translated into more than twenty languages.

CRAIG WELCH is the author of *Shell Games: A True Story of Cops, Con Men, and the Smuggling of America's Strangest Wildlife,* a finalist for the Pacific Northwest Booksellers Association Award. A journalist for two decades, Welch has been the environment reporter at *The Seattle Times* since 2000, and his work has appeared in *Smithsonian* magazine, the *Washington Post,* and *Newsweek.*

SUSAN WIGGS is a writer, a reader, a teacher, and dreamer, and #1 *New York Times* bestselling author.

cover design by Milan Bozic
interior design by Danielle Young

ISBN: 978-1-4532-5827-9

Published in 2011 by Open Road Integrated Media
180 Varick Street
New York, NY 10014
www.openroadmedia.com